W
FI

Wild Fires is Sophie Jai's debut novel. She was selected as a 2020 Writer-in-Residence and Visiting Fellow at the University of Oxford for *Wild Fires*, and was longlisted for the 2019 Bridport Prize Peggy Chapman-Andrews First Novel Award. Jai was born and raised in Trinidad and Tobago. She splits her time between Toronto and London.

www.sophiejai.com

Praise for *Wild Fires*:

'Sophie is one of the most naturally talented writers I've ever taught or mentored, and that talent shines from every page of *Wild Fires*. This is a gem of a book: beautifully crafted, emotionally insightful, and full of sharply-drawn characters who linger long in the memory. Sophie is a literary star in the making'
LAURA BARNETT, author of *The Versions of Us*

'It's an immersive story with everything I love in a book. It's an incredibly intimate, tender story about grief, mourning, silences and secrets, loss, identity, love, sisters/mothers, and home. *Wild Fires* is bursting with silences and thick with characters "emboldened by the dark, creeping in corridors at night, saying things they cannot say in the light." It reminds readers that families are often messy, tangled webs, thinly tied together with strings of the past that at any moment can unravel and leave us all spiralling. I'm hooked'
YVONNE BATTLE-FELTON, author of *Remembered*

WILD FIRES

Sophie Jai

THE BOROUGH PRESS

The Borough Press
an imprint of HarperCollins*Publishers* Ltd
1 London Bridge Street
London SE1 9GF

www.harpercollins.co.uk

HarperCollins*Publishers*
Macken House,
39/40 Mayor Street Upper,
Dublin 1
D01 C9W8
Ireland

First published by HarperCollins*Publishers* 2022

This paperback edition 2023

A catalogue record for this book is available from the British Library

ISBN: 978-0-00-838037-3

Set in Garamond by Palimpsest Book Production Limited, Falkirk, Stirlingshire

Printed and bound in the UK using 100% Renewable
Electricity by CPI Group (UK) Ltd

MIX
Paper | Supporting
responsible forestry
FSC™ C007454

"For even as you have home-comings in your twilight, so has the wanderer in you, the ever distant and alone."

—Kahlil Gibran, *On Houses*

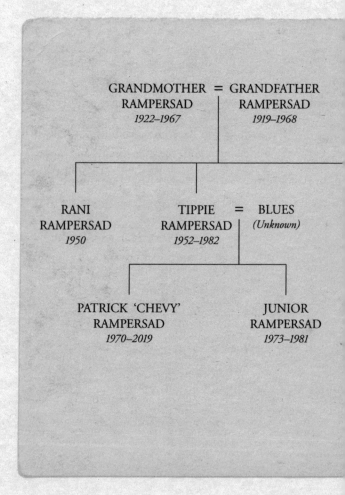

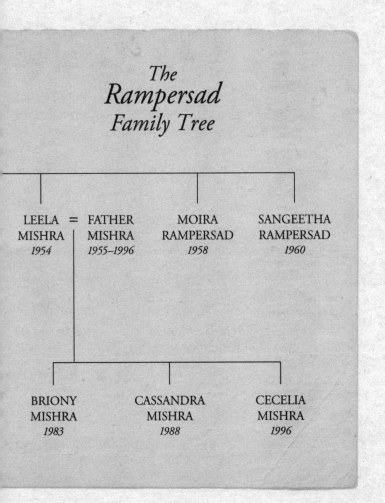

The
Rampersad
Family Tree

LEELA = FATHER   MOIRA   SANGEETHA
MISHRA   MISHRA   RAMPERSAD   RAMPERSAD
1954   *1955–1996*   *1958*   *1960*

BRIONY   CASSANDRA   CECELIA
MISHRA   MISHRA   MISHRA
1983   *1988*   *1996*

PART I

1

My cousin had Onions to thank for the name "Chevy". I was six years old when Onions first regaled me with the Legend of Chevy, and by the time I was eight and ready to leave Macaria myself, that humble street of my home in Trinidad, I had heard the story so many times that I could repeat each minute detail as if I had been there – the standstill of the clear, blue sky, the precisely five watchful birds on the electrical lines, the smell of exhaust fumes. There must have been something about seeing our small, vacant faces – my older sister and I, and whichever miscellaneous cousin was meandering around – that made Onions want to sit us down, neatly cross-legged next to each other like Russian nesting dolls, and ask, "You girls know how your cousin get he name? Is a real funny story. Come. I go tell you."

Every time he told the story, Onions described his younger self as a lanky, dark-skinned Indian as if these features had changed over time. He was eleven years old when the Legend of Chevy was born ("eh, that was a million years ago…" he would say) with hair so thin the boys played bets he'd be bald by twenty-five, and feet

3

so consistently dirty that we questioned the purpose of his sandals. Onions had gotten his own name on account of his epiphora, a condition that made his eyes water endlessly since he was a little boy. Unprovoked tears often leaked down his face, and the other boys, some girls, too, taunted him.

"Eh, Onions! You crying again?" They could barely stifle their giggles, but young Onions could not stifle his tears when they replied on his behalf, "Then stop chopping onions, Onions…!"

And then they were gone, their falsetto cackles and hurried footsteps fading into the echoes of fugitives through unmarked alleys. At some point, real tears mixed with fake ones, but when the others eventually earned nicknames through their own flaws (like Stinkmouth, Jumbie, and Long Foot), sticking to them so hard throughout the entirety of their lives that even to their own ears their given names sounded like that of a stranger, Onions was glad not to be called by his first name like Sunil, whom they excluded from everything.

Onions told us that on the day the Legend of Chevy came to fruition, he had declared to everyone in the front yard of a snacket that my cousin, officially known as Patrick from birth, had won a race running against a brand-new Chevy Nova II.

A true storyteller, patient and passionate, Onions would lean forward in his seat and segue into the weather and other orbiting elements he thought cataclysmic to his plot, seeing his life in third person as if already dead.

"It was a day in June 1982 – a Friday. The high-noon sun beam a gold spotlight onto the yard," he would say, as if the Legend of Chevy couldn't have been conceived on any other day but one with sun. The divine role of weather was lost on our young minds, and it was only when I grew older and began documenting the story of my family that I wondered how triumphant the Legend of Chevy would have been had the skies been grey.

4

We listened eagerly every time though, trusting each word as a pearl of truth, for stories were our only family heirlooms. We re-imagined the very Macaria we sat in through Onions' sepia filter of time: the one- and two-storey houses erected decades earlier by our great-great-grandfathers painted the hues one found on summer nail polish palettes – Coral Crush, Water Orchid, Blue La La. Roughly cut sheets of galvanized metal laying on rooftops that pelted the heat back to the sun, and when it was rained on sounded like gunfire. Dozing guard dogs beneath the sills of open windows and billowing cream curtains. Fuchsia and cotton bougainvillea petals spiraling down to front yards like the wings of butterflies. And stray dogs sniffing the streets' open drains for scraps, their skin sliding along their ribcages, heads bowed low. All this Onions said to us, his open palm moving across the room in panoramic scope as if from the center of it he wished to project the sights of his story onto the walls, even though we were sitting right there on the island, and none of those things had really changed.

The only time the story stopped was when the smile dropped from his face and he suddenly turned somber. "Listen, eh, you have to remember that Chevy wasn't some ordinary boy. I ain't only saying that because he's my friend, but because of what happen to him. By the time he was twelve years old, he live three lives already: first, being born into this world, second, as a suddenly only child, and finally, as an orphan."

Later on, when I would be in my twenties in a country much further north, and when I sensed it was my turn to tell a story, I told the greatest one I knew. I channeled my inner Onions and suppressed the accent that for years pleaded to be flung free from beneath my tongue. Often, Ines would be there. "Listen, you guys, listen," I would say. "It was a day in June 1982 – a Friday. The high-noon sun beamed a gold spotlight in the front yard of a snacket

– that's what we call little convenience stores back home…" For the most part, eyes would smile and bodies would relax, and if they didn't, I gave the abridged version. Ines would be smiling having heard the story countless times since the fifth grade. She never listened less with each retelling.

*

The story of my family is one of potholes and cracks that I have tried to fill over the years for no reason other than my own need to neatly pen a narrative – a beginning, middle, and an end, a sequential flow of things happening to my relatives over the course of time – so I cannot deny how I came to be. Why I am the way that I am.

When I am sitting in a chair with an unturned book in my hand, gazing out of my London flat; when I am in the late-night grocery store and a group of people bustle in and out in comfortable jester; when a good man asks why I cannot talk to them, why can't I just *open up,* and when I plead with a bad one to *let me in*; or, when finally in the company of someone I should be enjoying but my only wish is to be alone, I look to my past that first provided me these early, solitary linings: my home within that house, and my home within my mother.

I thumb through old family photographs and try to decipher the sideways glances in them, the three people out of ten not smiling. Fine-tune my hearing to the after-dark whispers, long after the lights have been turned off. Read into the swollen silence after someone enters a room, and another soon exits. Forget about what happened the night before – it never happened. This is how my family talks.

My attempts to fill in the gaps are forced and eager, overreaching into the past and present, blurring fact and fiction. Like Onions, now I am the storyteller. I, too, narrate life in third person as if already dead. I am outside of my body all the time; I travel atop the shoulders of everyone who has lived in the Florence Street house. I see the bones of their feet and the arcs of their backs wear brittle as I walk alongside them, years and years and years before I was born, in an effort to decode us: what my Auntie Rani is really doing, and thinking, cooped up in her room. Why my sister, Cecelia, can only be in the presence of our family for thirty minutes at a time before quietly slipping away. Why my Auntie Sangeetha uses the corridors as confessionals at night, pulling us into breathless, near-silent words, as if she were running out of time. Why a grainy picture of the little cousin I never knew, the glint in his eye immortalized at eight years old, sits atop our mantel, but his name, like his mother's, is said only in whispers. Why Briony, my older sister who lives at home at thirty-six, adorns herself with expensive things, sometimes with the price tags still attached, but never bothers to dye her greys or conceal her blemishes. Why my mother, Leela, is a levitating orb of influence, the tenacity of her single motherhood trespassing into other realms of life where there is no need for it, and if she knows the power she exerts over us all.

Why we couldn't help Chevy.

Of these things I know, yet cannot confirm, I try to put to shape the mass of my family's stories, a bibliography of reference and reason, genetics and geography, so that I may run my fingers across its structure – our Great Disperse – and know this palpable thing that has settled and taken its form in me, long before I was born.

2

I take my time rolling my luggage up the pathway. Under a cloudy
sky where the sun comes and goes in weak beacons, I see my
breath in gaseous bursts in the remnants of a relentless Toronto
winter. I see the frosted relics of weeds and forlorn tulips in the
hard March soil I walk along, and when I look up, I am further
devastated to see not much has really changed of our house on
Florence Street since I left for England five years ago. The brass
metal of the numbers 4 and 8 are bolted into the beige-bricked
wall, lusterless and permanent. The mailbox, once a presidential
red and gold, is coarse and stained with rust. The royal blue paint
of the porch has almost completed its slow descent into disinte-
gration; flake by flake, the front steps are entirely stripped of their
colour, and its ashen planks laying warped and unaligned like
decaying teeth. A single table that looks entirely made of cork,
put out for recycling by someone down the street and picked up
by Auntie Sangeetha years ago, still remains planted on the far
end of the porch, junk mail shoved under one of its legs, a full
ashtray its centerpiece. A brutalist porch swing, all edges and dull

iron that has drawn blood from me and my sisters over the years, sits motionless and frozen.

I make my way up the steps and look down the line of front porches to seek out a familiar face when I realize that I'm squinting through that brown reed screen and there – a synapse sparks. It's the same screen the neighbors put up years ago to obscure the view of our house from their peripheral line of – I want to say – not vision, but living. The man of the house had put it up right after their daughter was born. He was a burly, kind-looking man whose cheeks were rosy and eyes always soft. One day – it must have been at night when everyone was asleep – this soft-spoken man had put up the screen, and in the morning when we saw it, none of us said anything, not even to each other.

We knew. We knew that when their daughter got older, old enough to know that something wasn't quite right with the family next door, the screen would quell her questions. "Why do they swear so much? Why are they so loud, then so quiet? What kind of name is 'Chevy'? Why doesn't he say anything back when you talk to him?"

Why are they the way that they are?

We understood, then. So that even when Chevy met the little girl's father at the edge of the lawn to roll out the garbage bins in the early hours of the morning, when dewdrops were still teeter-tottering on blades of grass and the sky slashed a synthetic pink against a pale lavender dawn, each would give a cordial nod to the other, understanding that life was hard, and neither meant offence nor judgement, they just had to do what they had to do, before walking the path back to their own house where the screen divided them once more. We were the last house on the block, and like a limb rendered useless, we were surgically removed from the rest of a healthy, functioning body when that reed screen dropped.

Amputated, in one clean cut, and cast into the wicked shadows of otherness.

I remember this feeling. I remember home.

*

Yesterday, my younger sister called.

"Cas," she said. "Cas, oh… uh…"

It went on like this for some time.

"Cece," I said. "Cece, what's wrong? Why are you whispering?"

"Cas, you have to come home. You have to come home now."

From my London bedroom, inches beneath ground level where my window ran parallel to the sidewalk outside, I stepped into the slant of a shadow as if seeking privacy from the sun. Coils of fine dust like decorative tinsel collected in the corners of my room, and stones dangling from threads of gold necklaces chimed against my ceramic teacups as I bumped into the bookshelf from where they hung. A few pages of my manuscript fluttered about, and a book slammed to the ground.

"What happened?" I said. I felt the air drop from my throat to my stomach. In my head, I scanned a list of everyone in the house. Sangeetha, Rani, our mother. Ma? Ma!

"Chevy," she said. A long pause on the other end, then, "Chevy, he's gone. Come home, Cassandra. He's…" Then a gasp, as if realizing what she had just said.

"How, Cece? What happened? Cece, how?"

"In his sleep…" She began to sound distant, as if she were falling away. "In his sleep…"

She told me to pack my grip sole boots, there was still slush on the ground, and I began to cry.

I knocked on Ines' bedroom door, and seeing my face in my hands, she rushed me in. Black water swarmed my eyes. Blindly I followed her to the bed. I was thankful when she didn't ask me what was wrong; old friends know these things. She helped me pack, and then I ran and I flew, and on the plane I did what people in movies do; red-eyed and stunned, I stared blankly down the aisles, indifferent to hurried stewards, crying babies, crinkling bags. I closed my eyes and saw Chevy's empty room. I saw my huddled family watch the medics take him from the second floor to the ground floor, struggling down the steep, curling staircase, the very one that Chevy had climbed the night before. I saw him wheeled through the front door into the blast of daylight, away from his second home.

I saw that I was not there.

"Don't worry about writing," Ines had said before I left. She had both her hands on my shoulders. "Don't worry about the book. Your editor can wait, I'm sure. Drop her an email on the plane and put an out-of-office on for everyone else."

I nodded my head.

She snapped her fingers in my face, loud like cracking wood. "Okay?"

"Yeah."

"Message me when you land."

A light turbulence jolted me out of the memory. I took my notebook from my bag and felt the safety of the pen in my hand. It wasn't long before I drifted back to the past, and when I brought pen to paper what should have come out was some sentiment of melancholy, a deep, nonsensical dive into how I felt, or the dead weight of my hand dribbling a long mark down the page, which it was wont to do. But in my grief, in seeing Chevy's face turn away from mine when I closed my eyes, the only word that my pen could sputter out in long cursive tail was:

Why?

*

And now I find myself standing outside the second house I grew up in, decades after the Legend of Chevy, Chevy who is now dead. I am thirty-one years old.

I have a key, but I think about knocking. It feels strange under the circumstances to let myself into a house I have not stepped foot in for years. I put my ear to the door and hear nothing. I poke my finger through the mail slot and like an intruder peer through it, my eyeballs rolling from left to right like those of a thief in the night. I take in a waft of cigarette smoke and old dust and close my eyes. When I open them, there is another familiar scene: a dark hallway void of life. It occurs to me that one does not knock on their own door. I slide the key in, and instead of finding my family sitting on the living room couch, clustered together for warmth at a time like this, or roaming around the kitchen awaiting my arrival, there is no one. I hear no one and nothing except a low electric hum. The lights are out, and the blanched daylight barely filters through the tawny curtains of the living room. I look down at the shoe rack, and unable to tell who is home, I feel like a stranger. Shoe upon shoe clutters the rack: men's loafers and house slippers, women's flip flops and flats. The same disorder applies to the coat wall: windbreakers and coats, an assortment of spring, fall, and winter layers, hang in musty abandon. I take off my shoes and feel the cold of the hardwood floor drain my warmth.

Yet I know everyone who should be home is home. We are not the kind of family that takes walks. Not together. I know they have heard me enter the house. They have not come to greet me. They do not know what to say to me, nor I to them. They each sit in their rooms with their walls.

Upstairs I hear a creak, too faint to be from the second floor. It is coming from the attic, my mother's room.

I go to her.

3

I must say it now before going on. There is one particular pothole in the story of my family that will not be filled, prodded, or examined up close, and that is the one of my father.

I will go no further than this: my mother and father married young, both at twenty-four years old. They were in love, a rarity in the year 1979 for a Hindu wedding in Trinidad. I know from the loose pictures we brought with us to Florence Street, doubled over and over in plastic bags and labeled "SuperSuperMarket", that my father wore a grey, clean-cut suit, and my mother a crochet-lace cream dress whose humble flare pooled like milk at her feet. There was picture after picture of my parents smiling, the whites of their eyes and teeth more baring on this day, so much that it bordered lunacy, and their fingers intertwined and snapped into place like that of a lock and its key. It was only when I got older and understood the movements of this house that I noticed my Auntie Rani, the eldest of the sisters, was not smiling in any of the pictures. Not only this, but she stood distanced from my Auntie Tippie as if she feared catching a cold. I thought that if I brought the pictures closer to my face, I could see Auntie Rani grimacing, for when I tilted the photograph from left to right, her lips became sneers, and were I able to tune into the sounds of photographs, I was certain I would hear the grinding of teeth.

Fifteen years into my parents' marriage, then with two daughters – one just beginning to ask questions (me) and another entering teenage angst (Briony) – my father began to grow bored. The Great Disperse was still in effect. He yearned to shed the inertia the hot sun and long winding roads Trinidad bored into him. He would lie limp across the linen hammock in our small living room in Macaria – a room I can now only remember in a blur of colours and objects – hanging a slender leg and arm off it as though posing for a promiscuous picture. He would say to no one in particular, though always within earshot of my mother, that he could feel his youth and ambition and potential slipping through the crevices of the Caribbean. The snacket wasn't enough, he said, and selling simple things made him feel simple. He longed for North America and the promises he'd heard of it. The world was changing, and they were not changing with it, he said. The year was 1994.

"Leela," he would say. "You doesn't get bored here sometimes?"

But my mother, treating dreams as exactly what they were, would smile, kiss my father on his forehead and carry on with her everyday chores.

My father continued to dream. In a haze that became clearer each time he heard of another Trinidadian's success in Canada – Boya's successful roti shop, Shirlee's new car as a result of a steady office job, and Kamla buying a big house after being in Toronto for only four years – he envisioned himself there in the kitchen of his very own bakery. Lining the windows with cupcake tiers he could only describe as "fancy", and in hanging antique bird cages, would be Trinidadian sweeties and pies labeled as '*Real* Caribbean Desserts', glistening on a street that didn't bar itself up like jail cells when the sun began to set.

When he painted this picture to my mother – the elegant dishware, the sweeties, and the setting sun – she didn't quite feel the same way; she wanted to remain firm among her roots, dangerous dusks, jail cells, and all. Ashes of her family sat on our modest mantel next to pictures of their beloved bodily forms. Her sisters lived just down the street, and Briony was doing well in school. The tree they had nurtured for all these years, finally, was bearing yellow fruit.

But, I'm told, my father was insistent. When romanticism wouldn't work, he switched to rhetoric. He asked my mother of opportunity, freedom, and safety for Briony and me. He said to look at all those people living a good life over there, look how good their children were doing.

"We stupid not to take the chance," he would say.

"It does get real cold there, you know," my mother said.

"What is a little cold if you living a good life?"

"It safe?"

My father raised his eyebrows. "Leela, you think Toronto would ever catch fire like Port of Spain?"

When my mother and I fight now, she will often say, "You just like him."

Eventually she threw in the dish towel. My father proceeded with the process, filling out form after form, even going so far as to carrying them around in a manila folder wherever he went, mistrusting open windows, grubby little hands, and his wife's temper. On his breaks at work, he checked off boxes in deep, confident lines with blue ballpoint ink. No, he did not hold a criminal record. No, he was not seeking refugee status. No, he did not have a communicable disease.

After a year and a half of paperwork, interviews, weekly phone calls with others he knew in Toronto ("How thick a coat we need?

17

How much is rent so? TTC? What's that now? It safe?"), and scrupulous living to build our financial credibility, the four of us set course for Toronto. When my mother extended the invitation to her sisters and Chevy, they all said no, never, with the exception of my Auntie Sangeetha, who only began to cry and nod in acceptance, the kohl on her eyes giving way to black tears.

We flew in February. My father's carry-on luggage consisted of little relics of Canadian life friends and cousins had mailed him over the months as motivation to stay positive – a snow globe, miniature bottles of maple syrup and a red and white toque with moose antlers on either side which he foolishly wore from departure to destination. My mother took with her the ashes of her parents in urns sealed with Scotch tape. Briony and I squealed at the dreamlike prospect of riding in an airplane for the very first time, sailing among the clouds and flying close to the sun, only to arrive in a land of snow, naïve to the fact that we were leaving our friends, family, and home behind.

We lived in a basement apartment rented to us by one of my father's cousins in the deep east end of Scarborough, one room for four people – five, if you counted prenatal Cecelia, who caused my mother to take up more space each day. With the money my parents had from their savings – selling the Macaria house and my father's snacket, plus the job he held as an assistant at a bakery in North York – they took out a mortgage on a three-storey detached home in West Toronto, in the Junction. Three months later we had a basement, a kitchen, a living room, two bathrooms, three bedrooms, and an attic. And, about a week later, my father, finally content with setting foot on Canadian ground, slipped on black ice, hit his head, and died.

This is where I stop digging. This particular pothole is one that collapses under my feet, and leads to a tunnel that leads to a cave that leads to a lair that leads to the depths of depths of depths that lead to the core until finally, at the crux of it all, I am alone, with so many questions, so many questions, that I cannot –

I cannot find my way back. I cannot say his name out loud. I do not talk about him.

I suppose, in some ways, I am like my family, after all.

4

The space in between things: these are telling. The distance of a chair thrown askew from a desk. One shoe from the other of the same pair. How close someone stands to another in an empty train. How long it has been since I last spoke to Chevy. Or, how long it has been since I've had a real conversation with my mother.

I know my mother inside and out: the schedule of her day from the weight of her steps, her mood from the scent of her breath, and how much she cares about something from the number of words she uses in a sentence. But the one thing I do not know is who my mother is when she is alone.

Light beams from beneath her bedroom door, casting a gold blade across the hardwood floor. At the end of the hallway, the wooden beads of the curtain tap against each other like a light rain beginning to fall. I shudder as a wintry draft sweeps past my feet and snakes up under my clothes. I think if I press my ear to the door, I might hear the turning of pages. My mother is always in possession of several notebooks – plain and unnumbered, unsentimental – detailing what she has to do and who she has to call. She always has someone to call. Over the years, I would see her open to any blank page in the middle of the book, write in "Call Vidya" or "Check with Boya", or a long phone number starting with 1868 – no dashes between the numbers – sometimes with no name next to it. When Cece had bought her a proper phonebook for her birthday, glossy and stacked with alphabetical tabs and mindfully designed spaces for notes, our mother was only momentarily seduced.

"Do what?" she had asked Cece.

"What?" said Cece.

"I can do what?"

"What are you talking about, Ma?"

"The front cover says, 'You can do it.' I can do what?" said my mother.

My phone vibrates in my pocket. A message from Ines says she knows that I landed even though I didn't text her, she checked my flight status on Google. She tells me to be strong and kind, and to have patience. She says she will call me tonight. I turn off my phone and place my ear against my mother's door, but instead of hearing silence, I hear whispering, and though I am sorry, sorry for my poor mother, sorry that this, *this* is what she does when she is alone, I become angry and push open the door.

My mother sits at the edge of her bed, un-jarred, in blue high-waisted cotton panties, legs crossed.

"Cassandra." Her hands are folded in her lap. "You make it home."

Sorry again now, seeing the goosebumps on her bare breasts raised from the stingy heat of the radiator and the slight hunch of her back, I click the door closed behind me.

"Of course, I made it home, Ma." I want to ask, "Why wouldn't I have?" but instead I say, "Are you okay, Ma?"

She does not reply. She is looking at a point on the floor between us.

I want to say, "I'm sorry," but that is something someone says when it is only the other person's loss.

The room, like the rest of the house I surveyed in my dark ascent to the attic, remains the same. A too-large Victorian dresser peeling at its edges takes up most of a wall, and a tall plastic laundry basket cracked in the middle sits in the corner, its contents of lilac nighties, high-waisted jeans and paisley tops neatly folded and piled. The queen bed is blanketed with its "Saturday sheets", and another smaller dresser stands opposite. Its top drawer, I know, is for bed sheets, the second for towels, the third for miscellaneous linens, and the last empty. "Just in case," my mother used to say.

The wallpaper, though yellowed, still shimmers when light hits its cherry blossoms. The curtains are drawn apart, and thick mites of thistly dust dance in the sunlight, like dandelions that do not know they are weeds.

I want to say, "Who were you talking to?" but I don't want to embarrass her.

"You talk to Cecelia?" she says.

"Yeah. Yesterday morning. Where is she?"

"Downstairs in she room." She closes her eyes and shakes her head. Thick tears roll down her cheeks.

I swallow and look at the floor.

"That one – she," she says, pointing to the floor.

"Cece?"

"Cecelia? No."

"What?"

"What?"

She stands up and turns away from me, grabbing a white bra hanging off the bed post and clasps it around her chest. She wipes the tears from her face with the back of her hand. A few minutes pass where neither of us speak, and she takes a sweater and a pair of pants lying on the faded leaf-print bedspread and dresses herself. She tucks her hair behind her ears and brings her hands to her collarbones, bowing her head. Then, as though realizing I am still there, straightens up and turns to me. "Cassandra. Come."

I do not go to her, she comes to me. She moves the hair from my eyes with her index finger, drawing a line across my forehead as though casting a protective spell. She kisses my left cheek, then my right. I smell the gardenia and jasmine of White Shoulders she has dabbed in the crook of her neck.

"Unpack your things," she says, playing with the ends of my fine hair. "Stay up here in the attic with me. Cecelia room messy, and Briony is, well, Briony. Go and bathe, then take a little sleep. How was your flight? You looking tired. Look at the lines under your eyes."

My eyelids droop as she leads me to her bed.

"Your Auntie Moira is on a plane right now," she says, draping a blanket over me. "She ain't seen allyuh in years. She go be here tomorrow evening. Sleep now."

She pulls the blanket up to my shoulders and her hair falls into my face. The notes of her scent are threaded in the sheets, the pillows, the room, the house. I sink into a dreamless sleep, the deepest I have had in years.

*

I wake up late the next day to the sounds of life in the kitchen. As I go down the two flights of stairs, I remember that every time I walk into this house, I am in another place and another time. Toronto is behind the front door and I am back home, in Macaria. I see a cocoyea broom made from coconut tree leaves propped up against a wall, a cockset burned at its end sitting on a window ledge, even though it is not mosquito season, and tiered paintings of pastel gods on the corridor walls. When I pass Chevy's room on the second floor, I do not stop, I keep walking with my eyes cast downward. His walnut door is shut, and like the ring that traces the moon during an eclipse, a celestial sunlight halos the frame.

Cece's room is next to Chevy's. Her door, too, is shut.

Auntie Sangeetha lives in the basement. I hear her in the kitchen with my mother preparing for Auntie Moira's arrival and I smell something I haven't smelled in years: red beans and stew chicken. I want to fall to the floor and cry. I poke my head in the kitchen and heat dampens my face. Before me is a scientist's laboratory; liquids are bubbling, appliances are hissing, steam is filling the room, iron-cast pots are clanging against glowing burners and metal implements, and there is a frenzied woman cursing beneath the whirring of the stovetop fan. My mother is pirouetting in worn slippers and a lilac nightie between the oven and sink, telling Auntie Sangeetha, her loyal assistant and younger sister, to stir this, poke that, chop this, shake that.

I go to the living room before I am noticed and asked to help, only to find Briony there, crying before Chevy's picture on the fireplace mantel, which is next to a portrait of his mother, which is next to a portrait of his brother. I watch my sister cry in front of their faces, these people who are more shapes and stories than breathing bodies who once put clothes on in the morning, had jobs, cooked in the evenings, loved. Briony is wearing her jacket and boots and a small Guess purse is buoyed on her elbow. She is still crying when we embrace, iridescent tears so thick they fall not in streams, but spheres. We have not seen each other since I left.

"Auntie Tippie was like was a movie star, wasn't she?" I say.

She lifts her face from my shoulder, leaving a damp spot in the shape of a butterfly on my hoodie. She nods and new tears begin to swell. "Yeah," she says. "Her hair and lips."

The black and white portrait that hangs dead and center over the mantel looks more like that of an actress whose signature should be scribbled in its corner, the *i* of her name dotted with a heart. This is how we were taught to remember Auntie Tippie: not of this world, but an angel from heaven, the place she looked toward when she posed for this very photograph, up and away as if the light from above was already beckoning to her. She wears a lace dress and is sitting slender and tall, her complexion waxen and lips matte and nude. Her nose is rounded at its tip, making her look younger than she really was, and her eyebrows are waxed down, thick and curved and not a single hair out of place. Atop her eyelids is a perfect mark of eyeliner from where her lashes sprout like palm fronds. And her hair – oh, how I envied all my family's hair, having inherited my father's flat and lifeless wisps – was high and glossy. Soft to the touch, I was once told.

"I'm sorry this is how we're seeing each other after so long."

"I just can't believe it," Briony says. "I just can't believe it."

Looking at Briony's face now, she looks older than I remember, and she is beautiful. She has let her grey run past her roots, well into the middle strands of her neck-length hair that is thick and voluminous. From the inside corner of her cat eyes to her high cheekbones run two lines that are beginning to deepen and branch. Her teeth are an off white and her pillowy pout arched by a Cupid's bow makes everything she says sound sexy, or cryptic. Her jeans are too baggy around her ankles and her wool coat is pilled with lint. I look down to her boots that are salt-stained and wrinkled.

"Chevy—" she says. Both of us turn our heads to the wall when the floorboards creak in the bedroom behind the wall. And then again, a weight shifting.

Briony gestures with her eyes toward the porch.

Outside I tug at her coat sleeve. "Were you going for a walk or something?"

26

"Yeah," she says, wiping her nose and eyes with her sleeve. "I was just going to buy some smokes, but…" She ruffles around in her purse and pulls out a cigarette. "Knew I had one in here. Sit with me?"

Briony is four years older than me which means that when we were growing up, she was always cooler first. Everything she did cascaded down to me; I shed glittery, cherry-flavored lip-gloss in favour of nude pearlescent tones. I traded Backstreet Boys for Mariah Carey. I mimicked smoking with white candy sticks when I had seen her behind the school with boys during lunch, blowing smoke out the corner of her mouth. Once, I even went so far as to dye my hair after Briony came home with honey highlights, a then-toddler Cece cooing at me as I massaged Bronze Bombshell into my virgin hair in the laundry room of our basement.

Sitting on the porch swing with her now, we slowly begin to sway. Its bolts screech against the metal like the shrill wince of a guillotine. For early March, the air is mild, but without jackets we shiver and tuck our hands beneath our legs. Next to her, I feel like I always have: small and childlike. The origin of Briony's build is unknown; unlike either of our parents, she is sturdy and strong. She is a woman built of valleys of curves and hills of flesh, whereas on my own body the pinnacle of each joint protrudes through my clothes, fragile and lithe like my mother's. My kneecaps are pointy, my elbows too sharp. My hip bones are angular and suggestive of an unhealthy diet, and my collarbones, so jutting, leave a hollow dip just below my throat.

"I heard you come in yesterday," says Briony. "I'm… sorry I didn't come down to see you. I…" She shakes her head and a tear falls.

"Brie, you don't have to say anything."

She flicks my leg and smiles.

"Cece is still in her room," I say.

"Yeah, she hasn't really come out since yesterday. Leave her be, I guess."

We look out to the neighborhood. It is a Sunday and no one is out. In the Canadian spring, greens and reds and yellows begin to peek out from their buds against the grey slush left over from a dead winter.

"Did you get time off work?" I ask.

"Yeah, two weeks. But some of it cuts into my vacation time."

"That's not very lenient of a *travel* agency."

"Yeah, well, that's what we get, Cas. Doesn't help that I'm part-time. They give you, like, three days of bereavement leave, then expect you to come back in a few days and sell vacation packages to happy couples and cozy families."

I want to ask, "How come you're not working full-time?"

"Whatever, I'll take it. Don't want to return back to work a mess," she says.

"Yeah. I get it."

"I've missed you."

"I've missed you."

We sit in a silence that is neither awkward nor tense. Truly, she is my sister.

"I'm hearing whispers again," she says.

I nod.

"It's been a long time since I've heard whispers," she says. She brings the cigarette to her lips and rummages through her bag. Crumpled receipts, wrappers and bus transfers fall from it, and she shoves them back in like they're confidential.

"Well," I say, looking to the street, "Ma says Auntie Moira is getting in soon."

She pulls a lighter from the bag. "Moira," she mutters, catching sparks from the lighter, "Moira has always been a bitch."

Briony pushes her heel against the porch floor, thrusting the swing and us both into a startling force. I grasp the armrest with both hands, the blunt edges of it pressing into my skin. "Briony!"

The whoosh of the cold breeze makes me hunch over and the smoke of the cigarette stifles me. I hold my foot down firm on the ground, and yelp when I feel a stiff splinter impale the arch of my sole.

"You're such a baby," Briony says, nudging me hard with her shoulder. I bite down on my lip and hold my foot. "You've always been such a baby." She winks and snickers then the smile drops from her face, and we sigh and sit there swaying in silence.

*

Auntie Moira, in shape and age, is somewhere between my mother and Auntie Sangeetha. At sixty-one years old, having the imagined body one would expect time to mold for a woman her age, she moves through the general public unregarded. Neither possessing my mother's string-bean frailty nor Sangeetha's papaya girth, Moira takes the form of a Bartlett pear, her small upper body widening at the hips to thick thighs. A vain woman, her hair, though limp, runs long and box-dyed black past her waist. Though Sangeetha is the youngest of the sisters, Moira possesses the least wrinkles, the skin on her face taut and smooth and shiny. "It's because she doesn't smile," Briony once said years ago. "But once I saw her laughing. It was like watching an accordion fold and unfold."

In response, I had offered a weak, consolatory laugh after Briony's cackle and felt guilty at once. Though I've never had an intimate relationship with Auntie Moira, on account of her being the only one of us to still live in Trinidad, I've always enjoyed the homely presence of her visits. It may have all well been in my mind, my own

29

projections of what I wanted her to embody, but I thought whenever she came to visit Toronto, she smelled of ripe plantains and fry bake. I thought her skin trapped a radiance that no northern country or cosmetic could give me. When she hummed songs from *1942: A Love Story*, a Hindi movie all the women in our family had seen together in the theatre back home – even Auntie Rani – I wanted to say, "Stop, it's too much." But the cruel thing about Briony's comment was that even when Auntie Moira had massaged coconut oil into her hair to keep it shiny, wore ironed pants with a perfect, stark pleat down the middle, and painted her nails that Sally Hansen punch pink, she was still in the backdoor of conversation reduced to a fat, old lady.

Now at dinner, eight of us are sitting around the kitchen table made for six, seldom used but for holidays and death. It is the first time in years I am seeing these faces, and I grow anxious. I feel guilt and shame well up inside me, then realizing that I'm only thinking about myself, the shame deepens. I pick at my cuticles beneath the table, scanning my family's faces. Next to me Briony swipes something across her phone, and next to her, our Auntie Sangeetha, her eyeliner heavy, and a mole that today is dotted at the corner of her lips. She is a voluptuous woman and is pulling her V-neck sweater to her collarbone to conceal her cleavage, her breasts a lifelong burden that was always on the verge of spilling out. Across from us are Auntie Moira and Bass, the man she never married, looking about the room at its walls and ceilings as my mother sets food on the table. Cecelia, my twenty-two-year-old sister, sits directly across from me, and it's like I am looking at myself ten years ago.

"Cece," I had said earlier that evening. I had caught her going to the bathroom from her room. Everything about us, physically, is almost the same; we are gangly women, except that instead of a heart-shaped face, hers is oval, and instead of my father's and my

30

weak hair, she has bounce and body. In the typical manner of a younger sibling to the older, she is two inches taller than me. She had put her arms around me, exhaled loudly into my neck, and I kissed her cheek. "Cece," I said, and then she released me, pushing me away, before running back to her room.

My mother places the last dish, her macaroni pie, in front of me. She pulls out a chair at the head of the table opposite from Auntie Rani who sits at the other end. Rani, the oldest of my aunts at sixty-nine years old, and who I've only communicated with through creaking floorboards since my return, is a woman cloaked by a stern air. She has a jawline that is sharp and defined, and her hair is still cut in the pixie style she's had for years, every hair silver-grey. Her body is that of someone who might have once played a man's sport – though she never did, not as far as I know – exceeding both the width and height of an average female. She is wide, but not fat. Formidable, but not muscular, and with the hunch of her back beginning to take form before her seventies, she now reaches five foot nine. She has almond eyes, elfish ears, and high-arched eyebrows like Briony – her only feminine features. I glance at her from the side, too cowardly to turn my whole face to her, and with the exception of her back, she looks the same as I remember her. She catches my eye and unable to look away, I smile from the side of my mouth to disguise my thoughts. To my surprise, she smiles back.

"This all looking real good, Leela," says Bass. Bass, who runs a family-owned auto shop back home, is an otherwise normal looking man with an average everything, and had gotten his name due to his remarkable deep voice from a young age. Every time I see him, he has grease buried deep beneath his nails. He squeezes Auntie Moira's fingers on the kitchen table. Auntie Moira, being the only one of my aunts in a relationship, looks disapprovingly at Bass' hand over hers, as if she is embarrassed to be loved, as if, she doesn't deserve this display of affection. She moves her hands beneath the table. Bass, not seeming to take notice, says, "How early you had to wake up to make all this food, girl?"

My mother appears to not have heard him.

"Around seven," I say. "Not that I was any help." I force a chuckle and cringe inside.

"Is only such a shame that we had to come for this reason," says Bass. "Boy, when Moira tell me, I couldn't believe my damn ears. Chevy was so young – what? – only forty-something years old?"

"Forty-nine," says Auntie Moira.

"And to go so soon?" he says. "Why God doesn't take the old first? Why He does make the old suffer so? Who—"

"Eat," says my mother. "Before the food get cold. We don't have to talk about all that. We know why we all here." Her hand shakes as she lowers a spoonful of channa to her plate.

Sangeetha exhales loudly and begins to fan herself with a paper towel. Cece and I look at each other, then look away. Moira shakes her head. Rani and Briony say nothing.

"Let we just eat, please," says my mother.

Hands begin to reach for roti, channa, mango achar, macaroni pie, stew chicken, red bean, and coleslaw. Spoons and forks clink against the dishware and Briony's bangles clank against one another with each bite she lifts to her mouth.

"Those are nice," I say to her.

She smiles, chewing. "I got them from Pandora. At Yorkdale Mall. Matching earrings, too." She moves her hair and shows me blue round sparkle studs. She stops eating and smirks at me. "Do you remember Pandora? Or do you only know *Bri-ish* brands now?" She wiggles in her chair with her index fingers pointed up as she says the word "British".

"Ha-ha," I say. "They look expensive."

32

"They are," she and Cece say at the same time. Briony throws a red bean at my sister, and Cece, picking it off her sweater without looking at either one of us, eats it.

"Leave she, Briony," says our mother. "Like allyuh is still children." She steupses. "Have a little respect, nah. Have a little consideration." I look back down to my plate while Briony helps herself to another piece of macaroni pie with her fingers.

"Leela, your red bean tasting different," says Moira, her lips tight and wrinkled as if they were holding her face together like the knot of a balloon.

"How you mean 'different?'" says my mother. She turns her narrowed eyes away from Briony.

"I don't mean 'different' in a bad way. It taste good," says Moira, shifting in her seat.

"It ain't different. Is the same recipe I using for more than thirty years."

"Nah, Leela, girl," says Bass, making a fist to his chest as he belches. "It taste real nice."

After a long minute, Auntie Moira says, "Cassandra, you looking so thin these days. Look at your collarbone. They does say if you could see your collarbone that mean you starving yourself and you not eating enough food." She smiles at me and reaches across the table for my hand. "How life in London there?"

"It's good, Auntie." I reach for her hand, but too far away from each other, we do not touch. "I'm not starving myself," and not knowing what to say next, I say, "It rains a lot."

She laughs, withdraws her hand, the smile drops from her face.

"No, she not looking too skinny," says Auntie Sangeetha. "She looking nice and pretty like always. She does write she books in London. Tell them how you does write your books, baby."

Auntie Sangeetha is my favorite aunt. Not only because she moved to Toronto within weeks of my father dying to help my mother take care of us, but for all her attempts to mend tense moments and vapid conversation with compliments and tenderness. For her perfectly winged eyeliner that took up more of her eyelid each year, the finely dotted mole that moved around the lower equator of her face, and for the bathetic poems she wrote and kept stored in her basement room. I thought of all the women in my family, I might grow up to be like her the most. It was she who gave me my first book in Trinidad.

I thought Auntie Sangeetha was as perfect a creature that she could be – that is, given the circumstances of her life, she turned out more than all right. She could have been cruel, she could have been vile. She could have turned hysterical and run into the wild never to return and no one would have blamed her. Instead, she was delicate and malleable and, yes, melodramatic at times. She would bring her face so near mine that our noses almost touched, whispering something veiled and eerily predictive. The two phrases she has said the most to me and my sisters over the years in the dark hours of the night were: "They does leave and they doesn't come back" and "Who of we really know why?" Then she would retreat into one of the many shadowy nooks of our house, leaving behind the scent of peppermint or citrus from her breath from the pots of tea she consumed each day. Still, it was she who gave me my first book.

"I'm not writing anything new, Auntie," I lie. "It's just the same old, really. Still freelance writing for actual money. Exploring the city whenever I can. You'll have to come visit," I say, knowing the last part is a suggestion that will never come to fruition.

"I will," Auntie Sangeetha lies back. "How Ines going?"

"She's good, Auntie."

"Ines is a real nice girl," she says. "It nice you have someone there you know."

"Yes," I say. "It is."

"Okay, baby," she says.

"You get time off work?" asks my mother.

"Yeah," I say, reminding myself to email my editor tonight.

Auntie Rani coughs and simultaneously, my mother and I look up at her.

"Good," says my mother. "And Sangeetha, you too. Ask the pharmacy for four or five weeks off, nah. Tell them what happen."

"Four weeks?" Sangeetha says. She lowers her spoon onto her plate. "Leela, they ain't going to give me four weeks off. They tell me I could only take two. And is only because I working there for so long that the store manager give me that in the first place."

My mother stares at her younger sister. "Why not, Sangeetha? Why only two weeks? Tell them what happen. Tell them you are not able to come in. How they could say no in a time like this?"

"Ma," says Briony, picking red beans from her plate one by one and tossing them into her mouth. "We're not retirees like you guys." She waves a hand at my mother and Auntie Rani. "Flight Centre's only giving me, like, four days off and then the rest cuts into my vacation time. It's not like back home where everyone knows everyone and they say, 'Take the month off and come back when you ready.'" She drawls out the words, exaggerating the Trinidadian accent when she says this, flicking her hand on the last words. "It's not like that here."

Auntie Moira says, "Oh oh," and Bass says, "That's a real shame," at the same time.

Auntie Sangeetha closes her eyes and hums.

My mother looks down at her plate without lowering her face. The rest of us chew slowly. I think about saying something, like asking Auntie Sangeetha if the people at the pharmacy are still getting on her nerves, but my mother has not yet moved. The phone rings and none of us get up to answer it. It rings eight times before going to voicemail, and when my mother brings food to her mouth, I feel the change in the air, and our shoulders drop. The clock on the wall begins to tick again.

"Sharif and them say they real sorry to hear about Chevy," says Bass. My mother puts a finger to her temple. "When we tell Onions – allyuh know how close Chevy and Onions was – Onions ain't say anything. He just hear the words, look past me, turn around, and walk into he house, close the door quiet, quiet behind him, and that was that. I don't think he will come to the funeral."

My mother pushes her chair out from behind her and walks to the kitchen counter. As if letting dice roll from her hand, she lets her plate clash against the tin iron of the sink. Auntie Moira elbows Bass and he says in his deep voice, "What I say? I say anything wrong?"

"When allyuh finish eat," says my mother, turning to Moira and Sangeetha, "let we gone sit under the tree."

"Leela, is too cold for we to sit outside," says Bass.

"Is not too cold," she says. "We have coats. Moira, when you finish eat, come. We have plenty to do. If you not too tired from your flight."

"Nah, I ain't tired," Moira says. "I wouldn't be able to sleep, anyway."

Auntie Rani clears her throat, despite not having said a word. She takes her plate and glass to the sink, and with her back to us all she looks like a man, her shoulders and arms jerking in small movements as she washes her wares. After, she walks past my mother, who does not look at her, to her room down the hall.

Rani's room door clicks closed. My mother says, "Good," then, "Sangeetha, put on your jacket and you come, too."

"It's cold though," she says.

No one says anything and then Auntie Sangeetha says, "All right, all right." When my mother turns back to the sink to wash the dishes, Auntie Sangeetha looks at me, juts out her lower lip, and brings her fists to her cheeks, mockingly crying while looking upward to the ceiling like she is one of my sisters at the table instead of my much, much older aunt.

5

I was made to understand that something was amiss with Chevy when I was seven years old. It was one of the last times I would taste the freshly roasted peanuts of Macaria my mother used to buy for us before going to the temple. I was a wearing a heavy, white frilly dress, the only dress I wore to the temple and loved so much that I cannot recall anything my mother wore to the temple, ever. I don't know why Briony or my father weren't with us, but I remember my mother and I holding hands in the early hours of that Sunday morning before most people had yet risen and there were cars on the street. It felt special and sacred, not because we kneeled before gods adorned with gendas and lotuses and flickering flames under a high-ceiling dome that stretched to the sky, but because it was just the two of us. Like teenagers, we put on our best clothes without saying a word to each other and snuck out, carrying our shoes to the door before slipping them on, and clicking the door closed behind us. The sky that morning was not yet fully lit by the sun, a thin sliver of a left-over crescent moon could still be seen, and for the tropics it was a crisp dawn.

As we were leaving the house, my mother cursed to herself, and went back upstairs to fetch her purse. In the large, dark open space of the main room downstairs, the hammock held an ominous bulk from which leaked curls of smoke. In the rarest of moments, Chevy and I were alone in the same room, not by intention but natural circumstance, and whenever I had found myself only in his company, I would scamper away uncomfortably. Now, on this morning, something else seized me, a kind of quiet courage and daring, perhaps the idle curiosity of a child-in-waiting, that caused me to walk to him.

At the hammock, I found Chevy sleeping, except that he could not be sleeping if he was smoking a cigarette. Here was the Legend of Chevy, I thought, whose legs had thundered alongside a car of the same name and thus labeled him henceforth. Here was a man I had heard more about than talked to, even though we walked past each other every day. He was in his early twenties then and looked it, except for the slight folds in his face beginning their permanent settlement – one on his forehead and one under each eye – that Onions had once attributed to a long life rather than a long night. I wanted to poke his cheek, as children are wont to do, but I knew that would be further crossing a line. He smelled of tobacco and sweat and laid with his arms folded across his chest as though angry at someone. His lush hair was held in a low bun with a beige rubber band. He turned to me and opened his eyes.

As though expecting it, I said, "Why you not sleeping in your room like everybody else?"

He looked past me to the dawn out the window.

"You want to come to the temple with we?"

He took a pull from his cigarette and blew it away from my face.

"We could buy them roasted peanuts Ma does buy. You ever had them before? They good."

When he said nothing, I waited and said, "Can I try that?"

40

He looked to the cigarette, then back at me and smiled. He shook his head.

"I wouldn't tell Ma," I said, and just at that moment a bodiless hand grabbed me by the elbow and pulled me out from the darkness and away from Chevy. My mother pinched my neck and I began to cry.

Once we had walked some way from the house, my mother bent low to my face and wiped my tears. "I had to pinch you, baby," she said, blowing air on my neck where it had turned red. "How many time we tell you and Briony to leave Chevy alone, don't ask him anything, don't bother him. He does like to be by himself and don't like to talk too much. You understand? Come, baby, I didn't pinch you so hard."

I rubbed my neck and looked away.

"Why he don't like to talk?"

She took my hand and we began to walk again. "I don't know why, Cassandra. That is just how some man is."

"Like how?"

"Just silent. Strong and silent they does be."

"And ladies, too?"

"No. Sometimes. Mostly man."

At the temple, my mother and I walked through its halls and kneeled before Lord Shiva and Mother Lakshmi. We clasped our hands together, and when my mother started whispering her prayers, I closed my eyes and did the same. I heard bare feet brushing against the ground, the striking of matches, more whispers and wishes. I basked in it, this peace, this quiet, this feeling of being good and obedient, this incensed air. It was there I learned that silence was holy. And later, that it was deadly, too.

6

After dinner everyone went their separate ways. Hypnotized by the water I swooshed around in a small pot, I knew exactly how my family, like debris, would divide to their corners of the house. I knew that Uncle Bass, who said he could feel "this wicked cold" settling into his old bones, would go to the spare room to get some rest. He ascended with Cece to the second floor, where she headed straight to her room with a tall glass of water, a leaning tower of cookies on a saucer, and an entire roll of paper towel as if rationing for an unforeseen amount of time. Briony went for a walk. Auntie Moira waited for my mother to lead the way to the backyard, standing there and peering through the window as though readying to embark on a great pilgrimage. Sangeetha, believing she could make her way to her room in the basement without anyone noticing, but feeling her sisters' eyes on her, kicked a stout leg up and made a sharp U-turn toward the foyer where they grabbed their jackets. Through the window, I watched them tread through slush and dirt to the backyard, and Auntie Moira, unaccustomed to winter boots, walked like a duck, catching herself twice when she slipped on ice.

Hot tap water runs over my hands and its heat spreads to the rest of my body. From the kitchen window, I am watching my mother, Auntie Sangeetha, and Auntie Moira under the apple tree. When they turn their faces back to the house, their lips are moving.

My phone pings. There are no new emails from my editor or clients. Ines has texted me again, asking how everything is going, how is everyone? She adds that it doesn't look too cold in Toronto, so at least that's a plus. Her last text says that she hopes I am handling everything well. She ends it with a formal, somber period.

Ines is a good friend, the only one who has cared enough to stick around for more than twenty years. We met in school when we were eight years old, I having just moved to Toronto, she from Ireland. From there we went through childhood to adulthood, through awkward teenage phases of wobbly eyeliner and heavy metal, bad boys with good hair, to the convoluted decade of our twenties thinking our lives were over because we didn't have men in them, then to entering our thirties and not giving a fuck. We went from vodka to wine, lip gloss to lipstick. She has red hair and hazel eyes, and freckles on her cheeks and arms. She is extroverted, blunt, and forceful, and it has not always been an easy friendship for her with my long withdrawals, sad spells and innate cynicism. I tell her too much that were we ever to meet at our current junctures in life, we would not look at each other twice.

I close my eyes and shudder from the pleasure of the tap water's warmth, but of also seeing these yellowed walls again. Of seeing the radiators' black iron beneath their flaking paint, the chandeliers in the kitchen and living room missing half their lightbulbs. Of creeping down to the basement for no reason other than to feel its darkness again, the navy carpet spongy under my feet. Of walking to the brick-exposed laundry room and remembering how violently, how wildly, the washing machine shook in its spin cycle. Of reaching, on my tip toes still, for the cookie tin, a time capsule preserving our historical artifacts of Kinder Surprise toys, clothes pins, Monopoly pieces, Canadian Tire money, single strands of long sewing threads should we ever need seven centimeters of it in red. Of walking back up the basement steps, conditioned by Auntie Sangeetha to lean to the left on the sixth, seventh, and eighth steps near the top because they creak and wake her up, leaving her to pace the halls at night because she can't fall back asleep, not when "they walking up and down, up and down like jumbee."

Once when I was a teenager I had found her crying at the bottom of the basement steps in the middle of the night.

"Auntie?" I called from the top of the stairs. I flicked the lights on from above. She turned and looked at me and I gasped. Water splashed out from my glass and onto my toes. Without her eyeliner, lipstick, and floating mole, in my sleepy stupor I thought I was looking at the moon – pale, naked, cratered and veined with deep lines. I did not recognize her and she hissed at me like a wild animal and told me to turn off the lights, turn them off right now, and with my hand still on the light switch, I put her back in the dark, leaving a small puddle of water in my place.

"Ignore her," my mother had said when I woke her. "That is how she is." She was falling back asleep. "You know how much time Ma and Pa had to ask she why she sad, why she sad?"

My mother never talked about Grandma and Grandpa. "What did they say back to her?" I spoke quickly like I was losing the signal. "What was she sad about? What did they say?"

"Oh, I don't know, Cassandra. Nothing, really. Gone and sleep, nah…" Her mouth froze like she was singing the *oooohh* of a choir verse, and then she was gone.

Outside under the backyard tree lay dozens of frozen apple cores. In the summer and fall, pale green bulbs of Granny Smiths dangle on high branches whose arms reach upward in cheer. When Chevy moved up to Toronto with Auntie Rani to live with us, even though he was a grown man by then, he used to keep watch for when the apples came into bloom. When pink and white clusters of flowers peeked out from their stems, so, too, did Chevy's face from our kitchen window, and like a ball boy at a tennis match, he would dart out into the backyard with a small red pail that I never saw any other time but for this sole purpose.

One summer, he had assigned me, a then angsty sixteen-year-old, and Cece, to hold buckets under the tree while he jostled the branches with one of its limbs. Through the language of quick, pointed nods and offhand flicks of his wrist, we had long become fluent in his manners of communication, translating immediately where he wanted us to stand and in what position. Cece made a game of it, saying that whoever could catch the most apples in their bucket on their side of the tree won, though we never said what. I was too cool for the game, I thought, in my Nirvana t-shirt and black plastic bracelets stacking up my skinny arms. But without realizing I was enjoying it – sprinting from side to side with my face turned up to the sun when an unsuspecting apple loosened from its stem – I started to lose myself in it, I forgot that I was playing. I yelped and dove and got dirty.

This went on for the whole summer, and at the end of it Cece won, catching a total of twenty buckets, myself catching only seventeen. I blamed the loss on the fact that I was left-handed and standing on the right side of the tree. Cece said that it made no sense because there was no left or right of the tree. "Then define 'sides'," I had said. Chevy was sitting at the picnic table and he began to laugh. When Cece asked if what she said was stupid, he smiled, and shook his head.

The first three weeks Cece and I captured the young apples, the house smelled crisp and perfumed like fresh linen. Buckets, crates, and cardboard boxes piled into the corners of the kitchen against the walls, and when they were full, the kitchen pantry, wobbling against each other. We were giddy with gold; every time we hauled a bucket into the house – our bony shoulders staking out from our small backs like axe blades, arms stretching downward and quivering from the weight of the treasure, and our knees pointed outwards like bow-legged pirates – we giggled and muttered among ourselves, madlike.

Of course there were bad apples, too, deformed with bulges under their skin, sour to the taste when we gave them a chance. Some had deep brown holes with worms crawling out of their ends. Once, Chevy picked one up and in a perfect arc threw it into the Einhorns' backyard, a few houses down from ours, on the other side of the brown reed screen. Chevy tossed three, maybe four apples, into their yard, and the last bad apple he threw to me. I caught it and turned it around in my hand. I pulled my right arm back and catapulted it. It went clean through their back window, punching a hole dead through the center of its pane. Chevy looked at me, let out a scoffing laugh, and we ran inside.

My nostalgic smile drops from my face and suds sting my eyes when I wipe my tears. I slide a sponge around a plate in weightless circles. At the backyard's picnic table, Auntie Moira is zipped all the way up to her chin, her eyes darting between the house and my mother. Auntie Sangeetha parts her mouth to say something, but my mother holds up her index finger for her not to interrupt Moira. Auntie Sangeetha looks down to her folded hands in her lap.

The phone begins to ring – its quick trilling tells me it's long distance – and on its fourth ring when no one answers, I tut, wipe my hands on my pants, and run to the corridor landline.

"Hello?"

"Hello, good evening." A pause. "Who's this? Cecelia?"

"No. No, this is Cassandra…" I can still see a sliver of my mother and aunts through the window.

"Cassandra, this is Charlie mother. You remember me?"

"Um… I think so…" I don't.

"I know you since you was a little, little girl here," then, "Oh, God, I was real sorry to hear about Chevy, girl." She begins to cry. "Your mother there? Put she on for me, please, baby."

"They went for a walk, Auntie. I'll tell them to call you back, okay?"

Through sniffles, she gives me a phone number even though I tell her we have call display, and ends the call by telling me I must pray every night.

In the corridor, through my slanted view of the backyard, their lips part and unpart, faster and faster until they are speaking all at once, fast, fast. When each turns her face back to the house, her mouth remains pointed in the direction of the tree like the arrow of a compass, their words moving quickly and spreading like the crackling of a quiet wildfire.

*

I send my editor a cryptic two-line email that implies death and privacy, and do not set an end date for my out-of-office reply. I eat the cake half sitting up, half lying down on the pullout couch in the living room attic, waiting for my mother to come out of the shower. Just after I had hung up the phone, someone knocked on the front door bearing a cake on a platter and the shyest of smiles. The woman said they (whether she meant her family or the whole of Florence Street, I don't know) were sorry for our loss and hoped this helped in whatever small way it could. Confused, I accepted the cake, and stuck my head out the door to watch her turn down the sidewalk. She must be one of the newer neighbors.

On my way up to the attic, the entire house is dark, pitch black as it always is in the winter after 5 p.m. I walk confidently into the shadows – I could do so with my eyes closed and my hands tied behind my back. I pass Auntie Rani, who presumably sleeps since no light leaks from beneath her door, up to the second floor where Uncle Bass, Cece, and Briony have their bedroom doors shut. I balance a slice of cake on a saucer in my palm as though it were a candle in a chamberstick lighting my way. The third flight of stairs groans beneath my feet making my nearness known.

When my aunts and my mother had come through the backdoor and back into the kitchen, I was wiping the already clean kitchen table. They were out there for a little more than fifteen minutes. They walked across the room in single file with their faces to the floor as if trying not to lose focus. My mother's face was stern and confident, like she had made an important decision. None of them fidgeted, they didn't touch their pockets or shudder from the warmth of being inside. They did nothing characteristically human, only moved mechanically, one foot in front of the other, to get in and get out. Auntie Moira had a soggy apple core stuck to the heel of her shoe, and like a snail it left a thin film of sleet trailing behind her.

"Cold outside?" I had said.

"Yeah," said my mother.

I looked to Auntie Sangeetha to roll her eyes at me, loll her tongue out, tell me I missed a spot, wink mischievously, do something, say anything. But nothing. She was the last in line and kept her eyes on the floor until they reached the corridor, where my mother climbed the two flights of stairs to the attic in perfect slaps of two seconds per step. Moira, close behind her, shuffled. Sangeetha, ever so slowly, had descended the basement steps to her own room where I heard the door shut and the industrial deadbolt slide across it.

Now, my mother comes out of her room into the narrow hallway. She is wearing a pink bath robe and unravels her wet hair from a towel.

"Did you guys have a good catch-up?" I say from my bed. I put the empty saucer on the ground next to me. "You guys were out there for so long." She says nothing. "It was cold."

"I didn't know you sat outside in the cold now," I say, throwing my legs over the bed. I get up and walk to her. Drops of water land on my face as she thrashes the towel through her hair. She goes back to her room and pulls out a blow dryer from the closet. "Is everything okay?" – a stupid question.

I step into her room and close the door behind me.

"Ma?"

She turns the blow dryer on high.

"Ma?" I say louder. She looks at herself in the wide mirror of her vanity chest and flips her hair.

I shout this time. "Ma!"

She shuts off the blow dryer, pulls it from its socket from the middle of its cord, and throws it on the bed.

"What!" she shouts. She looks behind me to the door. "What you harassing me for so?"

I remind myself that she is grieving.

She begins to breathe heavily and shake. She brings her fingertips to her face, as though she has been in a horrible accident.

The sound that comes from her mouth is that of an animal, a shrieking, a spirit set free from her body that pierces the night. It is the loneliest sound I have ever heard, even more than no sound at all. I have heard it only once before, at my father's funeral.

She lifts her face, now damp and red, from her hands. She clears her throat.

She moves away from me and pumps lotion into her calloused palms, sniffling and sitting on the bed. I sit next to her, and like a cushion upon impact, feel myself deflate. The bed springs creak under us, and downstairs, someone shuffles in the hallway. There are two inches between us. I feel the warmth of my mother's leg creep into my own, trickling to the edge of my skin like a ripple of tepid bath water, comforting and haunting at once.

7

In my high school chemistry class, I took care to write down and underline twice that in order to split an atom, a neutron had to be traveling at just the right speed to hit the nucleus. Under the right conditions of impact, the nucleus split into two pieces, and energy – *voom* – dispersed. When that 14-wheeler hit Junior off his bicycle – traveling at just the right speed to kill him instantly – it also set into motion the Great Disperse – that is, my family's slow descent into division, then a rather rapid drifting into an arresting silence. A week after Junior died, Auntie Tippie – his and Chevy's mother, and a figurehead evanescent to me – was hit dead on the very same road.

My sisters and I know these things. No one has ever sat us down and told us exactly what happened, not like how we knew the Legend of Chevy word for word. We learned about it in whispers, when someone had too much wine, or when my aunts or mother felt a memory coming back to them like a premonition and one of us happened to be within range. Each of us – Briony, Cece, and I – have heard different parts of the story, and when we were younger, full of vigour and curiosity, and not yet dampened by the shortcomings of adulthood, we tried to glue it together like a broken vase. In the end, our questions only led to more questions, and too afraid to ask anyone, we let silence fill the cracks, which later would prove to be faulty caulking. All we knew was: a truck killed Junior, Junior's death killed Auntie Tippie, Chevy stopped talking. These words, like "I love you," needed to be said only once to be remembered.

*

In Trinidad, my grandparents died relatively young, my grandmother of an untreated cancer, and my grandfather of arrhythmia, a condition that made his heart beat too slowly. When Auntie Sangeetha spoke of her father, the sole breadwinner of the family, she made a point to always mention that he was a strong, strong man, one who was marked with the decades of Trinidad's "real ripening" all over his body.

His feet bore the markings of the year 1923; his baby toes grew inwardly from wearing tight shoes until he was six and child labor was (mostly) dissolved. Indented on his left calf was 1935, where a bullet grazed him in one of the riots when they used to "strike with they life." Two years later, when he lost his best friends – twin brothers from Penal's bush – in a "people's riot" ("nah, them police crack they head open," my grandfather had told Sangeetha), he quit the oilfields as a motor mechanic and locally became known as the "Any-ting Man". Whatever odd job needed doing – fixing doors, painting houses, driving trucks, "anyting, anyting" – he would do it, as long he worked alone. 1941, the same year he met my grandmother, was a translucent scar etched on his ribcage when he got into a scuffle with an American solider after telling him to go back home. When the American replied, "You wouldn't want to be calling mother 'mutter' now, would you?", my grandfather had cuffed him in the face (and attracted to his patriotic zeal, my grandmother married him that year). He entered the fifties on a stiff back; he had thrown out my grandmother's and his sixty-pound Zenith television set on impulse, sick of hearing election news, every hour, every day. Already exhausted by the world in his early thirties, he turned his attention to more personal affairs, welcoming the birth of his firstborn, then four more daughters within the decade, during which he lost all his hair. In 1962, he allegedly spoke of more ethereal happenings in his body than on it; finally, he said, they were slipping out of the womb, when Trinidad gained independence from the United Kingdom. Six years passed, and when my grandmother's heart slowed and stopped, so, too, did my grandfather's only a few months later.

"Isn't that romantic?" Auntie Sangeetha had said to me. "He died of a broken heart."

At the time of their father's death, Rani was eighteen years old and Sangeetha, the youngest, was eight. There was a period of mourning of which I know nothing, other than a few unprompted sentences Auntie Moira once said to me when I was very young. (I thought I was becoming quite the confidante in our family, getting used to being pulled into dark corners by one aunt or the other to lend me another piece of the puzzle, until Briony told me they had done the same to her when she, too, was young, and stopped when she started developing breasts.)

It was on one of her visits to Toronto when Auntie Moira said, while watching a *Mama's Family* rerun, that not only was Mama wearing an obviously fake wig and "fucking up she lines", but the only greater pain than losing your mother and father within months of each other was losing your little boy in the same lifetime. "That is what Tippie had to go through, my poor sister, so you can't really blame she for she state of mind when she die. You know?" I didn't.

"There is only so much the body can take. You know what I saying?" she said. Then she let out what sounded like a gasp and a sob, cut short by a belch that made her cheeks puff out and her lips flap like coattails in a breeze. A stench of vomit and barley traveled across the room. "Excuse me," she said demurely.

She went on. She said that once you had stayed alive – no, *remained* alive – to witness this happen to your family, when you realized that you could never truly be happy for the rest of your living days, only then were you free because the worst had already happened. To be happy, she said, was to forget. "And forgetting is a sin. Is a selfish thing. Jesus giveth and Jesus taketh," she said, which I thought was strange because she was wearing an Om pendant around her neck. It was a mess of words; an empty wine bottle was at the foot of her chair, and she was slurring and talking about everyone and everything at once. I was awkward and alone with her and did not know what to say. "She's trying her best," I said about Mama on TV. Auntie Moira steupsed and threw a beer cap at my face. She asked if I shouldn't be in bed by now. I went up to my room with the beer cap in my fist. In my notebook I taped it down to a page and wrote down, "The lord giveth and the lord taketh" and "The body can only take so much???"

After their father died, my aunts, in mourning, isolated themselves from the outside world, including that of extraneous family who may or may not have been blood related. They took it upon themselves to make their house a home again. They could not cry forever, Rani said, and Sangeetha, as young as she was, had arched an eyebrow in defiance as if to say, "Watch me." Under fresh portraits of Grandpa and Grandma, framed in purple wood and held up by twine on a single nail, the sisters held a meeting in the living room of their humble bungalow in Macaria. They did not sit down, but stood in a perfect circle invoking their duties. Rani spoke. She said she would go from part-time to full-time cashiering at the Macaria SuperSuperMarket, and Tippie would quit school to join her. Tippie, glamorous even in her grieving, her hair full and high even before she rolled out of bed, and her skin dewy and flushed pink from hourly tears, nodded at her younger sisters as if to say, "Yes, it's true." Moira, who did not yet have a gut; bare-faced Sangeetha, who would not discover her signature eyeliner until her teens; and my mother, who had no excess of proportions, even in her adulthood, nodded in subservience.

Everyone else would stay in school until they were at least fifteen, Rani said. Moira, who was gifted with a green thumb, one she had cultivated under the guidance of her mother, would tend to the garden, ensuring that their tomatoes, cucumbers, squash, carilli, and herbs came from their own backyard. Sangeetha, who was said to have her head in the clouds, sauntering to and from rooms, running her fingers along the walls, took long, searing showers, and reacted moments after a question had been asked, would be best suited to keep the house clean. "Keep two pillows on the living room couch," Rani had said. "And make sure to always fluff and beat any dust out of them."

"But Ma and Pa always keep three pillows on the couch," said Sangeetha.

"I know," said Rani. "But they not here anymore and we have to stop living like they coming home any day now. We have to change it up. We have to build something new." None of the sisters said anything.

Rani continued. The shower curtain was now to be pulled to the left, not the right, when not in use, and the mirrors wiped of steam. There should be no unwashed dishes in the sink at any time, and laundry was to be done every week, hung, ironed, and folded on the same day. Rani said that when my mother turned fifteen, she would join her two older sisters at the supermarket. Until then, after school, she was to keep an eye on Moira and Sangeetha to ensure things ran smoothly, that Sangeetha did not lament around the house all day, that Moira did not sit in front of the television eating too much, and that none of them at any time, went outside the house and wandered the streets alone. My mother, the middle child, and now, middleman, nodded once in agreement. Moira shrugged her shoulders. Sangeetha did not react.

"But," Rani said, "Moira alone cannot maintain the garden."

"Yes, I can," said Moira. "Ma show me how and Pa always let me do it on my own. I could do it. I could do it on my own."

"Yes," said Tippie. "She is perfectly capable."

"She is not 'perfectly capable', Tippie," said Rani. "She is ten-years-old. If Moira mess up the garden, a whole season of food gone. It will cost we more, both to buy food and to make the garden right again. Leela could help she."

"Leela don't know anything about gardening," said Moira.

"I know a little bit," said my young mother. "But I don't want to be in the garden, anyway. It does get too hot. I could keep a watch on she from the kitchen self."

"Everybody who think Moira can deal with the garden on she own, raise they hand," said Tippie. Everyone but Rani raised their hand.

Rani steupsed. "They's just children," she said to Tippie. "They don't know."

"We cannot do everything weself, Rani. Moira wouldn't mess it up," said Tippie. "Let we trust she. You wouldn't mess it up, would you, Moira?"

"No, I good," said Moira.

It was in small sieges such as these that Rani, the new matriarch of the family, began to lose control, and of all the elements she craved in her life at that moment, like all those who discover in death's cloaking shadow that they do not dictate to life but life dictates to them, control was the one thing she needed to take back. Her father, the person who had stood just as tall as she and taught her how to survive this world, and more immediately, Macaria – fixing the house, paying the bills, how to sweet talk her way into another job, with dignity, in case she lost her current one – was gone. How many times had he prepped her for when "the time" came, taking long walks with her down the road, and in his later days, stopping to clutch at his heart, keeping her at arm's length as time stopped, and the heat swelled and shrunk as he breathed in and out? How many times did he tell her that this heart one day would stop beating, and that her own pulse, as the eldest of the sisters, would compose the circuitry of their future, as his had done, and his father's before? In truth, knowing that these words would reverberate inside her head the second they were said – Rani being the attentive, rational, dutiful daughter – he had only to tell her twice. And though it felt to Rani like he had spoken the words dozens, hundreds, thousands of times, because of said reverberation, she was still not ready on the last walk when, at one last grasp at his heart, her father crumpled to his knees, fell into the gravelly side of the road, and set free one large breath of final life before surrender.

Her mother, on the other hand, was a figure with whom there was an unnatural distance she could never really traverse. Everyone – her sisters, her father, even herself – had deduced that mother and daughter's flimsy relationship was due to Rani being so close with her father, even in their physicalities – the dominating height, the boyishly cut hair, the tendency to look weak and ashamed if a smile lingered on the face too long. It was assumed then – as much as my indulgent imagination can conjure – that as the space between Rani and her father closed, the one between mother and daughter gaped and stayed open until my grandmother's last days.

And so, in those dark days, as Rani fell asleep and felt the tribulations and regrets of an old woman hedging within her, and he came around – yes, *he*, that nameless man who was not nameless at all, *he*, who my aunts would be bewildered to learn that we children knew of, when *he* entered my family's orbit on that overcast day in 1969, he unknowingly, with the cigarette he ground beneath his two-toned dress shoe before entering the SuperSuperMarket, set ablaze a path through time like the snaking long wick that leads to a pile of dynamite.

He had asked Rani her name, the spark took off. When she told him, he asked if she was the daughter of Rupi Rampersad. She said yes, the burning was quick. He said his own name was Blues, because he liked the blues. She laughed, saying she had never heard the music. The track before them was laid in flames.

"*What?*" he had said, and both began laughing at her cash register. Had she had hair long enough to fall in her face, she would have tucked it behind her ears.

Once Blues learned that her father had recently died, he brought her wildflowers he'd picked in the savannah. One of them was a dandelion, and when he told her to blow it out like birthday candles, she watched the spores scatter to and past his face, one of them catching in his stubble. He had the same jawline as her father and his smile was lopsided the same, too. The grey from his sideburns peeked out from under his cream Panama hat, and at just the right angle, like when he flipped through his wallet to find a bill, he looked like her father when he was deep in thought; faraway, unreachable, separate to her. Seeing the faintest of her father in Blues, she was unable to take her eyes away from his face. She quickly said thank you, cashed out the oranges in his basket, and excused herself to the bathroom to cry. When she returned to her register, Blues said that if she wanted to go for a walk after her shift, he would wait outside until she was done.

It was past eight o'clock when they began walking. They headed east, the shadows of streetlights, trees and houses yawning before them as the sun set. Spellbound by the melody of Blues' words, Rani felt at ease in his presence. There was an immediate recognition not only in his face, his eyes, his smile, she thought, but also in his being. She thought if she closed her eyes, she could still see him without any features of his body being visible at all – like he was someone from a long time ago, so long ago that perhaps they had forgotten they'd once met, and now found each other again. It was all she could do to keep herself from resting her hand in his, but she did not want to scare him, or be rejected. She was in agreeance with everything he said, and made shy because of the things stirring within her. She had few words when he asked her questions, and listened to him talk about the blues, acted impressed when he mimicked its sounds, and exclaimed when he said that music was the only thing he could rely on in life.

"Music is the *only* thing you could rely on?" she asked. "You feel so?"

"I know so. Very much so. And I lucky to find something that make me feel free. Or maybe it find me," Blues said. She smiled. "Music ain't ever going to leave me, cuss me, nag me. Everybody have to have one thing they could rely on."

Rani thought about her father and fell silent again.

After an hour and a half of walking, they arrived at the house. Blues bowed his head good night and wished aloud to see her again.

In the shower, Rani cried, off again, on again, both from the evening's magnificent stranger and the face of her father in him. She felt the tightrope beneath her loosening – that is, the loss of further control, and falling, far and fast, so soon into death's wake. She was falling and felt free; she was falling and felt trapped. The neurons of her brain jolted in each and every direction and instead of routine and schedule keeping at bay the extremities of life, the true forces of existence – love, loss – took hold. What the body was capable of fermenting now overflowed. She collapsed that night into her bed as though she had journeyed for days.

The next day, she called the SuperSuperMarket and asked for three weeks off to grieve once and for all, to get it all out of her system. The next time Blues visited, she thought, she would be a happy, laughing, unburdened girl. She may have only been eighteen, and Pa may have been the only man in her life, but she knew, by instinct, or some slow nurture that took its place in whatever modicum of womanly sense she had, that this was what men wanted. She would bring with her no baggage of her brokenness. She would keep her emotions under control. She would not challenge him, and thus, change him. In other words, she would not need too much other than his attention, and only then, sometimes. She would not need him to make her feel better having never felt bad in the first place. Yes, she would be a happy, laughing wife – should it, praise God, ever reach that point – oblivious to the wears of adulthood. Healed, she would engage with him, *reciprocate*, listen to him talk about his evening walks in the savannah, and ask questions, like where did he suddenly come from, what his father's name was, how come she hadn't seen him before, did he mind if she was two inches taller than him (then giggle), what did he want to do with his life, which blues musicians he liked, and many, many more.

It was said that in those three weeks, Rani let her sisters be. Tippie finished off the last term of her schooling, Moira tended to the garden and Sangeetha to the house while my mother supervised. Rani woke before the sun rose and came back in the early evenings, retiring to bed no later than seven o'clock, sometimes without dinner.

"Where she does go so early in the morning?" my mother had asked Tippie. Having shared a bedroom, they had woken up early and laid still in their beds. When they heard Rani leave, they ran to the front window and watched her recede into the morning mist as if she were entering another realm. She carried nothing on her body – not a bag in her hand or a fine sweater round her shoulders.

"Walking," said Tippie.

"Walking where?" said Leela.

"Everywhere. I ask around. Through the savannah, down quiet streets. Downtown. Just walking, walking."

"But for what so? She take time off just to walk up and down Trinidad?"

My mother was very young.

"Is good," said Tippie. "Is solved by walking."

The person who divulged this last bit of information to me – inadvertently, of course – on the porch of our Florence Street home, sitting with a cigarette in one hand and a Molson in the other, was none other than my cousin Chevy, though he did not know my young ears were listening. He began talking to Uncle Bass who was visiting that summer with Auntie Moira. Nearby, caught by the sound of my cousin's voice like the rare calling of a bird, I bounced a basketball in slower intervals, wide-eyed.

Uncle Bass, listening as one does to an old sage breaking his monastic oath of silence, his face leaning close to Chevy so as not to miss the spectacle of my cousin uttering full sentences, said, "Chevy, boy, how you know all these things? I just saying – don't get mad, eh – I just saying, *I* know these things because, well, everybody back home know these things. It wasn't a secret with your mother and all, you know what I saying? Let she rest in peace." He looked behind him through the open front door and down the darkened corridor as the kitchen sent forth a clash. He lowered his voice. "But you wasn't even born yet. Who tell you all these things? It wasn't good of them to tell you, I sorry to say."

Chevy looked out to the street past me. "You does get to know things. So much time does go by, you forget how you even know," he said. "But you know. And the more you think about it, the more it does make sense when you asking yourself years and years later: how life happen to me so?"

8

I am sitting in the reception on a bench by myself. My feet are crossed at my ankles and my body clenches in spasms every time a draft whooshes in through the door when someone enters. Wearing a knee- and wrist-length black dress, sheer black stockings, and little black flats topped with a shoelace bow borrowed from Cece, I feel like a little girl. People are passing and nodding to me, entering the main room where Chevy lies, and I smile politely back, thinking that they do not know what is going to happen at this funeral. I want to grab Jackie and his wife by the elbow, pull them aside and say, "Just brace yourself, okay? We're all going through a hard time." But I let them, and Susie and Luna and a few kind others from Florence Street walk on by and take their seats. I can see from here the bottom half of the coffin in the room ahead. I ask the director or assistant or whoever he is if, please, he could, please, close the door just a bit, please. He sincerely apologizes. Before he closes the door, I see people filling the seats at the back first, and the more people that come in, the closer to the coffin they're forced to sit. I think to myself, they should not have been late then, if they have to look around to see if there's anywhere else to sit, like they're at the movies. They should not be late if they do not want to see his face. But they are not late. I am not in a good mood. There are eight red-velvet Baroque seats, tall and wide, tufted and unoccupied, lined before the coffin. Today we are Florence Street royalty.

I do not know where my family is. On the twelve-minute walk here, on this brilliantly sunny day that makes the tree icicles drip and mounds of snow turn the streets into shallow rivers, it seemed an ordinary walk, except for the fact that we were all walking together. Briony had tried to say something wry, but even she could not keep up the façade. Halfway through the sentence, her voice had cracked.

On entering the funeral home, a two-storey brown brick building with vines sprouting up its walls and coiling around its corners as though it had sprung up from the earth that very day, everyone split in different directions. My mother, Auntie Sangeetha, and Briony went down a spiral staircase to the bathroom, and Auntie Moira, in her supportive wedge heels squeaking on the white marble floor, perused a corkboard of the neighborhood's recently dead. Uncle Bass trailed close behind her with his hands in his pockets. Auntie Rani stepped inside and only seeing two ways to go – down the staircase or into the main room with Chevy – retreated outside. She pulled a cigarette from the sea of frills of her white blouse. She wore gold studs on her lobes and no makeup, and her boyish hair blew in the wind.

When I turned around, my sister was heading to the main room.

"Cece," I had said, but she kept straight on, she did not hear me, or she pretended not to hear me. We were wearing the same outfit and catching a glance of us in the mirror at home before we left, I thought we looked like *The Shining* twins. In the funeral parlour with Chevy, she took her place on one of the red cushy seats, and her feet not touching the ground and only the top of her head visible, looked ten years old from where I sat. People began to touch her shoulder and whisper things to her. Her composure surprised me – she turned only her head from left to right, smiling and nodding, but kept her body poised toward Chevy.

"Miss," the funeral director says to me in a hush. I look up at him from the bench.

"Miss, your pandit has arrived. He's just parking out back. Would it be all right if you gathered your family into the main room?"

I nod and stand up and brush the creases of my dress. I turn to look at Auntie Rani who is already looking at me from the other side of the window. Neither of us has said anything to each other beyond small talk since I arrived. What was there to say? There was nothing to say. I nod at her, and she nods back, takes one last drag from the cigarette, drops it to the ground and grinds it with the toe of her boot. A few more people trickle in, touch my elbow, tell me they're sorry. I tell them thank you, and feel free to take a seat in the main room, forgetting to mention that screaming at the top of our lungs and thrashing our limbs before collapsing to the floor and being dragged out of the room by the underarms is completely acceptable and normal at Trinidadian funerals, and there is no reason to be alarmed. Just take a seat until it's over.

*

The old pandit takes off his shoes at the door and walks barefoot to the podium. He opens to a bookmarked page in a torn, tattered book and clears his throat.

"Our souls never die."

A spirit throws itself from my mother's body and she is flung from her chair.

"As a man passes from dream to wakefulness," says the pandit, "so does he pass from this life to the next." A terrible, bloated pause. "Today, we mourn Patrick 'Chevy' Rampersad."

My mother is crawling on the floor, inching toward Chevy. Sangeetha is rocking side to side in her chair with her eyes closed. Moira, whose head is bowed in prayer, clasps her hands so tight at her stomach that they have gone red. Auntie Rani sits straight and stares ahead to the middle of the room. A spirit then leaves Auntie Sangeetha; she, too, crumples to the floor. She and my mother moan, their howls fill my ears and haunt the room, shaking on the floor as the pandit goes on, paying no attention to the women he sees at every Hindu funeral. The walls contain their sorrow, making the air heavy, stifling. At the top of each of their shrills, my sisters and I flinch. I look over my shoulder and see white faces drained of blood, brown faces knowingly pained. The funeral director – one of the paled faces – brings in a basket of eight stemless flowers – one for each of us – and gently places it at my feet as though in worship. At the end of the service, we are to place it at Chevy's feet all the way up to his face before the cremation. I hear a choked sob at the back of the room, and turn around to see Onions with his face in his hands. I turn back to find my mother at the base of Chevy's coffin, reaching up for him on her knees, and that is my cue to leave.

*

The story goes, according to Onions, that nobody believed him at first.

Back in Macaria, Briony and I are eleven and eight years old. Onions is a grown man giggling, giggling as he tells us about the Legend of Chevy for the umpteenth time. In the distance, pots and wares are clinking against each other, spices are crackling in hot oil, my aunts are bickering. The television is on, but no one is watching. A car with a speaker attached to its roof is announcing the neighborhood's new marriages and deaths of the week. They are the sounds of life I never knew I would miss. Through the window beyond Onions, Chevy is doing pull-ups on a pomerac tree's branch.

"We was around twelve years old then," said Onions. "When I tell the boys at school that Patrick beat a Chevy Nova II, all of them did think I was lying. They turn and look at me and say, 'How Patrick could beat a Chevy Nova? Look at how thin he legs is.' It was true. Pat had thin, thin legs. All we had thin legs when we was that young. Well, okay, except for Chubbsy – but it only look like Pat legs was *real* thin because he was always wearing them khaki cargo shorts with them bulging kind of pocket, even though they was always empty.

"Anyway, I say to the boys, 'Allyuh, is true. I see it with my own two eye. We not calling Patrick 'Pat' or 'Patrick' anymore. He new name is 'Chevy.'

"One boy say to me, 'But how, Onions? You keep saying he win, but you ain't saying how.' A next one say, 'Onions' eyes always running water. He vision blurry. He can't be sure of what he see.' They saying one thing after the next and taking cheap shots at me – bam, bam, bam – but I ain't pay them any kind of attention. Allyuh think I lying?"

We shook our little heads at him.

"Ain't we does call Pat 'Chevy' now?"

We nodded.

"Right."

When the mocking subsided, Onions explained to the boys that Avi, the young policeman who had joined the Macaria Station only two years ago, had seen him and Patrick circling his new car outside the SuperSuperMarket in the back parking lot.

"Avi call to we, 'Psst psst psst' like we was stray dogs, and when we look up, he see that it was me and Pat, although Pat barely raise he head to look up at Avi. This car had Pat *real* shook, boy," Onions said.

"Allyuh must realize too, that at that time, everybody with ears and eyes did know who Pat was because of he *situation*, and thus," he held up an index finger, "they know who *I* was. Even when we was that young, Pat and I did go everywhere together.

"So, Avi see we. He wasn't in he police uniform – in fact, he look like a normal man that could have been we older brother, wearing he short pants and a t-shirt, holding a bag of tomatoes, so there was no need for we to run, even though we wasn't doing anything wrong. Plus, Avi was always real nice to we because of what happen to Pat – which Pat didn't like. Nobody want to be known as the boy who lose he brother *and* he mother in the same week. Nobody want to be known only for their loss. But Pat had a soft spot for Avi – and Avi for he – because Avi was the one that take he and your Auntie Rani home in the police car after the accident with Junior. And then after that, Avi *burden* heself to deliver the news about Pat mother a few days later. The rest – allyuh know. You young, and your aunties don't talk about them kind of thing, but allyuh know. And the truth is: it have to be spoken. You cannot just sweep something like that under the rug. What Avi did do for your aunties and Pat is not something that could ever be repaid. He wanted someone to tell the news to your aunties soft, soft, and not just report it like a next death in Trinidad. You cannot forget what Avi do for your family, with he gentle ways. Because after that day Avi come to tell your aunties that Pat mother dead, Avi never look the same again. After that day, he walk around like he lose a fight he wasn't looking for. The man was twenty-something at the time, and he was looking twice that."

When Avi saw my cousin and Onions circling his car, he said, "This catching too much eye from allyuh young boy. Why allyuh not in school?" He checked his wristwatch. "Is one o'clock on a Friday."

"School out today, man," young Onions said. Avi shook his head and laughed under his breath as he fumbled with the car keys.

"Patrick, boy," Avi said, studying my cousin's face. "How you doing?"

"I there, I there," said Patrick. "Avi, this is a real nice car you have here."

(Briony and I, transfixed by Onions' impersonation of Chevy – the full sentences that had once come forth from our cousin's mouth, and not the grunts and nods and flippant waves that we knew – thought he seemed more myth than the Legend of Chevy itself. Had our cousin really once spoken in full statements, the highs and lows of his voice conducting the singsong of our accents? Had this muted figure that moved among us once posed questions? Asked what was for dinner? Wished someone well? Had opinions? Held *conversations?* No, it couldn't be. But yes – it was once so).

Patrick was circling the car. His loose, light waves stopped at his shoulders which, like his arms and chest, were starting to take a defined, trim shape. His eyes moved over the silver sheen of the words *Nova II* that flashed against its scarlet red paint. The tires were tight and glossy, plump under its brooding frame, and when he flicked it with his index finger, the flesh under his nail pulsed like its own beating heart.

"If you want a car like this, you will have to do well in school, eh," said Avi.

"You telling me that studying hard get you this car?" Patrick said.

"That is what I say."

Patrick nodded his head. He walked to the hood of the car and placed a flat hand on the hood as if to imprint himself on it.

"Allyuh want to go for a ride?" asked Avi.

71

"Yes, pardna, yes," said Onions, rubbing his palms together. "Take we for a ride."

"Nah, forget that," said Patrick. "Why you don't show we how fast it is, eh, Avi?"

"What you mean?" said Avi.

"I go run against it."

"Now," said Onions to my sister and I, "Avi laugh when he hear Pat say this, but not me, boy. I only open my eyes wide and smile to myself. Because I know Pat. I know he wasn't joking."

"Race the Chevy?" said Avi. "Patrick, you smoking more than cigarette these days, boy?"

"For real," said Patrick. "We go start back there," he said, pointing about three hundred feet behind them where a palm tree leaned in its grove. "Reverse the car back to the tree. Me and the car will line up next to each other, and Onions go stand right here. When Onions signal we to go, you drive and I run. What you say?"

Avi looked to Onions as if for approval, then remembered that though Patrick was acting like a big man, he was still a boy. "All right, Patrick, all right," he said.

He looked behind him and back to the Chevy, then down the street, and back to the Chevy again.

"I go reverse and bring the car back to the palm tree." He looked back to the supermarket. "Onions, you stay here and make sure no cars go down that way by the tree. If they give you trouble, tell them the police say so and they have to go another way. We only need the road for a few minutes."

Onions nodded.

The Chevy's engine roared on ignition ("Wooooo, boy! If you hear that car," Onions said), while my cousin stretched his arms and legs. He jumped as high as he could ten times, then ten times more, bringing his knees to his chest. When he began to jog on the spot,

Onions rubbed his bare shoulders from behind like he had seen coaches do for boxers in the movies.

"You go get him, Pat, you go get him good," Onions said. Patrick tied his hair into a low bun.

"Okay, come, Patrick, come!" yelled Avi from his car. The Chevy growled in the distance.

Apparently, my cousin had walked to the car the same way he walked to the grocery store when our aunties would rush him to buy green onions for the weekend stew: with no real urgency. When he reached the Chevy, Avi revved the engine just for show and smiled at Patrick with his tiny, white teeth.

Once, I had interrupted Onions. "You did see them from where you was standing, Onions? You did see Avi teeth all the way from where you was?" Onions steupsed and ignored me. He wiped a rogue tear rolling down his cheek and said he could read their lips; Avi and Patrick had wished the other good luck.

"You ready?" young Onions screamed from his spot, both of his hands pin straight above his head.

"I ready!" Avi shouted. Patrick, one knee lunged back and one tucked to his chest, both his hands spread out on the ground, nodded at Onions.

The Chevy hummed in what seemed a suddenly quiet street. Behind them, at the SuperSuperMarket, no one paid attention to the boy who was standing in the middle of the road with his hands up in the air, and the other crouched next to a car. The five birds – some kiskadees and kingbirds – that sat perched on the electric wires refused to chirp or take flight. The water in the street's open drains gurgled indifferently, and a police siren a few blocks over blared twice then went silent. The heat off the pavement wavered in thick lines on the road ahead of Patrick, blurring everything into a mirage beyond it. Onions dropped his hands to his side. Both boy and car took off.

Now here is where the true storyteller in Onions emerged, his need for fable to override fact. For though he was far from Patrick and the Chevy, for the sake of having a good story to tell the boys in the yard, he had to imagine himself everywhere at once – running alongside Patrick *and* sitting next to Avi in the passenger seat. When he told us the story, he could see it in our little faces – mouths agape and eyes flickering in wonderment – the urgent need for pace and detail and redemption.

He would come close to our faces, and feeling his hot breath on us that smelled not like onions, but tomatoes and mint, explained that in the next fifty-one seconds, the man's and boy's senses were heightened. Like a clip from a movie, spliced and played back in slow motion, time decelerated and expanded on that short stretch of road. With less weight to carry than a ton of metal on wheels, Patrick bolted ahead of the Chevy, if only by a single millisecond. Avi kept his hands steady at ten and two, darting his eyes back and forth between the road and my cousin, smiling. Though Patrick and the Chevy were still far away from him, Onions dove into a nearby shrub. From behind it he showed his face and pumped his arms. "Run, Pat, run! You beating him!"

Patrick kept his head down, his upper body leaned forward, his arms cutting through the air. The curve of his bony shoulder blades moved in and out of his back, his arms propelling him forward like the wheel rods of a steam train. Avi's foot was featherweight on the pedal – not too heavy as to completely defeat the boy, but not too light as to blatantly trail behind. When the nose of the car reached Patrick, Avi could see that his eyes remained fixed on the cement below him, rivulets of sweat streaming down his face and into his eyes, unbothered. A pulsing string of veins had emerged around his temples, and with each impact of his feet, the developing muscles of his legs shook. When the Chevy reached just ahead of Patrick, Avi

74

let his foot off the pedal, and once Patrick reached the nose of the car again, he stepped down on the gas, spearing ahead. From the rear-view mirror, Avi did not see Patrick falter. The boy truly believed he could win.

With only three hundred feet left of the race – Onions' face getting closer and closer – the boy-ghost of Onions seated next to Avi saw the young policeman lift his foot off the pedal, press down on the brakes six or seven times, sending the Chevy into shuddered stops, flip on the windshield wipers, blast the radio on the traffic report, pop the trunk, and flick on his rear emergency blinkers. Patrick barely ran past the Chevy, reaching Onions in the shrub before it. He collapsed to his hands and knees, his breath deep and terse. As the Chevy strolled in just behind him, Onions danced around his friend, grabbing his shoulders and shaking him.

Avi stepped out of the driver's seat and left the engine running. "But what the ass happen here?" He scratched his head and kicked the tires. "Shit."

My cousin looked up at Avi. "You let me win."

Avi steupsed. "I ain't let you win. You can't see the car malfunctioning? Look the wipers on, the radio blasting, the damn trunk open on it own. Even the lights blinking at the back. How I could do all that and drive at the same time?"

Onions burst into laughter and slapped his thighs. Tears – though he did not clarify if it was joy or his epiphora – ran down his face. "Avi, it look like whoever sell you that car take *you* for a ride."

"Is true, is true," said Avi. "I go have to take it back and see what wrong with it." He looked down at Patrick. "You good?"

Patrick nodded and stood up.

"From now on we go call you 'Chevy', boy," said Onions. "Pat, that is your name now. Chevy. Che-vy! Che-vy! Che-vy!"

Avi laughed. "Eh, is not a bad idea, you know. Start up a new thing. Reinvent yourself." He looked my cousin straight in the eye as if to telepathically send a message. "Let the past be the past."

My cousin turned to face Avi, his breath still sparse. He wiped his nose with his wrist, untied his hair, then tied it tighter. Kiskadees from a nearby tree flew in the opposite direction, and three people standing on the sidewalk clapped in light applause. "Yeah. Yeah, they could call me 'Chevy' if they want," Patrick said. "But I ain't going to forget my name."

When Onions told the boys in the schoolyard what he had seen, by the end of the story, they, like my sister and I, had fallen silent. They kept asking for Chevy, where was he? They wanted to shake his hand. It only took seven of those boys to run in each and every direction in Macaria for my cousin, by nightfall, to be known as Chevy for the rest of his life.

"You have to understand," Onions told us all those years ago, "at the time, we really did believe he beat the Chevy. When we get older, of course, we know the story was just that – a story. Of course we know. Tell me one story that pass on and on that is clean to the bone. Eh, maybe some of we always knew it wasn't true but at least he *have* a story. And even more so since Chevy stop talking right after that car race. We needed them kind of things when we was young, them kind of fantasy. It make we feel like we could live forever."

8½

In truth, Chevy did not want to move to Toronto.

I was ten years old when I watched Chevy and Auntie Rani come crouching out of a taxi on Florence Street. From the living room window, with Briony, my eyes went over Auntie Rani, whom at first I mistook for Chevy until I saw her standing. Seeing her for the first time again in years, I was reminded how tall and broad she was, and wondered why she insisted on keeping her hair cut as short as a man's. She had a blue and gold shawl wrapped around her shoulders, readily prepared for the northern breeze. Her chest moved in and out, slowly. I believe she was assessing the foreign air. Approaching autumn, the sky was in a swirl of colours; orange, pink, and red, and the wind was blowing in hot and cold streams.

Then my eyes did not move from Chevy for a long time. His hair still stopped at his shoulders, light and airy, waving back and forth in the breeze. He tucked one side of it behind an ear, his jawline granite and his chin strong. I noticed then that he had a nose like Caesar's, flawed and commanding, of which I could only draw the comparison having walked past a book with his face on the cover every day at the school library. He was tall, but standing next to Auntie Rani, he seemed smaller than I remembered. With one bag on his shoulder and two in each hand, he looked around him. I saw what he saw – I had seen it too, years ago, although I had been smiling: renovated Victorian and detached houses on each side of him; preened front yards with cloud-shaped shrubs and not a leaf astray; a very tall or very short tree on each lawn; evenly leveled sidewalks that dipped onto a smoothly paved road. All the houses stood in the shade at this time of day and had triangular rooftops with stout chimneys, true to a child's drawing. There was one dog in sight and he was on a leash, and aside from the man walking it, there was no one else on the street.

Later that evening after Chevy and Auntie Rani rested in their permanently assigned rooms, I wandered into the kitchen to find my mother and Auntie Sangeetha grinding dhal. Attached to the edge of the table was a dull iron medieval-looking contraption with a lever on its side that my mother wound over and over as though rolling down a car window. She was hunched over the thing, and every time she reached the top of the rotation, it squeaked. Auntie Sangeetha scooped soft-boiled seeds into the grinder's gaping mouth that came out the other end like yellow soft-served ice cream.

Taking a break, my mother wiped the sweat from her forehead with a cloth hanging off her pants' waist. I walked over to her and looked into the grinder's well, the gears of it stuffed with fluffy dhal. "Don't put your fingers in," said my mother. I coiled my fingers back into a fist.

I sat at the kitchen table and watched them.

"Ma," I said. "Ma, how come Chevy and Auntie Rani living with we now?"

"Just so."

"Just so why?"

"Because everybody grow up with each other, so all of we should be together now."

She began to turn the lever round and round again. Auntie Sangeetha's arm jiggled as she shook the dhal in.

"But Auntie Moira and Uncle Bass ain't come up," I said.

"Well, they wanted to stay in Trinidad, Cassandra. We can't force each and everybody to come up one time."

"So they coming up, too?"

"I don't know, Cassandra."

She looked up at me while she turned the lever. "What happen? Why you asking so much question?"

I swung my feet beneath the chair. "Briony say Chevy come here because he was getting into big-man trouble back home."

My mother steupsed, still grinding the dhal. "Where Briony hearing this kind of thing?" she said. "And why she telling a child all that?" Auntie Sangeetha looked at me, then looked away. She kept her eyes focused on the grinder, mesmerized by the snaking dhal piling into the basin beneath. I tried to get her to look at me, I kicked my feet a little higher and looked into her eyes, teasingly, as if I were inviting her to come play.

"What 'big-man' trouble mean?" I said. I looked at Auntie Sangeetha when I said this.

My mother stopped turning the lever and stood upright.

"Come and grind this dhal." She put one hand on her waist, and I stopped kicking my feet.

"*Come* and grind this dhal. I have work to do and you asking me these damn question like I don't have anything else to do. Come and grind this dhal now." She pointed to the grinder.

Auntie Sangeetha stopped scooping dhal into its mouth, the hovering spoon shaking, her lips parted.

At my mother's hairline sweat was beading, bursting into slick streams down the side of her face. She wiped her forehead with the cloth once more, and said, "Whew, boy, it hot," and then said nothing for a little while. My aunt and I did nothing, said nothing, as though there were two children in the room and not one.

"Throw, nah, throw," my mother said. "We cooking air tonight?"

Auntie Sangeetha set back into motion; nervous, she threw a too-large spoonful of dhal into the grinder. The seeds bubbled and spewed from its mouth, half falling on the kitchen table, half falling to the ground. Auntie Sangeetha kept saying sorry over and over. "Oh, God, Lord, Father," said my mother. Like manna, they tried to catch the overflow in their hands.

"Silly child," Auntie Sangeetha said to me later that night.

I was washing a cup, the sun had gone down, and she had come from a shadow. Everyone was in the living room, asking Chevy and Auntie Rani questions about back home, who was still living and who was not, who had a man, who did not have a man but had a child, and so on and so forth. Auntie Rani balanced a baby Cece on her knee in an unnatural but trying effort. Chevy answered questions in monosyllables with his hands flat on his thighs – yes this, no that. Up close, I thought (and dared not to say this to anyone, not even Briony) that Chevy looked older than his twenty-eight years, perhaps thirty-five or even closer to forty. Nobody remarked on it, although my mother may have noticed as she had held his face in her hands and ran her thumbs over his cheeks, looking into his eyes as though searching for something missing. The two of them stood like this for some time as everyone chattered, pretending not to notice.

"What?" I said.

"You's a silly child," Auntie Sangeetha said, closer to my face.

I nodded at the faucet.

"You mustn't ask stupid questions if you want answers. Stupid questions does piss people off and you doesn't get the answer you want."

"It wasn't a stupid question," I said, looking up at her. "I just wanted to know what 'big-man trouble' mean."

"It was a stupid question," she quipped. She unwrinkled her eyebrows and smiled at me. She moved behind me and pulled my hair back from my face into a low ponytail. The tips of her fingers were wet and they dragged along my cheek.

"Auntie," I said. "Let me finish these dishes."

"Okay, baby." She gave me a kiss on my cheek that felt more like the lick of a puppy. I groaned and wiped it away with my shoulder, not waiting for her to leave, and she ambled out of the kitchen holding on to the wall with one palm as if making her way out of the dark. For the rest of the night, all of us together again, we talked to and over each other and listened to the crickets that came with the dusk when we moved from the dim chandelier of the living room to the single lightbulb of the porch. We looked back at the faces that turned at us on the sidewalk to see who the new voices belonged to, and thought maybe we were talking too loud. But it was an event of sorts, and we soon forgot who was passing us by when the night became black. Auntie Sangeetha did not say much for the rest of the evening. She laughed when everyone else laughed, nodded her head when everyone else did, and sometimes fell asleep for a few minutes, her chin touching her collarbone before rousing awake and crying softly to herself. Nobody said a word about that, either.

9

After everyone has come home and gone to sleep, my thumbs dance above my phone's keyboard. Ines has texted me saying it's fine that I'm not in the mood to talk, she know it's a tough time, but just a thumbs up emoji or a quick message to let her know that everything is okay would be nice. She says she can see me online every now and then. Wasn't the funeral today? she asks.

Slow, stalking footsteps percuss the wooden attic steps. It is not my mother, she is sleeping in the room next to me, and she does not bear that much weight, not in mass. It isn't Cece, either, she would not climb with such conviction. I raise my head from my pillow and steady the foot of my leg that dangles off the futon. "Auntie?" I say into the dark.

"Not '*Auntie*'. Me," says a low, croaking voice.

I unlock the door and Briony pushes past me.

"What was that?" Briony says.

I exhale, turn around, and flop back down on the futon. "Briony, please. I have a headache."

"'Briony, please, I have a headache' – *what*?" She is still wearing

83

her fitted black dress that hugs her hips and a little black sequin blazer that glistens every time she moves. She has three rings on each hand, each with a different stone, and a pendant of a tiger's head around her neck stippled with tiny silver gems. In the streetlight that comes through the window and bounces off her, bits and pieces of her shapely silhouette wink like stars in a night sky. She sits by my feet.

"I'm sorry."

"I can't believe you left," she says.

"I couldn't." I sit up on my elbows and look into her eyes. Her mascara is still thick. "I tried. But I just couldn't."

She looks at me for a while until, resigning, her eyes soften and she sighs and leans against the wall the futon is pushed up against. All the metals on her clink against each other, like the neighbor's door chimes that fill the empty night. "How did you try, Cas? How? We were sitting for, like, two minutes, the pandit barely said anything, and you just left."

I lie back down.

"Where did you go?"

"To the bathroom," I say. "I threw up."

On the way to the bathroom in the funeral home, I had smiled at strangers in the crowd to assure them nothing was wrong, despite being at a funeral. I had closed the door behind me using both hands before letting go. I took labored breaths. I was nodding slowly, as though to the tune of a song only I could hear, a tune that would eventually be over if I walked myself through its bars and scales, one beat at a time. I could hear the pandit's voice through the door, mumbles and murmurs, and in the background, moaning and wailing, the grueling tenors of my aunts and mother who were naturally sopranos, saying "Why?" and "Why not us?" and "Why?" Then I heard someone shouting something. I placed my ear against the door, then shot back when a voice crescendoed into a scream. When the pandit hit his handheld gong and I heard a thud hit the floor, I wondered what the faces of our neighbors looked like, whose jaw was slacked in stun, whose tie needed loosening, whose hand was reaching for the one next to them. Who was standing on their feet to leave as I heard another thud, then a crash, then a collective gasp.

"How was Cece?" I ask. I nudge Briony with my toe.

"Cece was fine." She pushes my foot away.

Through the window, we can see the other attics of the houses across the street, black and motionless like we were living in our time zone, stuck in a midnight bardo between the waking and sleeping worlds.

"Who put the flower on Chevy for me?"

"I was going to," Briony says, slinking lower onto the bed, "but then Ma took it from me and did it for you."

"What colour was it?"

"Red."

"Oh."

She sniffles her nose.

"And… the cremation?"

Briony looks up at me, shakes her head, and closes her eyes.

A lull of nothing passes.

"Was Ma mad?"

"Don't think so. I actually think she understood."

"Was Cece?"

"No, Cas. No one was mad. Everyone had other things on their minds."

"You're mad."

She sighs and looks at me. "I'm not *mad*. I'm just disappointed."

I fake laugh and say, "Okay, Ma," then, "Thanks for organizing everything."

She shrugs. "What are vacation days for?"

Another lull.

"Hey," I say, sitting up with sudden gusto. "I saw Onions. Remember Onions? I saw him. It's crazy that he came. I mean, not that crazy, considering he was Chevy's oldest friend. But it was surreal to see him again in the flesh. He probably wouldn't even recognize me now. I would have liked to talk to him."

After a bit, Briony says, "Yeah. Yeah, Onions wasn't there. At the funeral."

"Yes, he was. I saw him crying at the back."

"No, Cas. He wasn't there. If he were, we would have all known it."

"I saw him, Briony," I say. She looks back at me and smiles tiredly. "I saw him crying. He must have slipped in and out quietly."

She chuckles as if I'm not there. "Onions? Old-time Onions? Who has never been to Canada before? Yet alone in the winter? You think that Onions came to Toronto, all by himself, found out where the funeral home was, took a plane here, came to funeral for an hour, then left and got back on a plane? Without even so much as getting in contact with us? Is that what you think happened?"

"Sorry, kiddo," she says when I cast my eyes to the side. "It's been a rough day for us all. We've all seen things today."

Windchimes outside play a slow, distorted melody.

"I heard something crash when I was in the bathroom," I say. "What was that?"

"I was waiting for you to ask. I wanted you to ask first because you – *you* – are not going to believe what happened."

"I heard two thuds. Or was I imagining that, too?"

"No. You definitely heard two thuds, all right."

"Auntie Sangeetha and Ma fainted?"

"No."

"Auntie Moira and Auntie *Rani* fainted?"

"You can keep guessing all you want. You're never going to guess this."

"There's something more dramatic than fainting…?"

There's a shuffling in the main corridor downstairs, two flights down from the attic. I check the clock and it's already tomorrow.

"Try…" Briony says, taking a deep breath, "throwing yourself onto the ground and lying there as the pandit continues to read from his book without skipping a breath. I swore I saw him lick his finger before turning a page while she was writhing on the ground."

"Jesus. Auntie Sangeetha?"

"Of course."

"That's not so bad."

"Wait," she says. She pats her dress pockets for a cigarette. "Yeah, that's not so bad," she says, and when she finds one, she pulls a purple lighter from her bra. "It's not so bad to fall to ground and cry at a funeral. I would say one almost expects that at a funeral. Wouldn't you?"

She flicks the lighter. The small flare illuminates her face. I see that her mascara is not only thick, but smeared around her eyes like burned embers of coal, her eyes red and striated.

"But would you say that crawling on the ground on your hands and knees up to the coffin, and then attempting to crawl into it, until it slides off its stand and comes crashing down… is expected?"

I shoot up on my elbows.

"Would you say *that* was expected at a funeral?" Briony says.

"That didn't happen."

"That did happen. That very much did happen. I can't make this shit up." She takes a long pull from the cigarette, and blows smoke to the ceiling. "His shoes came off."

"*What?*"

"The coffin was completely open—"

"— okay —"

"—and his shoes came off because the coffin slid from the left to the right. It also took down a very lovely wreath someone sent." She takes another pull from the cigarette. "The funeral director came to pretty quickly, though. I'll give him that." She makes a cup with her free hand and ashes the cigarette into it. "He got some other guy to help her off Chevy while he put Chevy's shoes back on and fixed him back into the coffin—"

"Can you stop saying coffin?"

"—and everyone was pretty shook from it all. I mean, obviously. Nobody knew what to do. Even the crying stopped. It was like people were like, 'Whoa, this wasn't part of the plan.' You should have seen their faces. Our faces, too. Thank God for the director."

"Sounds like something out of a movie."

"Mmhmm."

I look at the wall, my mouth agape.

"Crawl? Like, fit in with him?"

"She was saying, 'Take me, too, I don't want to be alone with this kind of thing.'" Briony was whispering now. "She kept saying that, louder and louder until she tried to get in." Briony looks into my eyes, and she drops the hand with the cigarette into her lap. "I don't know what she meant," she says. "She never says that kind of stuff."

"She always says that kind of stuff, Brie."

"What?"

I brush her fingers that are holding the cigarette ash. "I'm sorry I wasn't there, Brie."

She waves my apology away.

"Ma found me in her bed when she came home," I said. "With my shoes and jacket on."

"Did she?" Briony takes a pull.

"Yeah. She undressed me from my clothes and put me in pyjamas and everything."

I lie back down and pull the covers up to my neck like a child having just heard a horror story before bed. The attic window isn't properly sealed, nor has it ever been, and a wicked wind blows against the glass. Gas-like, a draft seeps in. We both shudder and Briony lies down in the tight space between my feet and the wall, her body perpendicular to mine so that we form an upside down *T*. Her head falls to the side facing me and with her eyes closed, her long hair swept to the side, her eye makeup smoky and smudged, and her jewels twinkling in the dark, she looks like a slain starlet. I take the burning cigarette from her hand. It hisses in a glass of water next to me.

"I can't believe Auntie Sangeetha tried to crawl in with him," I say. "I mean, I know she's dramatic, but even that. That's… something else."

"Not Auntie Sangeetha," says Briony, sleepily. She turns on her side away from me. "Auntie Rani."

"Auntie *Rani*?"

"Yeah," she says. "Auntie Sangeetha fell to the ground first, then Auntie Rani. Then when the funeral director went to help Auntie Sangeetha, Ma told him to leave her. 'Leave her, leave we.' Then Auntie Rani started crawling and we watched and yeah, that was that. Auntie Rani was the one who wanted to get in." She yawns. Before I can demand more details – what did Cece do, what did our mother's face look like, what did Auntie Rani's face look like, tell me *everything* – I hear the beginnings of her gentle snores and the dead weight of her body on my feet.

*

Then my feet are cold because Briony isn't there anymore. In my sleepy fog as I wake up, I have not yet remembered the events of yesterday. I am lucky only for these few seconds of the day. But lodged in my stomach there is a phantom that evades my hands like smoke when I try to push it back down, creeping its way back into my recognition, my brain, my mapped anxiety. I look around the room and see a glass with a swimming cigarette, a pillow with two black smudges eye distance apart, a red flower which, when I focus my eyes, is really a crumpled plastic bag, and the door left ajar at quarter past two in the morning. How foolish I am, I think, as I return. How foolish it was of me not to be at the funeral. I could have learned so much. I could have been there for everyone.

But that is not what has awakened me. There is a rousing in the hallway or somewhere downstairs – I feel it as though it were movement within my own bones. The groans and creaks of the house that once disturbed and frightened me as a child have now tugged me from sleep. My open door invites me to walk through it. In the attic hallway, I tiptoe past my mother's room and peek inside. She is asleep with her face toward the ceiling and her hands at her sides like a wooden plank and I hear it again – there – a rustling. I hurry myself back out to the hallway and fold myself over the staircase banister, stretching my body to its lengths like I'm made of rubber. When I hear, "Auntie, I'm tired," and a few other words I cannot make out, I pull back a few inches. It is Briony.

I can see straight down to the ground-floor hallway from here. All the staircases are on one side of the house, each floor a copy of the one beneath it. Like an open-faced dollhouse, I try to imagine where everyone is positioned and fixed, except for this one phantom that moves through our haunt. If I dip my head and look to the left, I can see Auntie Moira's door on the second floor is shut. It is not she who speaks to Briony. I cannot see Auntie Rani's door from here;

she is on the main floor out of my purview. I hear more – hushes and exclamations, the words "Stop!" and "That's not true, shut up", and two shadows dancing around each other. Briony is trying to leave. She is making her way up the staircase back to her room, but the shadow grabs her and hisses things, the words coming out of its mouth like steam. Briony wrangles herself free, water splashes out of the glass she holds. She runs up the staircase and I step back into my own darkness should she look up. When I hear her room door close, too loud for this time of the night, I stand still. The shadow at the bottom of the stairs does not make a sound, and the thought of her upturned face looking up at me, her bulging white eyes, the black hole that is her mouth is enough to make me whimper for my mother. I do not dare breathe or move. The shadow wears slippers – I hear them slide against the hardwood floor and slap against the soles of her feet. As the sounds fade, another makes itself known: the creaks of the sixth, seventh, and eighth steps of the basement stairs. Everything echoes in this house.

10

For a couple of cents, Rani bought a notebook. She wrote on the inside cover the name of its soon-to-be owner: Moira Rampersad.

When she gave the notebook to Moira, she said that starting today – she pointed to a July day in 1968 in its tabbed calendar – Moira was to write down everything she did in the garden, including her mistakes.

"Mistakes?" Moira had said.

"Yes," Rani said. "Mistakes."

Auntie Moira had begun telling me the story on one of her autumn visits to Toronto (she had always wanted to see the maple leaves change). She was standing at the kitchen counter, looking for a number in my mother's phonebook. Its inside cover had a stenciled drawing of a garden in bloom.

"Yack," I heard her say. I was thirteen at the time and could peer over her shoulder with ease.

"This bringing back bad memories," she said. "When I was a young, young girl, younger than you now, Rani did make me write down everything I do in the garden back home." She flipped through the phonebook, fast, fast.

"She wanted to know where the sun was in the sky when the scotch pepper ready to pick, how moist the soil was if the cucumbers come out yellow, how hard on a scale of one to ten the tomatoes was." She steupsed. "If the tomatoes was higher than seven on this scale only she know, Rani would say it not good to make choka. Your mother and I used to eat them like apples just so they wouldn't waste. It real take out the fun of the garden for me. I just wanted to do what I know how to do, you know? You don't want to *write* about it. Because once I write it down, the next time I go to garden, I was feeling too much pressure, too much method. I was ten years old – what child want to learn like that? I just used to like feeling the cold dirt on my hands. Oh, God, that feel good. Mammy used to say that as long as the dirt get under your nails, all the vegetables would turn out good. But if you don't get dirt under your nails, you wasn't doing it right." She began to giggle then, as though she were a little girl again and I smiled. "But Sangeetha," she said, as she continued to flip through the phonebook, "Sangeetha and I did have a little fun with Rani. She and she boldface ways."

Young Moira did as she was told in the notebook, but only the bare minimum so as to proclaim that she didn't *not* do what Rani had asked of her. She wrote the sun was hot, the rain was heavy, the tomatoes were a four at most, they were fine, the bird peppers were fine, too, just a little yellow at their tips. Sometimes she drew houses with smoke coming out of their chimneys, cats with bowties, or smiling fishes with gills before losing interest in its pages and returning to their television's three channels.

One evening, Sangeetha saw Moira's notebook on her nightstand before they went to bed, and already fond of books in her rare chances of coming across one, she opened it. She saw the times of the days, the names of nocturnal animals. She saw how high shado beni would grow, and how much cool water to pour onto it. She asked Moira what was this book and since when did she write? Moira said she was keeping track of the garden. Sangeetha asked how do you keep track of a garden, and Moira said, rolling her eyes and making a face, that she didn't know, *Rani* asked her to do it so she could track her mistakes.

"You could make mistakes in a garden?" Sangeetha said.

"I guess so!" said Moira. "Mammy never say anything about making a mistake when we was planting seeds. But I guess you could make mistakes now."

"I see," said Sangeetha.

"I see," said Moira.

"I see," said Sangeetha, and they kept saying this to each other, snickering until they fell asleep.

When Rani next checked the notebook, in its contents she found drawn in deep pen leafy vines, bursting strawberries, fat droplets that may have been rain or tears, and little fairies fleeting from page to page. There were simple two-line poems about birds and rabbits, about their flight and fluffiness, their secret day meetings in the stumps of trees, and so on and so forth. In between Sangeetha's fictitious little stories – which Rani recognized as her cursive from reviewing her homework every night – Moira continued to document the garden, the positioning of the moon, the direction of the wind (which sometimes she wrote as "left" and "right" or "it come from the back of me" instead of the proper cardinal directions). It was only this Rani cared to see, if even she had to decode fiction from nonfiction on every page – that Moira persisted in her gift and did not lose it – and any literary vengeance the two sisters avowed was as lost as Moira's interest in recording in the book in the first place.

I think of this book now and what I would give to see this browned almanac of their defiance, the words they gave to the green boils of the carilli, the gentle arch of the baigan. I have often thought of this relic and where in the world it might be, whose fingers might have run across it or tossed it aside, and in my own diary (the one I have the beer bottle cap taped into that Auntie Moira once threw at me), I drew my own poor rendition of a fairy sitting atop a leaf. Somewhere, buried under dirt and dust there lies a book authored by my two aunts. A true book, too, that boasts joy and uninhibited imagination, one inscribed in rebellion to the duties bequeathed onto them, where, like the strawberries and vines preserved in its pages, their sisterly love lives, too.

*

In the three weeks Rani took off from the SuperSuperMarket, she walked out of her grief. When she left the house, knowing her sisters' eyes were hovering above the front window's ledge, she would turn left down the street, then right, right again, and again, until she was on the main road. Most stores did not open until eight o'clock and few cars were on the street.

On her walks she took with her nothing except some fine change she kept in her dress pocket. She did not eat breakfast before she left home, for once on the main road she bought herself freshly squeezed orange juice, whose natural sugars improved her mood. Then, without thinking too much, she went wherever her feet took her. Sometimes it would be down Main Street and inside its coiling streets until she reached all the way to Arima. Along the way, she sat in open green areas and little shops, keeping to herself. In between places, particularly when she stopped moving, greats wells of emotion overflowed and poured through her eyes. She remembered she would not see her father again, and all the words she never said to her mother; how, unspoken, they would remain with her forever. When tears ran down her face, she let them run. If she saw someone she knew, she quickly wiped them away, stopping to talk for a while before going on her way again.

She once found herself in the opposite direction, in Port of Spain, down by the water. She sat on the port's hot concrete ledges, watching old and new water technology come and go – cargo ships, little rowboats, and two new large vessels: *Scarlet Ibis* and *Bird of Paradise* – carrying people to and from the sea bridge. People were happy by the water; families gathered, lovers necked, but the foamy white streams left behind by boats made her sad, how they lapsed back into nothing in the big, blue sea. Children threw rocks and men their anchors, paralleling her own sinking within. She imagined it – just for a few seconds – harmless – surrendering the weight of her being to water, sinking to a kaleidoscopic, all-consuming darkness. Then, suspecting that the sea's tropical but murky depths made her feel terrible things, think terrible things, she left, and did not return to the port again.

Another time, she went to Empire Cinema to watch *Love in Simla*, a Hindi slapstick musical harboring a plot she knew nothing about. How the stars sometimes align: the main character, a recently orphaned, plain girl, taunted and mocked by her family, vows to make her cousin's fiancé fall in love with her.

The theatre was speckled with more couples than friends, and like her, loners; in the dark they all looked the same. Rani smiled all the way through the film, tapping her feet while the male fiancé sang. "Who has very sharp eyesight? Whom does the wind kiss and blow? By whose words does the flower fall? By looking at whom does the moon feel jealous?"

He sang to both women.

*

When the three weeks were over and Rani had finished pitying herself, she brought Tippie to the SuperSuperMarket to seek a part-time position as planned. On the first day, the eldest sisters walked alongside each other. They had nothing to say, not because one was angry with the other or being spiteful, but because they had been opposites their entire lives. They seemed not two years apart, but ten. Rani was of a dignified calm, Tippie was more aloof. Whereas Rani liked everything at home to be in its place, Tippie remained indifferent, believing that everything was already in the place it needed to be. Whereas Rani had taken after their father, Tippie was their mother in print, bearing the same grace, demure, and naivete. They passed by the savannah where Blues had picked the bouquet of flowers for Rani. On seeing the dandelions, like the one she had blown across the stubbled artistry of his face, the details of it branded into her brain – the roughness of his skin, the smirk of his grin, the shadow that fell across his face from the tilt of his Panama hat – she smiled to herself. She had told no one about him.

Rani presented Tippie to the store owner, a spindly man with a pubescent moustache. Momentarily made dumb by Tippie's delicate beauty, he cleared his throat and told Tippie to come with him. He showed her to the back of the store where the fruits and vegetables were on display and handed her a hose that sprayed an atomizing mist. He said that every two hours, a new cart of produce would be wheeled in from the back and all she had to do was stock it. She said okay. He said the pumpkins were heavy and if she needed help call Maco, the stock boy, who not only promoted discounts, but unsolicited local gossip. He gave her a black smock with deep pockets and reminded her to spray the produce every ten minutes, so that when customers were browsing the bodi, dasheen, and oranges, they would look like they had just been plucked from the motherland itself. And, if she could also mention the on-sale items at the front of the store, that would be nice, too. She said okay and smiled and thanked him.

With aisles of canned goods, laundry detergent and boxed foods between them, from a bird's eye, the two sisters worked at opposite ends of the store. Rani, whose view of Tippie was obscured by two cement pillars, could see her sister moving back and forth between them, spraying the produce with the flick of her wrist, piling guavas atop each other into a pyramid, then stepping back to admire her work. Rani watched Tippie, who, like Cinderella, swooshed her broom across the dampened floor collecting sodden leaves, and redirected customers back to the front of the store to the sale items. It was in this way the sisters represented the start and end of the customer journey, *the flow*, the store owner said each morning, moving his noodle-thin arms in sea-like waves. Rani welcomed customers who bustled in with empty baskets and plastic bags they brought from home, Tippie guided them back to the front to the discounted toilet paper and baby food. In between logistics and strategy though, Rani hoped only to see one customer, and after two weeks, she saw him walk through the double glass doors. He came to her immediately.

"My, my, my. Just my luck. Long time no see, girl," Blues said. He cocked his head to the side, like a dog hearing a strange sound. He put a brown paper bag on her counter. Under her skin, she was blushing, and she felt her eyelids get heavy.

"I know, I know," Rani said, looking into his eyes. "I take some time off. I… I had to take care of some things."

Blues nodded. "I understand. How allyuh doing at home?"

"We there, we there. You know how it is."

"I know how it is. I forget if I did tell you, but I lose both my parents when I was a young boy, you know. It was rough."

She mirrored his smile, his gazes, the ponderous moments he looked away.

"But yours is a different situation," he said. "Ain't you have some sisters?"

"Yeah. I's the oldest one. So is up to me to make sure everything is in order. Otherwise, who will do it? Can't have them running wild."

"Is true." He scratched his cheek. "Boy, I was lucky not to have any brothers or sisters," he said through a laugh. Rani laughed, too. "Once my parents gone, I just take off from school and just kind of float around with the boys in the place, going from here to there, here to there. I think by the time I was nineteen years old, I see the whole of Trinidad."

"That sounding like adventure, boy."

"Jamaica, St. Lucia, Grenada. All them places I see, too." At this Rani gasped. She had never been outside of Trinidad, not even to Tobago.

"Well, that really sounding like adventure!"

Blues winked at her. Behind him the line was growing – neither had noticed – and the store owner tapped his watch at Rani. "I getting you in trouble it look like," said Blues.

"Nah," Rani said.

Over the next week, Blues came into the store every afternoon. In between screaming children, the clang of registers opening and slamming, and the scurry of workers following the shatter of glass, Rani developed a sixth sense for Blues' arrival. If she was cashing out a customer, she would feel the hairs on her arms rise, and as though channeling a psychic message from beyond, she tuned out the noises around her only to turn and see Blues, like a vision, walk through the door, which was no less illuminated by a wardrobe of what seemed to be entirely white clothes. He never failed to wink at her upon entering, and in return she would smile, quick to look away. Over time, she came to learn that Blues, like most people,

100

bought the same handful of items on each visit – cigarettes, some type of sweet juice, a hygienic product, and always his baseball-sized oranges.

One day, he came to her register (out of the five women working, she noticed) with cigarettes, papaya juice, deodorant, and the largest oranges they had in stock. Were the store owner not keeping a watchful eye on her, she would have charged Blues nothing. Blues said he would be back in a few days' time and hoped that it would not be so long until he saw her again. Rani smiled and said, "Yes, that would be nice." He put the groceries into his wrinkled brown bag and tipped his hat goodbye.

On the walk home that night, the moon was full and lit the path home. The sisters partook in light banter from the good mood of a day worked hard.

"You don't find Devon a little crazy?" said Tippie. "He always running around like a chicken with he head cut off."

"Devon like that from day one."

"You see how he shock heself from replacing the lightbulb in he back office? I say to he, 'Devon, boy, like you have smoke coming out of your mouth.'"

"You say that to him?"

"Yeah, why not? Devon is like a little boy. You want to know how I know?"

"Nah, I don't want to know."

The sisters laughed into the night.

Rani gave herself a moment, then said, "You does see that man that coming in every day? He kind of oldish. He does buy them big oranges."

"Which man?"

Rani did not want to say that she knew his name; they had never talked about men. "He does wear them kind of linen shirts and pants and he have that white hat like Pa used to have, with the blue stripe around it."

Tippie kicked pebbles ahead of her.

"He nice," Rani said.

Tippie shook her head. "No, I never see that man. But I see Devon bend over today to stock a pile of rice bags. He does wear little boy jockey shorts," she said, giggling.

The next day when Blues came into the store, Rani's heart quickened when she saw that in his fist he held a bouquet of wildflowers and dandelions. He seemed to be in a rush; he winked and held up a finger to indicate he would be with her in a minute, as though she were the customer. He made his way through the aisles hurriedly, and returned with two big handfuls of chenette.

"Is only this you come for?" she said. "Chenette?"

"In a way," he said, and he smiled that smile that always made her turn away. Too scared to meet his eyes (what would happen if she met them? What would happen inside her? Could she undo what was already undone?), she focused with great intensity on taking the fruit from him, each motion deliberate, careful not to touch his hand. She walked herself through the transaction in steps as if it were her first day on the job. She placed the fruit on the scale (*Okay, good, now punch in the weight*, she thought to herself. *First 5, then the decimal, then 1. Good, good.*) The cost appeared on the screen and flatly, she told him how much he owed. Blues counted the change in his hands, she counted six lines on his left palm. She put the fruit into a bag and he hung it in the bend of his elbow. He took off his hat and ran his fingers through his peppered hair.

"I finding myself in a good mood today," he said. "So I say to myself, let me get the sweetest fruit." She thought she might die right there, right then. She felt herself stagger backwards, though her feet had not moved. She cleared her throat.

102

"Rani," Blues said. "You have the eyes of a saint," and he tipped his hat goodbye. Her whole body, like a ballerina in a box, turned and saw him out the door. He turned around and waved goodbye once more.

She placed the "not available" placard at her register and stepped out from behind the counter. She made her way down the health aisle to the produce, untying her smock from behind so she could move freely when explaining to Tippie that that was the man, that was the man she was talking about last night. Some feelings are whole universes – the body cannot contain them. She needed it out of her.

A little boy ran into her stomach face first, she steupsed, gripped him by the shoulders and moved him to the side like a box. She saw between the pillars the back of Tippie swaying from her left heel to the right, misting the corn.

"Tippie," she said. She felt her heart in her throat. "Tippie," she said, placing her hand on her chest.

"Yeah?" said Tippie. She turned on the heel of her foot, and caught off guard, sprayed a couple caught it in the mist's crossfire. She laughed, apologizing, and the couple looked each other up and down, saying why go to the beach when they can just come here, wiping their faces and laughing, too.

"Okay, wait, nah," Tippie said to Rani as she ran to back room for a cloth. She bounced past her, carrying no weight at all. Leaning out of a pocket of Tippie's black smock was a stippling of white on green shoots; a burst of yellow and red flowers; two full dandelions, thick like clouds of cotton; and one standing upright and bare, its spores blown out and gone.

11

The morning after the funeral, my makeshift bedroom is cold and bright. I quickly scan a text from Ines ("Remember me?"), and a few emails from clients offering generic condolences. I leave my phone on the bed, and when I look out of the window, I see that a fresh blanket of snow has sugared Florence Street into a quaint and scenic Swiss village. From the third floor, the neighborhood looks like a child's diorama of picturesque gingerbread houses, the knobs of doors like candy buttons, the perfect geometrical snowfall on rooftops that only nature can lay. I make a visor with my hands; the snow reflects all the sunlight, its whiteness beautiful and blinding. It is mid-March, and should not have snowed this much, but none of us have been watching the weather channel.

Ten in the morning and everyone is awake. In my pyjamas, an old t-shirt and a pair of jogging pants that doesn't reach my ankles, I make my way down the two flights of stairs, passing Chevy's and Cece's rooms. Past the guest room, Uncle Bass' feet peek out from under a blanket, his brittle toenails long and pointed like the Wicked Witch of the East. Down below I hear Auntie Moira in the kitchen with my mother and Auntie Sangeetha talking about all this snow and how they won't go out the road in this weather, no way.

"You always wanted to see snow, now you seeing it," says Auntie Sangeetha.

"I never wanted to see snow, I just wonder what it look like," says Auntie Moira.

"Now that you seeing it, what you think?" says my mother.

"Oh, it beautiful, beautiful."

"Sometimes it does get so, so cold outside, that when you walking, your eyelashes and tips of your hair does turn white. And then it does thaw out when you come inside."

"No!" says Auntie Moira.

"Yes," says Auntie Sangeetha. "I telling you."

"Nah, I can't believe that," says Auntie Moira, then they are all talking over each other at once. I stand in the corridor and lean my head against the wall, listening and smiling to these sounds of innocence from long ago. My mother peeks her head from the kitchen. I nod at her and she nods back, waving her hand for me to come here, she wants to show me something. I stand there like a scared animal. "You coming?" she says. She is not mad about the funeral and I will love her forever for it.

I am surprised to see Cece sitting at the kitchen table. She is watching something on her phone and nods her head up at me. "Hey," she says.

"Hey."

She goes back to her phone and the tinny track of a video mingles with the shuffle and voices of my aunts. It's hard to believe this is a day after a funeral, that people – these people – are moving and speaking in accordance with each other like a— well, like a family. My Auntie Sangeetha brushes past me, pinches my arm and makes kissing noises with her mouth, and her slippers, which are made for

106

a man, slap against her soles. Then I remember. I remember the vision of her face last night, the naked, cold cream she fails to rub properly into her skin, rendering it pallid and ghastly, the white of her eyes and the black tunnel of her mouth, Briony escaping, barely, the creak of the basement steps.

"Good morning, sweetie," she says.

"Good morning," I say. I smile too wide, and she pinches my cheek.

"Cassandra, come," says my mother, ushering me to the kitchen window. "You see all this?"

"Yeah, Ma. I saw from upstairs." We look out to the backyard at the bare apple tree, each of its branches sheathed with snow.

"How long it been since you see snow like this? You does get snow like this in London?"

"No. Not like this." Looking at her face lit by the snowlight reflected off the pane, she looks like an angel. I give her a long, soft kiss on her cheek, and she closes her eyes.

"I fry plantain," she says. "Gone and eat."

When I turn around, Auntie Moira hands me bread and plantain already toasted and buttered, and a can of Coke. I sit at the table next to my sister.

"Did you eat?" I ask her.

"Yeah," she says. "We left the end pieces of the plantain for you."

"Where's Briony?" I say. I want to add, "Are you mad at me? Are you mad that I left?" but I'm afraid she'll ask, "Which time?"

"I don't know," says Cece. "Somewhere around."

"And Auntie Rani?"

"Outside, I think," she says.

I peer into the corridor and, like a grazing cow, chew on the plantain like a grazing cow. Its oil leaks past my wrists to the inside of my arms, and I wonder what everyone might think were I to lick it all up. I taste just my fingers and as the oil settles into my tongue, a Rolodex of memories spins through my mind: pieces cut like chips and left under a bowl after school. Seeing the plantains slowly ripen in a brown paper bag, hungry and angry that they were still hard. Macaria, in its entirety. My sister – and I start smiling to myself – splattering herself with oil when she first tried to fry it, and the homemade face mask and long-sleeved shirt she wore on the next attempt. My mother had called Auntie Sangeetha to come and see how Cece was frying plantain, then Auntie Sangeetha laughed so hard she had to run to the washroom. I let my feet swing beneath me as I finish my sandwich and have a yearning to ask my mother for my Flintstones vitamins. I tip forward in my seat, my aunts are moving from the fridge to the stove, from the window to the cupboards, cutting each other off like cars on a freeway. Down the corridor through the screen door, I see Auntie Rani feeding salt to the snow before it freezes and turns to black ice.

*

Briony is at the living room window. Her arms are folded and the billowing cup of coffee she holds fogs a small splotch of condensation on the glass. She is still wearing the same black dress and sequin blazer from yesterday, which feels like a week ago. On the hand that holds the cup, her thumb is sticking up like she's trying to hitch a ride out of here. Seeing her dress hug her hips and ass, one cheek a little higher than the other from the weight she places on one leg, I feel small and childish standing behind her in my too-short pyjamas. Her face is without expression – content, almost. The sunlight hits her rings and necklace. I watch them both: Briony's eyes on Auntie Rani, Auntie's eyes on the walkway outside.

She catches me from the corner of her eye. "What?"

"What?"

108

Her eyes move around the room. "What?"

I mirror her and look around the room, too. "Nothing." I shrug. "Nothing."

"Why are you being weird?"

"I'm not. I'm just standing here."

"Okay, weirdo."

I go and stand next to her and take an exaggerated whiff of her hair. I make myself tremble from its scent and with my eyes closed say, "You smell like summer."

She rolls her eyes and shakes her head. "Obsessed with me."

I join her in staring out of the window, first looking at Auntie Rani, then in the opposite direction, somewhere down the street. Like a general, I cross my hands behind my back and rock back and forth between my heels and toes. "How did you sleep last night?"

"Fine."

"That's good."

Auntie Rani breaks for rest, placing her hand on her lower back and stretching.

"Did you have any bad dreams?"

"No," Briony says. "Why? Did you?"

"No. I mean, I thought I was having a bad dream for a bit, but I think it was just someone walking around last night."

"What, like a jumbee?"

On any other day, I would have laughed and said, "Yes, like a *jumbee*", and widen my eyes, bare my teeth, and wriggle my fingers in her face. But it is the day after a funeral, and we are all thinking of ghosts and spirits.

"No," I say. "Just someone walking around, talking. You know."

"Oh." She looks away.

"It was probably Auntie Sangeetha pulling Cece into a corner or something," I say, staring at a house down the road. "You know how she is."

"Yeah, probably."

Salt and snow crunch beneath Auntie Rani's boots.

"Did you hear anything last night?" I turn to Briony.

"No," she says, holding her gaze on Auntie, twitching her nose and sniffling. "I was sound asleep the whole night after I went back to my room. Long day."

"Ah." I clear my throat. I give her a chance to say something; she says nothing.

"Maybe I dreamt it then."

"Maybe, it wouldn't be a strange time to have bad dreams."

"Yeah," I say. "True." I turn my face toward Auntie Rani. "True, true, true."

*

Briony started stealing, we think, when she was around fifteen years old. I say "we" loosely – I'm speaking on behalf of everyone, though we've never said it to each other out loud. But it became harder and harder not to say one or two words about it when two policemen were standing on the front porch for the second time in the first year Briony started her new hobby. When my mother opened the front door and they said they'd have to take her in next time, she replied, "Take she. Take she in."

As Briony and I watched Auntie Rani shovel the last bit of snow onto the sidewalk, Briony had said that she needed some air and she was going for a walk. I told her to at least change out of yesterday's clothes. She said fine, went upstairs, and descended wearing a dress even shorter, lifting it at its edges like she was a bride. My sister blew me a kiss.

"I'm going for a *walk*," she said, and she went out the door with her coat unzipped, tiptoeing over the salt and slush in her heeled boots past Auntie Rani.

Fine, I said to myself, I'm going for a walk *too*. My mother came up from behind me and told me to put on some warm clothes, we were going back to the funeral home.

On the way to the attic, I go into Briony's room. The carpet is still its baby pink from when we first moved into the house and Briony was thirteen years old. I can only see spots of it here and there as I step over flats and heels and boots, hosiery, shopping bags and totes – some with the price tags still attached: $199, $49.99, $349. The single bed, which I cannot fathom how it bears her now womanly weight, is dressed in its blushed silk sheets with wavy frills that curl at its ends. A pile of shimmery black dresses, silk and suede, drape over the chair in front of a vanity mirror with round bulbs lining the glass. When I walk over to the turn off its lights, my stomach sinks as my eye catches a $999 price tag on a pair of unworn Valentino heels. That's a big one, I think. That's a really big one.

I look out of her bedroom window to see what she sees. There is a clean view of the backyard, and from above everything under the sun and snow glistens like glass. The house is quiet now. After breakfast, Cece went back to her room and closed her door, my mother and Auntie Sangeetha sat in the kitchen peeling bodi, and Auntie Moira and Uncle Bass watched television on near mute in the guest-room. I did not once hear them say a word to each other. It feels like a December afternoon, close to Christmas when there's nothing to do but lounge, eat and stay warm inside, with the addition of a funereal mood.

I run my fingers along the silvers, golds and diamonds on Briony's dresser. They tinkle against each other like little bells.

Despite the police's warnings to my mother in Briony's teenage years, Briony was never taken into the station or charged. She was pretty and underage and she flirted. She knew all of this, too – the way she checked the cuticles of her nails, rolled her eyes, or looked laconically to the side as the police – almost always men – ran through a list of items they found in her backpack. I wouldn't be surprised if she said something inappropriate in the back seat of the police car on the way home, perhaps held eye contact for just a moment too long. Flesh on her moved at a young age, and like an artificial intelligence becoming conscious, she became aware of what was a dormant power. She had made grown men feel uncomfortable, and it made me uncomfortable when I was witness to it. I have seen her "activate herself" – a phrase we used to say when she was "ready to roll" – more times than I can count, the first being when she was fourteen and I was nine. We were walking to Tim Hortons and she said she wanted to try something, but wouldn't tell me what. Once we got inside, I sat at a table pretending to read a newspaper up to my eyes like an undercover cop. I watched her talk to the thirty-something-year-old cashier, smiling and tilting one side of her face toward him. When he sat down for his break, she sat across from him and rested her chin in her hand, smiling and gazing into his eyes as if they had been through something private together. I myself smiled and gazed at her from the other side of the shop, and every time we went back for the whole year and saw that cashier, we got everything for free.

She moved on from frappés and donuts quickly. From the success of the coffee shop experiment, she began to extend her talents to other parts of her body, like her sleight of hand. She began with little things – candy and earbuds – from convenience stores and pharmacies, but only when men were on their shifts. If they were too old, "like you could blow the dust off of their face," she didn't bother. They were more pissed than perverted, she added, and already suspicious of us young brown girls. Like her young protégé (not of stealing, but of the world, of wanting, of life to know risk), I nodded.

I hated when she moved on to local malls, and then to big ones like Yorkdale and Eaton. Not because of what would happen if she ever got caught, but because of what would happen if *I* ever got caught *with* her. Though I didn't yet know my dreams, I knew I did not want the capacity to dream to be taken away. The big malls had real security guards walking around in trios with their hands on what I thought were guns. Briony used to tell me not to make eye contact with them or anyone who worked in the store, and I always did, every time. I never knew how not to tell a secret with my eyes. Alas, it was a secret no one wanted to know, not from something so scrawny, so meager, with such flat hair, so obviously incapable of crime. The guards were mostly suspicious of young girls who wore leather jackets and dyed their roots red, or boys with bags under their eyes and both hands in their windbreaker pockets.

I never participated in the act of stealing – not once; there was nothing I wanted but books and songbirds, and those I could get for free if I sat near a window in the library. But whenever Briony asked me if I wanted to hang out at the mall, foolishly, I thought she meant to eat junk food, look at what other girls were wearing, finger clothes we had no money for, talk about boys. I thought we might step out and be normal. And though we did run our fingers through the denim and plaids and studs of the nineties, only one of us was slipping them into our bag. I remember watching her reach for a chartreuse cashmere scarf from behind an earring rack I spun round and round in The Bay. Her fingers were, and still are, long and bony at the joints, alienesque, so that when she reached for the scarf it was with such precision and fluidity, such machinelike confidence, that I thought she might have made an excellent surgeon.

When she let the scarf cascade into her bag, it was with such grace, as natural as autumn leaves falling to the ground, it would have been offensive to interrupt such a performance that only the cameras and I were privy to, or suggest otherwise, like she was a thief.

Waiting now, my mother and I spot Briony in the distance down the street and walk quickly to catch up with her. We begin to trudge through the snow to the beat of her jewellery. Jangle, jangle, jangle.

"Let we go this way," our mother says. She wants to drop off a handwritten note of thanks to the funeral director. "I feeling for a different route." Briony and I U-turn behind her.

Eventually we end up walking in sync, my mother between Briony and me. Ma has both of her hands in her coat pocket, and though it is not too cold, her shoulders are shrugged upwards to her ears. Between us and inside her layers of garments, she looks small, like she is sinking and shrinking with each step. I walk closer to her so that our elbows touch.

When we reach the funeral home, our mother asks if we want to come inside and say something. Both of us say no. Ma disappears behind the funeral home's door that's made up of little shards of mirror, showing Briony and I standing on the street, little clouds of air escaping from our mouths and noses. Traffic from further down the intersection hums along.

"Who would choose a mirror as a door for a funeral home?" I say, turning toward the door. "I mean, who would want to see what they look like as they walk into the worst day of their life?"

"Maybe the funeral home doesn't want people looking in. People are like that, you know," she says. "Nosy as fuck." In the mirror I can see Briony has her back to me.

"I guess, I don't stare into funeral homes. I just keep on walking by."

"Two kinds of people, I guess."

I walk to the edge of the sidewalk where she stands. She looks down the street toward the traffic.

"There are two kinds of people," I say. "Those who look without," I stretch my palm outwards like I am cradling a human skull and deepen my voice, "and those who look within."

Briony closes her eyes and shakes her head, smiling on the side of her face I can't see. A car drives by and both of our heads turn and follow it until it disappears around the bend.

"I'm not in the mood," she says.

"Were you downstairs with Auntie Sangeetha last night? Just tell me. After you left my room? I heard something downstairs."

"I can't remember."

"You were. I saw you."

She scoffs. "Are you really doing this right now? Because I'm not playing this game."

I shrug. "Okay." I make a tiny *O* with my mouth and puff hot air into the cold.

She pulls up her coat sleeve, checks the rose gold watch on her wrist, then pulls the sleeve back down.

"Just tell me."

She brings her middle finger and thumb to the bridge of her nose.

"Briony."

She says nothing.

"Nod once if it's a yes."

"Shut up. Just shut the fuck up."

She steps toward me and I flinch. We stand face to face, the tip of her nose red and her cheeks flushed pink. We are staring each other down, sizing each other up, except I am not staring her down, I am not sizing her up. I am looking at my big sister for the first time in five years. A white light flares at the center of her pupils. She breaks first; she looks to the left, licks her lips, and exhales up to the sky.

I put my hands in my coat pockets and hunch my shoulders. "Sorry."

We wait for my mother in silence.

12

In February of 1970, when Tippie became pregnant with Blues' son three months after he tucked wildflowers into her smock at the SuperSuperMarket, Rani began hitting her younger sisters. At first it was with wooden spoons on their calves for any and no good reason. Rani accused Moira of forgetting to water the garden, blamed her when the tomatoes were eaten by night creatures, or accused "she fat little mouth" of devouring them herself. She hit Sangeetha once after she had failed to fold the fresh laundry, and after seeing the youngest fall to the ground at the first light lash, shouting for their mother and father to return from their graves and save her, Rani left her alone. Upon walking away, from the corner of her eye she could have sworn she saw Sangeetha rise from the ground, unfurl her grief-struck expression, dust off the flaps of her dress and skip away.

Rani only hit my mother once. I know this for a fact, unlike much of everything else. I heard it from the mouth of a distant older "cousin" who was visiting Toronto for the first time. She told the story to all of us at the dinner table like it was folklore, as if the main characters were not seated next to her. "Leela did do something bad," said the old cousin, "and Rani make she go into they own backyard and pick out a piece of switchgrass."

We have had many "cousins", "aunts", and "uncles" visit us from Trinidad and the U.S. over the years, and with their luggage and exasperated bodies, regardless of the distance they traveled – be it five or ten hours – they brought with them stories of my mother's and aunts' youth that I have pinned up in the bulletin board of my mind. But this particular story I have circled and put at the center and crux of an unsolved case whose files and folders, blacked out sentences and redacted names, keep piling up over the years.

I will never forget the moment after this cousin finished telling the story. She explained, as she sashayed pepper sauce into her pelau, her sagging jowls moving with her hands, how Rani had hit my mother three times with the switchgrass, and when blood was drawn, threw the switch aside and left my mother on the floor. We stopped scooping food into our mouths, even Cece, who was an absent-minded teenager at the time, and Chevy, who, though always silent, appeared as if at a loss for words. To take the place of silence, a waft came in through the kitchen window and brought with it the smell of ripe apples. I remember my heart beating fast, and when I looked to Briony and Cece, I knew their hearts were beating with mine. *Who* was this woman, we thought, barging in and disturbing the quiet we'd made for ourselves? Who did she think she was?

It was a bad memory – the cousin should have known this, though, not really, they were all hit back then, and it was possible she was reminiscing on "the olden days". But it was a bad memory to bring up, not only because the suppressed event was a pivotal moment when something changed between my young aunt and my mother, but it also made clear that my mother, at some point, and more importantly, for some *reason*, had spoken to someone outside of the family about one of her own. The betrayal on my Auntie Rani's face at the dinner table was enough to turn her from accused to innocent before a jury, the way her eyes and mouth turned downwards and a single pigeon pea dropped from her spoon. No one said anything. My mother cleared her throat. Our spoons clinked against our plates.

After dinner, Auntie Rani sat on the front porch swing smoking a cigarette and beneath her tall and broad frame, the swing looked too small for her as though it belonged to a child. My mother was upstairs in the attic on the phone. My sisters, Auntie Sangeetha, and Chevy, not yet able to go back to their rooms with a guest in the house, watched television in the living room. The guest asked to use the washroom. I said I would show her the way.

The walk from the kitchen to the second-floor bathroom took a little over two minutes at the old cousin's pace. With no one close by, I knew this was my only chance of being alone with her, and feeling a little like my Auntie Sangeetha, seizing this otherwise unsuspecting person in a dark corridor, I asked her to tell me what happened after Auntie Rani hit my mother, and did it have anything to do with Blues. I said his name like I knew everything about him.

The cousin steupsed, and I looked behind us to see if anyone was watching. "Oh, Blues," she said. She began to wheeze and cough.

"What?" I said, looking behind me again, up and down, left and right, wherever someone in my family could pop up like a cardboard figure. "Blues was what?" I whispered.

In a burst of energy, she said something loud and incomprehensible, then, "Blues!" I had to restrain myself from cupping my hands over the old lady's mouth.

"When Rani hit your mother," she said, placing both feet on a step before moving to the next one, "that was when Sangeetha and Moira start to really pull away from she and move toward Leela. Power in numbers." She tapped her temple then she turned back and put her hand to her chest. "At least that is my opinion, child." (I

119

was in my mid-twenties.) Then, "I know what is like to have bully for sisters. I know, I know. When I was a little, little girl…" She went on about her sisters, my mind trailed.

We reached the bathroom at the top of the stairs and before she went in, I managed to get out, "What about Blues, though?" before she closed the door in my face. She spoke as she urinated; she must have been squatting as I had to place my ear to the door to make out what she was saying above the pour. I closed my eyes and bit my lower lip, and thought that should someone catch me listening to the hollow piss of a stranger, I might never again be trusted in my whole life. Nevertheless, my ear remained pressed against the door, and as she spoke, I focused on the ground ahead of me; with my mother's voice on the phone trailing from the attic and the blare of the television's explosions from downstairs, I found myself wedged between the sounds of the three generations, each of their distanced echoes dancing around my head like apparitions. The old cousin flushed the toilet and I cursed – everything she said in those last few seconds syphoned down the drain along with her waste, breaking up and shooting off in ten different directions in the pipes below.

She talked as she ran water from the tap, coughed and spat into the sink, and when she opened the door to find my nose almost touching hers, she said, "Child, some space, nah."

I took her by the elbow and led her back downstairs. She continued to talk. By the time we reached the corridor, I could hear my mother's footsteps coming down the attic stairs, and then the second floor's, and soon we were all three standing together. I told the cousin it was lovely to meet her and kissed her goodbye. My sisters and Chevy came from the living room, monotonously, and said the same. We left my mother and the cousin standing there, and after my mother took her onto the porch, this cousin, this leaked and firsthand source to a major event in my family's court of law, I never saw again.

120

That evening after having heard the first story at dinner, then the second muddled through the bathroom door, I thought of my poor young mother, who, unlike Sangeetha, did not falter under the shadow of a hand, but stood on both her feet until she could no more as the switchgrass came down from above. I thought, too, of poor Auntie Rani; I knew from the soft skin under her old eyes, and from the look on her face when the cousin told the story, that she regretted it, wholly and completely. She had never hit someone before, is what the cousin had said, and perhaps Rani did not know that grass, weightless like the apology she never gave to her sisters, could draw blood. She never hit any of them again.

*

What I learned from the old cousin was: Rani, at twenty years old, had become a hardened woman. When Tippie, cupping her belly beneath its sloping hem, had brought Blues to their bungalow to meet her sisters, Rani had to watch Blues take off his shoes. She had to watch the way he removed one loafer with the push of his index finger, and how he let it fall to the ground without a sound. She had to watch the way he took off his hat and held it to his chest as he ducked his head beneath the doorframe to step inside her home. Everything about him was magnified. Whereas before in the SuperSuperMarket he had presence, before her and her younger sisters now, he held the air of a demigod. She had never seen his hair without its hat for more than a few seconds, but had once imagined it when he had bought a tube of blue hair gel at the store. Everything he brought to her counter she treated as an archaeological discovery that transported her to his natural state of existence, his life beyond the store. She thought of the way he might have dolloped a dime-sized glob (the recommended amount according to the back of the tube she'd read after he left) into the palm of his hand and run it through his hair until it was slick. While he did so, the tune of a blues record might be playing in the background. She thought of the deodorant under his arms, the residue of sweat and talc left behind on his shirts. The cigarettes he stored in his linen front pockets, and where in Macaria, or Trinidad, he would stop to ponder and relish through a smoldering haze. The cinnamon toothpaste he used – emasculating for any other man, Rani thought, but endearing for Blues – and the kick of his breath. The oranges he placed on his kitchen counter and what else might be there – a breadbasket? A tidy pile of napkins? A bottle of rum which he only allowed himself to dabble in every now and then? Then, in her mind as she moved along the kitchen counter, she rewound back to the oranges, and zoomed in on the tiny SuperSuperMarket stickers that perhaps she herself had stuck on them, the ones he had walked to the back of the store for, the ones Tippie would have handed him, the ones where their fingers might have touched when they passed from her sister's hands to his.

On seeing the thicket of hair that was black and grey in undulating waves, Rani, as though feeling motion sickness, excused herself.

Tippie introduced Blues to her sisters, and Rani, once back in the living room, exerted a great amount of control to say yes, they knew each other. Everyone, Blues too, looked up at her.

"How?" Tippie asked.

"I working in the store longer than you," Rani said. She focused on Tippie's face so as not to look at her hand on Blues' elbow. "He does come in all the time, of course I know he face. I know plenty customers' face." (Did she fight back tears when she said "he face?")

"Rani and I go way back," said Blues, winking at her. She felt her throat close. "Ain't that right, Rani?" He put his hat back on and tipped it at her and she wanted to rip it off his skull, tear it in two, it was a stupid fucking hat, she thought; no, it was a beautiful hat, it was the most beautiful hat she had ever seen, she wanted to spit on it.

The old cousin had revealed that my mother, Moira, and Sangeetha were immediately besotted with Blues. All three were still under the age of fifteen, and the molasses of his voice, the tan of his desert-sand skin, and the grey threads in his hair lent him an air of wisdom. He said fatherly things, like how the girls should stay in school, and what a wonderful job Tippie and Rani were doing raising them and how much they were sacrificing, like Tippie having to quit school herself. He said that their father – my grandfather – had been a hardworking man, and that they should remain true to their values. Like meerkats, they all nodded. It had been a long time since there was a man in the house.

After he left and Tippie asked what they all thought, apparently my mother had said, "But this is an *old* man," and they laughed and laughed. There were questions upon questions, not in the traditional familial habit of dispelling Blues' worth and capacity to be Tippie's partner, but to find out everything – *everything* – about this charming man. What did he do for work, where in Trinidad was he from, how old was he, really, and when were they going to get married? Rani excused herself again.

Rani and Tippie continued to work at the supermarket. Rani made up reasons to leave home earlier or later than Tippie to avoid walking home together, and none of the sisters, including Tippie, seemed to take notice. It relieved Rani that she and Tippie worked on opposite ends of the store, but soon, even that became too much when Blues would visit her sister, only saying hello to Rani as he came in and goodbye as he left. She wondered why Blues needed to see Tippie during work hours, why they could not be normal lovers and embrace after dusk – not that their love was a secret, the way it protruded from Tippie's belly week after week. Rani asked for her shifts to be changed from late evenings to early mornings.

The old cousin had told me that, of course, people in Macaria were talking about Tippie. ("Oh, poor, poor Tippie," she had said in the bathroom as she unzipped). People gossiped about street dogs and ill-maintained gardens, she said. They were going to talk about an eighteen-year-old unmarried girl who was made pregnant by a man more than twice her age. "And especially because of Blues' reputation," said the cousin. I had my ear so hard against the door I thought it might give way. "But Tippie didn't know. How she could know? She was so, so young," she said.

At the end of the first trimester, Blues visited the SuperSuperMarket every day, sometimes even twice. He asked the store manager if she really needed to be working, hovering his hands around Tippie's stomach as though it were a crystal ball. Tippie interjected, saying that she wanted to work, she did not want to be a bored cow, grazing in domesticity in the heat of her home. At the end of her shifts in the evenings, Blues walked Tippie home, and upon their arrival my teenage aunts flocked to him as if he was their own father returning from work. Blues reciprocated the role, too; he brought them small gatherings – flowers from alongside the road or misshapen rocks he thought were unique. Sangeetha, ten years old at the time and easily seduced by all tokens of affection, adored him the most.

"He so handsome, Tippie," Sangeetha would say. She would kneel on Tippie's bed at the windowsill and place the rocks and dying flowers in alternating patterns as Tippie soaked her feet. "So handsome. When allyuh getting married? I could be in charge of the flowers?"

Tippie would shrug and smile, kicking her feet in playful flicks, splashing the water in the metal tub. "You could be in charge of the flowers."

124

The old women of the neighborhood began bearing gifts when Tippie ballooned in her second trimester. Some of them had been friends of my grandparents, faces they had only seen behind curtains and windows, or taking slow, solitary walks in the evenings with their hands crossed behind their back. Although my young mother and aunts continued to withdraw in the grief of their parents' death – a full year had not yet passed – the women of the neighborhood nonetheless presented their gifts for Tippie: ugly padded sandals for the extra weight, faded and floral muumuus to cover it all up, packages of beans and lentils for constipation, jars of shea butter for stretch marks, grated ginger for morning sickness. Tippie, seeing her body morph, let the gifts pile up and around a chair by the front door, and sometimes, when she went out on the veranda in the morning, gifts would be swaying on the rocking chair. She had my mother and Moira move the chair from the front to the backyard. The women began leaving gifts on the steps.

The women did not like Blues. When they saw him coming around – which happened less and less (he had taken up an evening job at a bar to support Tippie and the baby) – they gave him long, knowing stares and tutted their teeth loudly as though shooing away a dog (the old cousin herself was one of these women). Blues told Tippie he did not like the women either, how they looked at him from their windows or the side eye they gave him while sweeping their front yards, which they only thought to do once they saw him coming. Once, from the veranda, Tippie saw an old woman with long grey hair approach Blues from behind as he walked up to the house. The woman was holding a cocoyea broom, and from the blank look on her face and the quick flutter of her lips, she looked like she was delivering a message. This did not surprise Tippie – she came to understand that the women were only protecting her – but she felt a twinge of doubt sit within her when, instead of smiling sympathetically at the old woman and tipping his hat out of respect, Blues responded in the same manner. Only his lips moved and his eyes looked dead during what appeared to be a short monologue, which he ended by nodding his head up at the old woman. He turned away from her and walked toward the house, and the old woman, taking hold of the broom in both her hands, watched him until Tippie let him through the front door. Tippie saw that he stepped on a small package of oats that she had not yet retrieved with the heel of his foot as he walked up the veranda steps.

It was natural then that Tippie blamed the women of the neighborhood when in the eighth month of her pregnancy Blues left her. He stopped showing up at the house and the SuperSuperMarket, and when she tried to call him, his phone rang and rang. Sure that he was in danger, Tippie sent Rani to his apartment in San Fernando to check that he was all right, that he had not been robbed at gunpoint, or hit by a car and fallen into a ditch, sitting unclaimed in the emergency room. Hesitant as Rani was, she, too, was worried about Blues. At his apartment, the landlord said that Blues had moved to Caracas four days ago.

"Where?" she asked.

"Caracas," the landlord said. "Venezuela."

"Probably to be closer to he small son and them," the landlord added. When Rani choked on her spit, the landlord tapped her gently on the back.

On the way home, she thought: how a man could just pick up and leave like that? Really. How a man could just do that? Rani told Tippie the news, Tippie accused her of lying. Rani asked why she should lie, the landlord told her herself. Tippie said nothing, then, in a burst of movement, charged outside onto the veranda as though an eight-pound human was not buoyant inside her, flinging open the door with such force it bounced off the wall and slammed itself shut. She began cursing, loud. My mother and Moira and Sangeetha came to the front window and watched, their heads piled atop each other like a totem pole. Moira asked Rani what they should do. Rani said to let her be. They watched Tippie scream and yell crude things about the neighborhood women, about their private parts, and their mothers' private parts, and how they would all end up in hell for being witches. She accused them of casting spells on Blues, of shape-shifting at night, of coming to her and Blues in their dreams while they slept. She said she had seen the electric blue of a manicou's eyes in their backyard on the last night Blues came to visit her, and that she knew it was one of *them* in their true form, the soucouyants that they were. She spat on the grass. She traced her index finger across the neighborhood houses, and when she landed on the window of the woman with the long grey hair, the curtains were pulled shut. So potent was her fury that she picked up, with great ease, a small pillow with blue fringes left on the veranda steps and punted it into the neighbor's yard. In between grunts, she sent a bowl of cherries flying into the air like shrapnel, flung a fig-sized pair of socks behind her, scrunched dry peppermint leaves that fell between her fingers like ashes. She tore a hibiscus from the front garden and strangled it, screaming. At this Sangeetha had gasped.

And on that night, induced by grief and rage, and surrounded by her four sisters in a hospital room, my Auntie Tippie gave birth to my cousin, Patrick "Chevy" Rampersad.

13

I have thought about contacting this old cousin again, of course. The things I learned from her under auditory duress in a matter of minutes only left me wondering what more I could learn in an hour, eight hours, a day, a week. I thought maybe I could find her name – Rosel – in my mother's phonebook, call to tell her how much I enjoyed talking to her, ask how she was doing. She would not remember me, and I would say, "Leela's daughter – the middle girl." I would not need to say too much for her to start talking; she had no children or husband, and the sisters she did have, she was not on speaking terms with, not even on the day they died, she had said. I found this devastating.

I looked in my mother's phonebook for her name, marching up the attic stairs once upon a time, armed with my own notebook and pen in hand. In the phonebook, there were names littered and scratched out, the carve of ink ran deep like engravings and the back of pages bumpy to the touch. The pen must have been held by a fist; violent streaks sparked out of its raised welts. I flipped through page after page searching for the old cousin, deranged, as if I'd just opened an empty box that was once filled with treasure. I stopped on a page where I saw the first and last letters of her name on opposing ends of a black scar: 'r' and 'el'. In between the letters, everything was gone, including the phone number below it, except the area code, which I already knew. I closed the phonebook, and my eyes. I let my hand rest on the cover. I took a deep breath. I opened the book again and tears fell onto its pages ruining the last digit of one "Cherelle".

I could not tell who had once had a name.

I remember thinking: so much of our past had already been erased – official documents lost in transit, there was nothing on paper of my grandparents – whole people of lived lives, gone – must we do it to ourselves, too? And then I was forced to remember twice over, negotiating with myself up there in the attic, that some people needed to forget, and ink as it giveth, can taketh away, too.

PART II

14

> Ines... let me tell you... when somebody
> dies, other ghosts come to visit

That's cryptic...

What happened? How are you? Is everything okay?
Want me to call you? I'm at work but I can step out

Hello??

Cas

*

For the second time in a week, another ambulance is on Florence
Street. At one in the morning and a little below zero, about ten
people stand on their porches and the sidewalk in robes and oversized
jackets and undone winter boots exposing woolly carcasses. Toronto
is not a small city, but each neighborhood feels like its own town

with its own gossip; every time an ambulance blares down our street then goes silent, we peer out our windows and tell our family to come quick – someone is dead.

We stand on our porch – me, my mother, Briony, Auntie Sangeetha, and Auntie Moira. Auntie Rani and Cece sleep inside. It is unclear whether they were woken in the first place, then I remember Uncle Bass. So agreeable is the man and so rare have we crossed paths in the house that I often forget he's among us until the timbre of his voice hums from the guest room with Auntie Moira's trebled murmurs.

We clutch our jackets to our necks and Auntie Moira blows hot air out of her mouth. "If allyuh did tell me it was going to be so cold here," she says, "I would have buy a thicker jacket right at the airport."

Squinting through the blue-black night, we watch a stretcher emerge from the house across the street, two houses down to the right. The body is covered from head to toe with a white sheet and strapped down with three black straps at its chest, torso and shins, like it threatens to jump up to life at any moment. At the sight, my mother and Auntie Sangeetha put their hands to their faces and turn their backs to the neighborhood. I put my arms around my mother.

"Who is that?" I ask.

"I wonder if it's that old, old lady that living there long time with she daughter?" Auntie Moira says. "Ever since I coming up here, that old lady did live there. That's she, Briony?"

"Yeah. I think so," Briony says. "I mean, I hope so."

I raise my eyebrows at her.

"I meant to say," she says, "that I hope it's not the daughter. That would be tragic. It's the mother, I think."

Since she last confessed two days ago at the funeral home that Sangeetha didn't *not* corner her with words, words, words, things have been strange between us. Briony and I are not like this; we are not our aunts. Yesterday in the kitchen, we danced around each other as though we were in the other's way, bumbling over our words. Then this morning when she came into the living room to (presumably) watch television and found me sitting on the couch reading, she pretended she forgot something up in her room and never returned. Now, she keeps her face toward the street, cradling her elbows and shivering.

"My God, she's still living?" I say. "Is that Meena?"

"Nina," says Briony. "And the daughter's name is Posie."

"Is that her by the door?" I say. My mother loosens herself from my embrace and turns to see.

"I don't know," Briony says. "I haven't really noticed her in years, to be honest. Either of them, actually."

"Yeah," says my mother. "That is she. That is Posie by the door."

"But Posie looking so different!" says Auntie Moira. "She looking about the same age as the mother."

"Poor Posie," says Auntie Sangeetha through sobs. "Poor, poor Posie." She had put on a bit of makeup to step outside, a quick sketch of eyeliner, a prick of a stray mole and rosy lip balm.

In my twenty years of growing up opposite them, my family has only ever referred to Nina and Posie a handful of times, and then after that as "them two old ladies". The mother and daughter didn't have jobs, they did nothing. We would see them taking silent walks together, Posie trailing behind her mother, both holding fabric grocery bags or with envelopes tucked under their arms, or just their little purses slung across their chests for no apparent reason other than to walk. Aside from the initial curiosity we had about their dynamic – why they rarely came outside or acknowledged their neighbors, or how they managed to pay the bills for a three-storey Victorian house – nobody, at least not in my family, cared to ask after their business. They were quiet, our interest ebbed.

A wide and short figure – Posie – stands behind their screen door, and though their house is in much better condition than ours, at least ours maintains the appearance of habitation. The wood of their porch is a dark chocolate brown but appears blacker than the night. It has always looked vacant – no chairs, no plants, no welcome mat on the porch – and every slat looked like it might creak under the slightest weight. I imagined their kitchen to be neat and tidy, a strict no-children zone, and antiquely British for some reason, with floral teacups hanging from gold hooks under oak cupboards; fine untouched china sitting in a gilded locked cabinet; and a television garbling on low sound.

There are three lights on in the house; in two rooms on the second floor, and one in the hallway behind Posie, illuminating her figure that's drowning in an amorphous white nightie. Her hair is white, I think, but I cannot for the life of me guess how old she is. As one of the paramedics talks to Posie on the other side of the screen door, two others roll the stretcher – Nina – into the back of the ambulance. Posie, not turning in its direction, looks more like she's telling a canvasser that she has dinner on the stove and she hasn't time to talk. Posie and the paramedic exchange a few last rushed words. When the paramedic leaves the porch, I see that Posie is not wide at all, but thin, the joints of her knees and elbows outthrust at her sides.

The silence after the ambulance rolls away acts as a moment of remembrance, and after a minute everyone makes their way back into their homes. Two or three people from the pavement approach Posie's porch, but she sees them coming and closes the screen door, then the front door. From the small slated window above the door, the hallway light shuts off. The neighbors don't appear offended – it's death in the early morning, after all.

136

Back in the attic, I stand by the window. I've always been able to see Posie and Nina's house from here, but until now, thought of it as another house on the street and not theirs, not one with lives, stories, memories behind it. The lights of the two rooms on the second floor are still on, the edges of the maroon velvet curtains glowing. The curtains in every other room, also drawn shut, indicate nothing of what lies beyond.

I wonder what's going through Posie's mind. When she reached the top of the stairs, which of the rooms did she go to first? Which she will sleep in tonight – her mother's or her own? Sitting alone beyond the velvet curtains, shut up in the private amphitheater of her grief, what will be the first thing she *does* after her mother has died? Turn off the lights? Lie in the still-warm bed? Deny the last few hours and go straight to her room?

My mind trails to Auntie Rani.

Unable to sleep, I toss and turn in my bed. I get up and pull my old desk chair to the window and sit thinking of Posie and Nina, and all the secrets the house protects. I fall asleep siting up against the wall. Two hours later when I wake up, and the two lights are still on in Posie and Nina's house.

*

Since Chevy died, Cece only opens her bedroom door for our mother. When we had walked to the funeral home, my mother had gone upstairs to ask Cece if she wanted to come with us. From the foyer, as Briony and I put on our jackets, over the rustling of polyesters and zippers, we heard the distant exchange between them like amorous whispers between two lovers.

I mimic my mother's knock – two quick taps – on Cece's door. When she opens it, I hold up a brown paper bag. "Donuts?"

137

She turns around and leaves the door open.

The room smells like sweat and dust. Like Briony's room, though with far less glamour, and somewhat unusual for Cece, clothes are flung about the ground, over her desk and chair, over pictures of her and her friends, of her and me and Briony when we were children, and one of our father (she is the only one in the house to have a picture of him not tucked away). A toppling pile of underwear, socks, and sweaters sits at the bottom of the bed. She curls herself under the duvet and the pile wavers. On the bedstand next to her stands a column of saucers that Auntie Sangeetha has been looking for, cookie crumbs and cake leftovers, and no fewer than nine coffee cups, some with coffee and yogurty white clusters floating on its surface. The window is not open; particles of my sister's sadness drift through the air and sink into everything. I feel words rising within me, angry ones, but with Cece, more than anyone else, I have to fight my hot tongue. She isn't like us. Before I can stop the words from coming out of my mouth, I say, "Look at the state of this place."

She is used to it, she says nothing.

I sit on the edge of the bed and the pile of clothes topples over. Cece raises her head from the pillow. "Sorry," I say, then, "Cece, don't you want to eat your donuts? I got your favourite. Sour cream glazed. I didn't forget." I shake the bag in my hand and hate myself for it. She's almost twenty-three years old, for God's sake.

A mop of thick black hair like a Mardi Gras wig sits on her pillow. She's done this since she was a child – cover her whole face when she's trying to sleep because the light in her room, even with blackout curtains, is too bright. In the darkest of darks, Cece has sworn since she could talk that she could see light seeping into the room from the windows, outside the hall, from the digital clock in the corner. She will throw hand towels over the DVD player and wireless router, and in her worse moods, unplug them entirely. She has sliced a foam roller lengthwise into two and placed it under her door, and will turn off her phone at night rather than put it face down. When she was a child she would say, "Too bright," when my mother put her to bed. In total darkness, my mother would say, "Cece, baby, I can't see you."

"Okay, then," I say. "I guess I'll eat them myself." I crinkle the bag.

"Just leave them next to me," she says under the blanket. I mouth the word "where?" to myself and say, "Okay." I take two coffee cups from the bedstand, put them on the ground and place the donuts next to her.

"Do you want to eat dinner later together?" I ask. A sliver of skin shows from underneath the wig and I touch it. She does not move.

"Okay," she says. "Yeah. Yeah, I'll come down."

"Okay. Cool."

I take the pile of saucers in one hand, and hook three empty cups on to my other, emptying them into the bathroom sink down the hall and scrunching my nose as I flick the milky curds down the drain. Walking back to her room for the remaining dishes, I see Chevy's room door is partially open down the hall. I leave the dishes in Cece's room.

*

Fender electric guitar, 1998
Gifted to Chevy (source unknown) upon arrival to Toronto in aforementioned year to feed love of rock and roll.

Steel-toe boots, date unknown

Work boots as per construction and factory regulation. Placed at edge of bed as though owner might return any minute.

Photo, man, date unknown
Black and white picture of a man, framed in a simple gold picture frame. Man wears white shirt against grey background; is not smiling. Photo bears resemblance to passport picture.

Photo, Tippie Rampersad, 1967
Chevy's mother, fifteen years old. Lying in hammock in Macaria house, pretending to be asleep, one eye open, smiling.

Brown corduroy pants, 1990
Gifted by Leela Rampersad for birthday in the same year; worn until last living day. Zipper broken several times over years. Chevy would leave pants hanging over railing of banister; they would be mended by the next morning.

Cards, 1998 to current day
Every birthday card ever given him, stacked like leaflets on top of idle fireplace mantel.

Pamphlet, Toronto Humane Society, 2017
Shiny pamphlet with Golden Labrador and orange tabby cat soliciting donation. Chevy donated several times a year.

Passport, Trinidad & Tobago, 1990
Next to candle. Passport shows 22-year-old Chevy. Hair abundant. Jawline sharp, angular. Never went back to Trinidad again.

Unworn t-shirt, date unknown
Plain black t-shirt at top of pile of clothes. Price tag of $7.99 from H&M still attached.

Large white votive candle, date unknown
Next to pile of birthday cards. Burned a long time ago; cratered center gathers dust, wick snapped off.

Photo, Chevy Rampersad and Junior Rampersad, 1980
Brothers, Chevy, ten years old, and Junior, seven years old, riding bicycles. Taken one year before Junior dies, and Chevy witnesses it.

*

In the very early hours of the morning when it's still dark, I hear creaking coming from downstairs. Sick of it, I throw the covers off me, the floor like ice on my soles. Walking past my mother's bedroom, I see the door is wide open. Silver moonlight coming through her window shows me an empty bed, made up impeccably, its bedspread tight around the corners and tucked under the mattress. None of her things – creams, perfumes, ointments – are on the dressers, there are no clothes in the laundry basket. I walk to the window and slam it shut, its curtains caressing my cheeks before dying down. Shivering and rubbing my palms up and down my arms, I walk down the attic stairs, moonlight monochroming everything before and behind me to a steel inferno of metallic blues and greys. I stop when I see that Chevy's door is still open, too, his bedsheets laid with a fresh spread. His windows are open and the drapes flap wildly as if possessed. To my right, I see the same of Cece's room, except that her curtains waver gently. She too is gone.

I feel like shouting into the dark, like I'm in a horror movie, "Okay, you got me! The joke's over! Come out now!" But further down the hall, so frightened by what's before me, I begin to cry. All the doors are open – the bathroom's, Briony's, the guest bedroom where Auntie Moira and Uncle Bass are meant to be sleeping. I can't see Uncle Bass' feet sticking out past the edge of the bed. Moonlight is beaming through all their doors, even though there's no window in the guest room, and I hear nothing aside from a warping rush in my ears like I'm underwater. My hand searches and finds the light sconce on the wall. It flickers three times, like lightning, then the light blows out. In the brief flashes I'm given, I see downstairs, at the foot of the stairs, Cece pushing off Auntie… Auntie…

She's struggling. I can't move my feet. I still hear nothing except that warping sound, getting louder and louder. Their lips are moving. Leaning over the banister, I shout, "Cece, run!" but no sound escapes my mouth.

The figure of the aunt, like a beast, pins Cece down by the arms to the stairs. The aunt holds a wooden belna in one hand. She is saying something to Cece, over and over, and Cece is shaking her head from side to side, her eyes squeezed shut. She kicks the figure in between her legs; nothing happens. I hear the words the figure speaks. "Rani, Chevy, Junior. Me, Chevy, Junior. Rani, Chevy, Junior. Me, Chevy, Junior." And then rapid whispering.

"Don't listen to her, Cece!" I scream. "Cece, don't listen to her!"

One by one the doors slam shut, so loud that I have to cover my ears, and when they're all closed, I look down to my sister and aunt. Both of them are gone, as if they had not been there only seconds ago. A light comes from behind me, it is day now, and Chevy's door is wide open. From the hall I see everyone – Cece, Briony, my three aunts and my mother sleeping in Chevy's bed, curled up in the fetal position, their knees to their chests.

I wake up sweating. I sit up and drink an entire glass of water, steadying my breath, taking off my pants and shirt. I go to look over the staircase banister. All the doors on the second floor are shut, as is my mother's behind me.

15

If there's one person's history that is not lacking in my family, it's the childhood of Chevy. He was the first baby of my aunts' generation – I coo inside when I say this, to think of my tough cousin as a smiling cherub – and as such, he was the son of them all, even Auntie Sangeetha, who was ten years old when he was born.

I forgot this when growing up with him on Florence Street – that he was the first baby of the family – and waves of guilt and regret wash over me when I think how I whined to myself as a child, and well into my irritable teens, why he couldn't just *be normal* for the family. As time passed and I got older and more aware of how my family moved, and therefore how I moved, I felt his deathlike reticence to be a force that both bound and broke us, an invisible power suspending a large mass that was neither in full operation nor benign. All of us were hanging on to – or being hung by – something unseen, a threadlike nerve connecting and pulsating through us as one.

In my early twenties, before I left for London, I started leaving the house more and more for days and nights on end, staying with friends or a boyfriend's, not doing much other than lying on the couch watching television, helping myself to their food, talking to their mothers. It was only when I left for those days that I could see, with the distance between the house and I, that it was not that Chevy did not want to be normal, but that he could not. This will pain me for the rest of my life.

I stopped staying at friends' houses. My fury subsided with empathy. But the constant compassion drained me, and often I slept into the afternoon. If I could not tend to my own desires and needs – flitting across Europe in my gap year; introducing to the family a boy I loved and who loved me; proposing a career in the arts, like, say, writing, instead of the slow leak of the soul that comes with a desk and delegation – if I could not do any of this, lest I be deemed selfish, then I would keep to myself. And I did. In purgatory I remained.

*

When Blues left Macaria, my aunts busied themselves with newborn Chevy (who would not actually be dubbed "Chevy" for another thirteen years). The light in his eyes reignited life into their own. Tippie was almost nineteen when she had him, but in the weeks following his birth, said she felt eighty. She breastfed endlessly, said the child was not only suckling milk, but meat and blood. Sometimes she fell asleep in the act, and one of my aunts would run to lift Chevy's head up on her chest. She woke up late and went to bed early, had crying spells when she ate, took refuge in the bathroom, lashed out at her sisters for minute things. She lost weight too fast; her pre-pregnancy body, once small-boned and modelesque, was now withering to a sickly frailty, and her hair, once as full as a mane, began to look pared. When they called a doctor to the house, reading aloud both the physical and emotional changes Sangeetha had recorded in her gardening journal, he told the sisters that it was simply the stress of being a new mother.

"She go eventually snap out of it," he had said, "and be a mother."

Sangeetha, ten years old, said, "So what that make she now?"

On one night in particular, the sisters were awakened by Chevy's crying, gasps of deep breaths drawn from his belly before he broke the night with his screams. They gave Tippie the chance to be stirred from her sleep and go to him, believing that if they did so, with practice, she would assume the natural role of – as the doctor said – a mother. Minutes passed. The house next door turned on a light, a melodramatic steups escaped an open window. A car and its loud exhaust sped down the road and a dog began to bark. They could take the screaming no more when Chevy's shrills became high-pitched and sharp, painful to their chests. Rani tended to him, and Chevy, cocooned by touch, immediately was hushed. My mother found Tippie rocking back and forth on the veranda rocking chair.

"Tippie," my mother said. "You ain't hear Chevy crying? Come. He need he milk."

"I coming, I coming," said Tippie. She made no movement to get up, rocking back and forth, hypnotized by the basic black of night.

My mother crouched next to her, resting her hand on the chair to slow its rocking. "What happen, Tippie?" she said. "Is he you thinking of?" then whispered, "Is Blues? Forget he, Tippie. He's pig shit."

Tippie shook her head with her fists to her eyes and began to cry. "No, no, is not he. I don't know what it is. I sorry. I sorry. I's a bad mother."

"No, Tippie, no, don't say that. You's just new. Come. You have we."

Tippie began to sit with Chevy on the rocking chair in the evenings. The old women and some men, too, came to see him and how she was doing, quickly forgiving that she had thrashed their gifts all over hers and the neighbor's front yard only weeks ago.

"He go be a good boy," they would say.

"A healthy boy, you could tell he all there and he not missing anything, and for that you must thank God."

"Look at them pink, pink cheeks. That mean he born a happy baby, Tippie. You do a good job."

"A gift from God."

"Isn't he?" Tippie would say. "Isn't he such a gift from God?"

Amid new life, each sister carried on with her job with renewed enthusiasm. Moira planted more seeds in the back garden, blending fruits and vegetables into purees for Chevy. My mother and Sangeetha kept the house immaculate, not leaving a shoelace unstrung or a bottle unscrewed with its upturned cap nearby so that Chevy might choke on it and die. Rani continued to work at the SuperSuperMarket, and unbeknownst to anyone else at home (or at the store, in Macaria, in the world…) she fell into her own postpartum depression after Chevy was born, for though her sister was left by the man they both loved, Rani had not been given the chance to be left at all.

And worst: what special fool remembers moments that never were? His thumbs on her temples and her eyes still closed long after they had parted from a time-crushing kiss. The sudden grasp of her hand that brought on an instant amnesia of environment, language, the past. The unfolding wing of his arm enveloping her back to bed after she had gone to the bathroom. Scrutinizing a faraway foreign sea in complacent, quiet wonderment at how they both got so lucky – how, they had found what most people search for their whole lives and never quite find.

What fool, indeed? She felt rejected, and deceived, and worst of all, denied the decency of closure. As such, Rani could not seal the wound in her chest, and to the bottomless horror of this hellish love, even after everything, she still yearned to be seen by Blues again.

Six months passed, Chevy began to crawl, time held no power over the memories of her and Blues talking at the cash register, her blowing out the dandelion, their one, single evening walk. Within the year, Chevy was walking upright and confident like a little man, and whenever Rani saw a man wearing a Panama hat, she thought it might be Blues. Six more months came and went, Chevy was speaking full words, and she thought she might be sick in the head, because once or twice, she swore on her life that she had seen Blues.

The first time was on her walk to work, down by the savannah. A man was sitting on the bleachers drinking from a beer bottle. He was dressed in all white, and as she approached the high chain-linked fence that separated the road from the field, she looked at him until he looked back. She gripped the fence and as though imprisoned, curled her fingers through its wiry holes. The man locked eyes with her mid-swig, swallowed the rest of what was in the bottle, and rested it on the bench below him. He wiped his mouth on the back of his hand, climbed down bleacher stairs, and disappeared behind them. She waited for him to reappear; perhaps he recognized her and was walking around the savannah to come say hello. She was thirty-five minutes late for her shift.

The second time was one week later, in the evening when the sun was beginning to slip across the sky on an unbearably hot day. She decided to take a walk, thinking that a breeze might come with the humid night, and when that failed, she thought she might find solace in a drink – not water, not soda, not juice, but a real drink, a man's drink. "Is the heat," she told herself. "Is the heat that making me want to drink so."

She walked to a small snacket in the opposite direction of home, the one that had four stools raised before its open roadside bar, likely already occupied. She did not care – what reputation did an invisible woman have to ruin? She would stand to the side, and if anyone wanted to talk about how they saw her standing among men, drinking, drinking into the night on the side of the road, let them talk, let them talk.

At the snacket, she saw the man again, wearing the Panama hat and all white, sitting on one of the stools. His back was turned to her, but she knew the arch of his back (memorized from when he used to reach to the lowest shelf at the SuperSuperMarket). To her surprise, the other stool next to him was empty, and it seemed like fate was dealing to her its more divine cards; there: the man she loved, an empty seat, a sunset. In the shipwreck of anger and sadness she had drowned herself in for the past year and a half, desire like flotsam buoyed inside her. She began to feel nervous, she stopped walking. What could she say to him, the deserting father of her sister's child – her nephew – now that he was back in Macaria after almost two years? What were they going to talk about? Jazz? Dandelions? The SuperSuperMarket? Too much had happened.

Still. There was an empty seat next to him.

She leaned against a tree and feigned a pebble in her sandal. In this performance, should anyone be watching, she brought her heel to the back of her knee and turned her head to the road behind her, rehearsing line by line possible scenarios. She could say hello, he would be caught off guard. She would pacify him, calm his fears of being scolded, and ask him calmly where he had been, give him a chance to explain himself. She fiddled with her sandal's strap, and thought perhaps she should act angry instead – have some self-respect – so he could apologize. Then, once he did, she would forgive him at once, they could be nice with each other again. She dropped her heel to the ground and twisted her sandal back on, smoothed her hair and shirt, dabbed the excess sweat off her forehead with the base of her palm, and when she looked up the man was gone.

On the third sighting of Blues, sitting near a small lake by a mall, she saw him walking in the distance in an all-blue linen suit. She quickly turned away, told herself she was going mad, the sightings would stop, and if not – if she kept seeing Blues over and over, again and again – she would check herself into the hospital.

She thought the hospital might not be an unreasonable option, when one day after work, she came home to find Tippie, Chevy and Blues sitting on the veranda. Blues was squatting and walking a toy soldier toward Chevy – who was almost two years old – as though they had been a happy family all this time. Tippie rocked in the rocking chair, looking down at them. At the foot of the walkway, Rani looked at them, and saw her sisters' faces behind the front window. The curtain fell back in its place when she met their eyes. Tippie saw her, waved her over and Rani walked up the three steps as if seeing a person she once thought dead.

"Hello," Rani said.

Blues nodded his head at her. "Hello, Rani."

Rani looked down at Tippie, long and hard.

"He say he sorry," Tippie said.

"Chevy, come," Rani said. Chevy stopped playing with the toy and looked up at his aunt. She picked him up from under the arms and held him like a football before bringing him to her chest. He did not cry or make a fuss, but put one arm on Rani's shoulder, letting the other dangle at his side. Rani looked at Blues, he looked to the front lawn. She looked at Tippie, they only looked back at each other. It was quiet on the street; no one was sweeping their yard, hanging clothes on the line, watering their plants, or quarreling, but Rani knew that the women of the neighborhood were watching. From their windows, like her younger sisters, they watched her say something to Blues, they watched Blues say nothing in response. They watched Tippie sit between them, tilting forward and backward in her chair, looking into the distance as if alone at sea. Later, Tippie would tell Sangeetha that you could love a man twice. They watched Tippie grow in the belly in the coming months with Blues' second child. On account of the boy's premature birth and his limp, feeble body, Tippie named him Junior, a name that Blues would never know. He ran to Venezuela again, or Antigua, possibly St. Lucia. For the rest of their lives, none of them, including his sons, ever saw Blues again.

16

Down in the basement, seven in the morning. I half-sit, half-lie on the couch with the television on mute, whispering into my cell phone. Everyone is asleep except Auntie Rani who is watching the morning news in the upstairs living room.

"Ines," I say. I speak into the phone like it's a walkie-talkie. "Things are weird." I look back to Auntie Sangeetha's room. Her bedroom door is closed, I keep my eye on it as I talk. "I don't know how to explain it." I pause, keeping my thumb pressed too hard on the record button. "I feel like I never left here, you know? I feel like the house is playing tricks on me." I've had too much coffee, I'm talking too fast. "I thought I saw Onions at the funeral – remember? – Chevy's friend? The Legend of Chevy story I used to tell? But Briony said he wasn't there. So, yeah, there's that." I sigh. "It's like time has frozen over here. Briony and I got into a weird fight. I keep having these dreams. Some old lady died across the street from us. Sorry, I'm rambling. My head is a mess. You know how it is when you come back home. You turn ten again." I hear Auntie Sangeetha sneeze in her room. "Anyway, don't worry about me. No, I'm not thinking about writing or work before you ask. My editor gave me an extension on my deadline, though. So that was nice. Bye for now." I lift my finger off the record button and the voice note sends.

When I reach the top of the basement stairs, I hear below me sudden sounds of motion. Auntie Sangeetha has advanced from her bedroom to the bathroom. I am standing in front of The Room.

This is what Briony and I called Auntie Rani's room when we were young, not because we were made uneasy by the quiet that nested into the foundation of the house when she moved in, but because it was where our mother and father used to sleep. After my father slipped on the ice, our grieving mother moved to the opposite point of the house and stayed there forever: the attic. The Room on the ground floor was left empty, and the door was closed year-round like a business gone bankrupt. None of us – child or adult – ever went into The Room again; when my mother mentally boarded it up, so did we, and over the years we treated its door without regard as though it had been sanded into the wall – until Auntie Rani moved in.

A few months after she and Chevy moved in with us, Briony had asked me what I thought Auntie Rani's room looked like, which was code for Briony suggesting that we explore The Room when Auntie left the house. I was ten years old and afraid. I told my treacherous teenage sister that I was not crazy like her. She left my room and returned fifteen minutes later.

"Nothing out of the ordinary," she said. "Everything is *so* neat. Like, OCD neat. It looks so much different than—"

"But look what I found," she says after a pause. She unfurled her fingers, as though releasing a butterfly, and at its center was a small, dogeared black and brown photo.

I took it from her hands and gasped. "I never saw this picture of Grandpa before."

"Turn it around."

On the back of it was written "Blues."

"Look how it's ripped down the middle," Briony said. I ran my thumb over the fissure. "It's taped back together so well. It looks more laminated than torn." I nodded.

She said she had found it in a small cardboard box, and I slapped her on the arm and asked how she could do such a thing, and if she ever snooped around in my room. She said no, she knew everything about me and that I was boring.

"Well, go and put it back exactly the way you found it," I said. "Hurry up."

Standing in front of The Room now, I think of the photo behind the wall in its cardboard box and the letter hidden under its flap that Briony, in her clumsy haste, never bothered to lift and thus, never discovered.

From the living room Auntie Rani calls to me.

"Morning, Auntie," I say, standing at the living room archway.

She sips coffee on the single loveseat. In the chair's sunken lowness and her own old age, she still appears strong; on her two feet, one of her backhand slaps would send me flying. Her silver pixie hair is ruffled and her small eyes appear smaller, tighter, as if she hasn't slept for days, which may very well be the case. She leans to the side like an old weather vane, and she mouths a few words that I know aren't intended to be heard.

"You up early," she says, turning her vacant face to me.

"Yeah," I say. "Yeah, I can't seem to sleep past seven or eight these days."

She nods her head and brings the mug to her lips.

"How you feeling? You feeling okay?"

Taken aback that she has asked me something personal, I straighten up. "Yeah," I say. "I'm feeling okay. I guess."

She nods a nod that has no end, hovering the coffee cup above the saucer in her hand.

"It's sad about Nina and Posie, huh? So sad."

"Oh, yes," she says. "Very sad."

I almost say something painfully pedestrian like, "We all have to go sometime though," but she says, "Nina was very old. Very old. More than a hundred, if you could believe that."

I lean forward and drop my jaw for reaction.

"Yes, more than a hundred. Maybe even a hundred and five, self. But she live a happy life. She didn't have any other child but Posie, or a man to worry she so, and Posie was a good child. Posie was a good, good child. She live a long, happy life, and I feel Posie will live a long and happy life, too."

"That *is* a long life," then I laugh and say, "*Too* long." Immediately, I wince; sarcasm does not translate well to my aunts. "Sorry," I say, and scratch my arm like a child.

"Her mom just died, though," I say. "I don't know if she's going to be happy for the rest of her life now."

Auntie Rani shrugs and turns her mouth into a thinking frown. She scratches a spot on her head with a bony finger and her scalp moves with it. "I think so," she says. "When somebody get that old, the children know it's only a matter of time. Plus, they did look like they genuinely like each other."

I stand there while Auntie Rani slurps from her cup, fidgeting with loose threads of my pyjamas. I'm about to say how cold it is and how it probably won't snow for the rest of March, when Auntie Moira begins to come down the steps.

Beyond my understanding (and wanting to understand), the nighties my aunts and mother wear are so fine and dainty that when the sunlight or any light hits them, they're nearly translucent. As far back as I can remember, they've all always worn these fabrics to sleep as if they had all gone shopping together, split into teams and hoarded the summery-soft pastels as provisions. Through Auntie Moira's chiffon carmine pink nightie, a white Wonderbra and black high-waisted panties that cover the top of her paunch are on, by no means subtle, display. She takes her time, holding on to the railing with both hands, putting one foot down before the other on the same step. She has said on every single visit that without carpeting on these old stairs, she would surely "slip and break she neck and dead one time." Even in this cold, she wears flip-flops that slap against the wooden stairs. When she reaches the bottom, she looks at me and fans herself. She peers into the living room, and seeing Auntie Rani, pretends not to see her at all, and looks around the room as though for something misplaced. She goes to the kitchen. Auntie Rani sips her coffee.

As if in bridal succession, my mother soon follows down the stairs, but she descends steadily. Her nightie is of pale lime, one that has been washed so often over the decades that it appears jaundiced. She is wearing a woolly sweater over her nightie and clutching it at its middle. She does not need to hold the railing, she knows she will not slip, not even in the flimsy slippers she wears that hang off her feet, and she walks with such ease that it's like she's floating toward me. Still far above me, she is as tall as an alpine, and with each step she gets shorter and shorter until our heights even out and she is before me. I kiss her. She begins to say something, sees Auntie Rani, Auntie Rani sees her. My mother U-turns into the kitchen.

I tell Auntie Rani that I'm going to get coffee.

Auntie Sangeetha is already sitting at the kitchen table, her legs crossed at the ankles and her arms folded on her lap. She isn't wearing any makeup; the mole on her face is missing, and her lips are parched and drenched of colour like she's in desperate need of water. As with Auntie Rani, her eyes are beady and small. Everything she wears is too big – her sweater and sweatpants, both grey, look like a man's – until I realize I had seen them atop the pile of clothes on Chevy's bed. Her hair is tied into a low bun and strands of it fall into her face, oscillating my view of my poor old aunt. She stares listlessly at the cupboards, as though looking out the window of a retirement home, sedated in the mourning of what remains. Her lips are parted and her breathing is raspy. My mother and Auntie Moira make coffee, toast bread. Perhaps it's something they haven't seen before, perhaps it's too early in the morning, but I feel the instinct to wrap a blanket around my Auntie Sangeetha and put her to bed.

"What I want to know…"

The words come from the living room, loud, as though they've been spoken right into my ear. A knot forms in my chest and my arms go stiff at my sides. Auntie Moira lowers the coffee from her mouth, leaving a milk moustache behind, my mother stops buttering her toast. Auntie Sangeetha blinks once, twice, slowly.

"What I want to *know*," Auntie Rani says louder. I hear her coffee cup clash against the saucer. Upstairs there is shuffling; my sisters are coming out of their rooms.

"Is why," she goes on, "people treating me like this." She enunciates each word, I hear the periods at the end of one. The air stills as her padded footsteps make their way to the kitchen.

Auntie Moira doesn't know what to do. She stands there with her mug cupped at her chest, the film of milk above her upper lip starting to dry into a froth, looking back and forth between Auntie Sangeetha and my mother. My mother resumes buttering her toast, her back to the kitchen. She keeps spreading the butter over and over, its scraping in sync with Auntie Rani's approach, until a sinkhole forms at the bread's centre. Auntie Sangeetha sighs and makes a languorous motion with her hand as though she's brushing away a fly. I step aside from the doorway, the air of Auntie Rani brushes past me. I am behind her now, and when I look down the hallway, Briony is standing there with Cece behind her. My eyes wide, I shrug at them both. I put my back and palms against the wall and slide against it until I reach them.

"What the shit is going on?" whispers Briony.

"I don't know," I say, looking to her and Cece. "Let's go upstairs."

"What happening with all*yuh*?" we hear Auntie Rani say. None of us move. From where we stand, we can only see the back of Auntie Rani, and Auntie Sangeetha sitting in her chair, her face in profile, still staring at the cupboards ahead her. "*Allyuh* have something you want to say *to me*? Because it *looking* like allyuh have something you want to say *to me*. You think I don't know allyuh? What you have to say, say. Say it, nah, say it."

Briony and I lock eyes, Cece holds on to Briony's sleeves from the back. Cece looks confused, tired.

Uncle Bass makes his way down the stairs and peers over the railing midway down.

"What happening over here?" he says to me. So rich is his voice that he sounds ominous, but his face softens when he sees us looking back at him like puppies down a well.

"I don't know," I whisper.

"Girls, come upstairs," says Uncle Bass. "Leave them. Come. Come upstairs."

"Oh, you know what," says Auntie Sangeetha. All of us – Uncle Bass, too – turn toward the kitchen and peer in. I have never heard Auntie Sangeetha's voice, routinely saccharine, flatten to an octave deeper.

"You know what?" she says again.

"Sangeetha—" my mother says.

"Nah," says Sangeetha. She gets up from the chair, it screeches as she pushes it backwards, almost toppling over. "I tired of this," she says.

"Tired of what now," says Rani. The question comes out like a sentence.

"Everybody know," says Sangeetha.

"Everybody know what?" says Auntie Rani.

Auntie Sangeetha takes a step toward Auntie Rani, and a full six inches shorter than her sister, she looks up at her and says, as though they're her two last two breaths, "Everybody know."

"Sangeetha," says my mother. "Enough. Sit down."

"No," says Auntie Rani. "Everybody know what? Say it."

"Girls, I say come on up*stairs*," says Uncle Bass, but he says it without conviction, and we ignore him.

"Everybody know," says Auntie Sangeetha, "that you was always jealous of Tippie."

I bring my fingers to my lips and Uncle Bass groans.

"Always been jealous of she," says Auntie Sangeetha. She takes another step toward Rani. Auntie Rani does nothing. Her hands remain at her sides, straight and relaxed.

I can't see my mother, and I wonder how her body is holding her right now. I wonder how her face falls. Is she walking toward Auntie Sangeetha, ready to tackle her once at close proximity, as though my aunt's finger is on a trigger? Does she feel the need to muzzle her sister, like I once had with the old cousin? I imagine Auntie Moira at the side of the kitchen with her palms to her cheeks, or perhaps they run short and stiff along her sides, paralyzed. The stairs creak from where Uncle Bass stands, and it is unclear whether he is coming or going.

"Always jealous," says Auntie Sangeetha. She closes her eyes and shakes her head, furiously, as if to rattle away her thoughts. "Always jealous. You did like Blues – oh, you did *like* Blues – you did want to be with him—"

She stops here, and my mother's fingers, thin and long, come into view. She is reaching toward Auntie Sangeetha, slowly, like she wants to choke her, but her arms wrap around my aunt's shoulders. Auntie Sangeetha frees herself from my mother's embrace. "And you is the reason why Chevy was the way he was, why he never say anything, the poor thing, he see it all, and look – look where he is now."

"Okay," says my mother. "Okay." Auntie Sangeetha swats my mother's hands away.

A seething rage, an enclosing calm, a fantasia of disbelief – any of these could be coursing through Auntie Rani's veins. We still can't see her face, then she raises one of her arms and I feel my sisters and I collectively shrivel. Rani points a thick finger in Sangeetha's face. She holds the finger there. Auntie Sangeetha does nothing, though she appears to be holding a full breath in her chest.

Auntie Rani drops her hand back down to her side. "You can go now."

Auntie Sangeetha crinkles her eyebrows. "I can *go now*? Rani, I's a grown woman. I could come and go anytime I want."

"No," says Auntie Rani. "Leave. Leave the house now."

Auntie Sangeetha's face changes shape; her eyebrows fall loose, her jaw falls slack, and her eyes, suddenly in a turn of emotion, are doleful, big and wet, tremoring with the light of the kitchen's chandelier. Her face springs back in that which I know: an apologetic fear.

"Rani, I living in this house before you. You have no right to tell me something like that. I's not a child."

"Just go," says Auntie Rani. "Gone. Gone get your things and go."

Auntie Sangeetha opens her mouth to say something, she looks in the direction of my mother. My sisters and I lean against the wall of the stairway to get a better view like we're turning a sharp corner. We see nothing.

Auntie Sangeetha looks back to Auntie Rani, and Auntie Rani

turns around, not looking at any of the other sisters in the kitchen. Briony, Cece and I line ourselves up and flatten against the wall to make room for her to pass. She does so, as if we are not there, and returns to the living room. I hear the springs of the loveseat creak, and the low murmur of the television, which heightens as she turns up the volume. She clears her throat and the cup politely clinks against the saucer.

Like schoolchildren, Briony, Cece and I fall back in formation: Cece behind Briony, Briony behind me, and we look at Auntie Sangeetha. She looks down to the basement, as if really considering fetching her things.

"Sangeetha," my mother says, but my aunt holds her palm up, which is meant to be firm, but is trembling. We see my mother now, she steps into the frame of the kitchen doorway, and she looks reserved, upset, but also sorry, like my aunt should have known better than to say what she felt.

Auntie Sangeetha walks toward the basement stairs and goes down one step, her man-slippers slapping the silence. Then she lifts her foot and turns back around, shoulders back, chin up. She moves through the hallway down to the living room, and again, we line up against the wall to let another aunt pass. Against her will, her buxom body brushes us in the narrow hallway. Cece whispers, "Auntie, don't."

She does not acknowledge Cece and heads straight to the living room, all of our heads turning, Uncle Bass', too, up on his roost. She reaches the living room, but does not turn her head to Auntie Rani, she is in the foyer now, at the front door, opening it, then the screen door, and she walks through it, leaving them both open, placing one slipper in front of the next. She walks down the front steps, down the pathway, snow water soaking through her slippers and flicking spits of slush onto the back of her grey joggers. She turns right down the street. My sisters and I and Uncle Bass go out of the door to the front porch. None of us call her back. Soon, she is out of view. She disappears around the bend concealed by the bare, sturdy trunks of oaks and maples. An arctic wind howls into the house and a scarf is blown off its hook, mail is strewn from the front cabinet. Uncle Bass comes out of his hypnosis and shuts the door, returning to the porch rubbing his bare arms that stick out of his white undervest. He goes to the edge of the steps and leans his whole body forward, balancing on one foot, looking down the street.

"She gone," he says in his low, low voice. "She really, really gone."

17

Oh, but Junior's face was both heaven and hell! For in the infant's refinement, beneath the layers of baby fat as he grew into a spindly toddler, lay latent the spitting image of Blues.

On Florence Street, there is a photograph sitting on the living room's mantel of the little boy I never knew, smiling, as dead children do in pictures. In it, Junior is five years old. He is whooshing down a slide, both arms raised above his head, and squealing in an almost audible delight. My Auntie Tippie is crouching at the end of the metal tongue, waiting to receive the full thrust of her youngest. If there were ever a picture to be framed, slotted into a documentary, and moved slowly across the screen as an ominous narrator told the true account of their tragic deaths, this would be the one.

We do have photo albums. My parents had brought with them from Trinidad hundreds and hundreds of pictures, and at one point, when they moved to Toronto, had decided to organize the people of their lives, including themselves, into chronological order. But when Briony and I went through the albums, often in search of our younger selves, we found that each one, though started, was never actually finished. We found pictures laid under thin, sticky films at the beginning and middle, but in the last quarter, nothing – not even the films of the pages had been peeled back. There existed seven or eight albums curated like this with no logic to their endings; the last picture of one album is of icicles, zoomed in, hanging off a tree, and in another, three smiling faces blur into the background with a closeup of a startled and unidentified iris.

Briony and I used to make a game of it, reaching our arms elbow-deep into the box, churning the pictures around, saying that whoever we pulled out we'd have to live with for the rest of our lives. Once, I pulled out a picture of young Auntie Moira, and Briony had screamed, "Oh my God! No! Never!", and when she pulled out a picture of Auntie Rani, we just looked at each other and shrugged. If we didn't know who was in the picture and it was of a male, we took the risk that he was not related to us and said, "Your boyfriend." Another time she pulled out a picture of our father, and both of us – I had seen it in her face, too – had to try very hard not to cry.

Unless we were lucky to find the date was scribbled on the back of a picture, we never knew when a photo was taken, and most times, not even who was in the picture. Briony and I often mistook ourselves for the other, especially when we were babies and nothing but blobs and drool. We would fight and ask our mother. She would barely need to look at the photo before saying who it was, with the evidence of a story to back it up.

"Oh, that is Briony," she once said, of a photo of Briony lying naked at a couple of months old on a doubled-up quilt on the floor. "That is the old, old house, Ma and Pa's. Sangeetha was washing all the bed sheets that day and we had to put Briony on the ground. She didn't even cry once, you know. She was such a nice baby."

It was in this convoluted way we looked back on our youth, and with it saw the disjointed life of Junior. In one photo album there were three pictures of him, and even those were not in chronological order. The first was a duplicate of the one we had framed on the living room mantel; in the second, he was only a few days old in the arms of Auntie Tippie, who, after this birth, as with Chevy's, showed further hair loss. The third picture was of Junior on his eighth, and last, birthday. All other pictures of Junior were at the random mercy of the hatboxes; like a magician, I would pull one out, first making sure it was him, trying to guess the age, event and mood of the photo. Then I would pull out another, then another, get distracted by someone else I thought looked familiar, until finally, laid out on my mother's bed, there were too many photographs of differing times and tones to confidently trace their origins.

It was Briony who pointed out how much Junior looked like his father.

"Wow, he is definitely his father's son, that's for sure," she had said. (This was after we had seen the torn picture of Blues that Auntie Rani kept in her room. I never did tell Briony I found a letter; I didn't want her to feel outperformed.) I tried to play it off, like I had forgotten what Blues looked like, and she rolled her eyes. She went down the attic stairs and came back with the picture of Blues.

"Briony!"

"Oh, what's a few minutes. She'll never notice."

"Unless she looks at it undyingly every hour."

She looked to the side as though this might be a real possibility, then shook her head and scrunched up her face. "No, that's stupid. And crazy." She looked down the picture. "He's kind of hot."

"Oh my God," I said. "He's *old*. And a dick. What kind of a man does what he did?"

"I know, I know," Briony said. We were whispering now. "Okay, but look at his face and look at Junior's face."

Junior was a little more light-skinned than what we could make out in the picture of Blues, but aside from that Briony was right. Junior was, uncomfortably so, a mirror image of Blues. We held up the picture of Junior, where his hands are cupped around his eighth birthday cake, taken off guard by an anonymous paparazzo, and held it next to the picture of Blues. It is true to say once you see someone's face in the face of another, you can see nothing else. The corners of their jaws were slightly sunken as if a bolt lay hinged beneath the skin; the slim slits from which black irises shone through; the shallow carve in their chins, which, in Junior's young face, gave him the air of a boy that would be athletic in the teenage years he would never live to see. We could see, too, from another picture we pulled out of the box, the dual colour scheme of their lips, the lower one full and pink, and the upper thin and brown.

"Yeah," I said after a while. "That's crazy. They do look exactly the same."

I put the pictures laid out on my mother's bed back into the box. Briony went to return the picture of Blues to its rightful owner. As I piled face upon face of people I didn't know but probably knew *of*, I imagined in sore, empathic detail how hard it must have been for them both – Auntie Rani and Auntie Tippie – to cope with Blues' second, unforeseen abandonment.

Perhaps, I wondered, even more so for Auntie Rani.

In Junior's toddler years he had looked like Tippie. He had her abundant head of (pre-birth) hair, winnowing long lashes, the effeminate frame. But as Junior grew more into himself, shedding blubber and gaining speech, my aunts soon noticed how the cut of his jaw and lop-sidedness of his smile bore so strong a resemblance to the man they came to hate that, in Junior's early years, they could not look at him without staring at his face and feeling a strike of sudden sadness. Despite their efforts and desire to forget Blues, they would never be able to deny the origin of Junior's being.

This included the women of Macaria, too. From a great distance (though none greater than mine), anyone looking in on a conversation between Junior and one of the women would note that they listened to the young boy with great attention while he spoke, when, really, in the privacy of their thoughts, they were receding into the past, thinking how children truly did not know anything that came before them – and more: what lengths they would go to protect that peace, namely by means of disregard and gaps in plot-logic when questions were asked. The men of Macaria often disrupted this peace, telling Junior how much he looked like his father, what a heartbreaker he was, and with a face like that, he would break hearts, too. The women told the men to hush their mouths, and whether Junior questioned the whereabouts of Blues is not something I have given much thought to or dared to inquire about. Like all of the women, I hated Blues, too.

I am to understand that Chevy and Junior, three years apart, were close, but not very close. Where Chevy stood like a man right from the minute he could walk, my aunts and mother felt that Junior hesitated to do so, preferring to be held by Tippie and stay within close proximity of my young aunts. By the time he could walk and talk and understand instructions, Auntie Tippie had long since returned to the SuperSuperMarket to work alongside Auntie Rani again, and Junior, with his bone-thin legs and long arms, remained at home miming the household duties of my mother, Auntie Sangeetha, and Auntie Moira. When my mother hung laundry in the backyard, she strung up another line at his height where he was assigned to hang the socks. When Moira tended to the garden, she put him in charge of the fruits and vegetables that were ready for picking, and with the heist of his aunt's arms, Junior plucked them from their stems with great accomplishment and placed them into a basin. When Auntie Sangeetha swept the house – an incompetent staging of housework, there'd barely be any dust in the pan – she would steal moments to nap or read or look out a window, and if Junior was watching her, he would put a finger to her lips, then his, place a pillow next to her, and pat it. They each – my loving aunts and mother – made Junior to feel as though he were running the house, and that a male, no matter how young, could be taught to uphold the home in more ways than one. It was this loyal modesty, which lasted until his last living day, that made his death even more tragic; that a boy – so angelic, so pure, so quiet and indrawn and who wished for nothing more than to be with his aunts and feel his mother's touch – should be taken away so cruelly.

"To me, it make sense over time," Auntie Sangeetha once said to me. "He was too good for this world. So it only make sense that an angel live in heaven."

Chevy never bullied or mocked Junior for his shy disposition (as one would expect of an older brother), nor did Junior seek validation from Chevy (as one would expect of the younger). For all the rites of passage brothers were to go through together, neither partook and simply surpassed them. Chevy did not help Junior with his homework because Junior did not need it. Junior did not copy anything Chevy did (like tying his hair into a low ponytail, or leaving the house wearing nothing but short pants and flip flops), or pay any special admiration for his brother's more masculine features. Chevy never told Junior how the boys at the school found him too quiet and dumb for it; he defended him with fists. And most of all, unlike growing children, Junior was never tempted by the allure of being away from home. He was an innate homebody, they said. Auntie Rani once wondered aloud if this was natural, if maybe they were sheltering him too much. Junior never once pestered Chevy to take him along with him and his friends when they knocked about in the neighborhood, instead preferring to lie at home in the hammock

Auntie Sangeetha nailed up for him in the backyard, or slapping muddies together in a pile with an imaginary friend.

Worried that imagination might become Junior's only friend, Tippie urged Chevy to take Junior with him to meet some of the other boys. To appease their mother, both did as they were told, but returned home soon after, no different than if they'd been asked to run to the store for milk. Tippie asked Junior if he had fun, Junior shrugged, saying that it was boring sitting around, talking, doing nothing all day in the sun. When Tippie pressed him for more answers, he said that being outside made him tired, and he really did not have anything to say to the other boys, nor they to him. After that day, to neither brother's offence, Chevy and Junior spent little time with each other, except when they were watching television and eating dinner, laughing at different parts of the same show and when they were riding their bikes.

It was strange, Auntie Sangeetha said, how indifferent they were to their differences, as though they had fully known themselves through and through and carried within them no insecurities. "If only all of we was as confident as them little boys," she said. "I don't know where they does get it from."

On a rare occasion, my aunts were all seated in the living room of Florence Street, including Auntie Moira. From the basement steps I heard them bickering as my laundry barrelled round and round in our archaic dryer, about who Junior took after in the family, each one convinced that he had had the traits they didn't perceivably notice as their own. Auntie Rani said that he had been the strong, silent type. Auntie Sangeetha said that he was a melancholy romantic. Auntie Moira said that he was a utilitarian, and that he took every day as it came and nothing more (she surprised me – a cocky under-grad at that time – knowing that word). My mother said that he was an academic, and like Tippie, found the general population boring.

He could have been something, really something, she said, and in the end they unanimously agreed he was a little bit of everything, without flaw and better than them all.

That same day in the evening after everyone had eaten and retired to their rooms, Auntie Sangeetha sat in the living room with the lights off just after the sun had set. She saw me coming down the stairs and waved me over. We both sat there, sighing a few times in the summer's stifling heat when she told me without prompt that Auntie Rani never kissed Junior more than five times in his whole life. I remember this moment perfectly; it would be the last time Sangeetha ever told me anything about Junior. She said so much, so fast, that I had to look away from her face to really hear what she was saying. Much like the summer when Auntie Moira had thrown a bottle cap at my face, Auntie Sangeetha had had too much too; when she belched, she hunched her shoulders and elongated her mouth, and a deep rumble quaked in her chest and unleashed a putrid peachy gust in my face. She had just gotten into a petty quarrel with Auntie Rani the previous day, and I don't know if this had anything to do with the way she had drawn on her eyebrows – dark and thick and curvy like inverted bullhorns so she looked demonic – but she said, leaning over the couch and coming close to my face, "Rani – your Auntie Rani – she could never kiss Junior, you know."

She put her feet, which looked like swollen loaves of crusted bread, up on the coffee table, and collapsed backwards into the loveseat. I pulled up my pants mid-thigh like a man, switched on the record button in my head and readjusted myself. In the humidity my clothes stuck to my skin. I saw that not even the truth serum that was alcohol could make my aunt say, what she wanted to say, unfiltered. She began instead to talk around that enigmatic thing, like how when Junior was first born, Rani took care him like he was her own, even though, even though, even though... and she trailed off, her last ounce of soberness flashing its red lights to indicate that she was in danger of saying something that could not be unsaid.

"Even though, what?" I had asked, trying my best not to lean forward in my seat – that, I was just a passive listener hanging on to the last hours of the day.

"In any way," she continued, "once baby boy reach about four years old and he lose he baby fat, all of we did start to see how much he looking like that next muddahcunt and none of we say nothing. What we could say? What we could *do*? Junior couldn't help it. How Junior could help something like that? Junior didn't even know he look like he father – he never see a picture of him, nothing. We never used to show him or Chevy a picture, and when they did ask where they father was, we used to tell them not to watch that, look ahead, not behind, and all the pictures we had of that manbitch we tear up and throw away in the rubbish with the rotten food and trash.

"But it was hard for Rani. I really feel for she, you know?" she said, gesturing an open palm toward me. I nodded. "Not only because she had to see Junior face every day," she said, (without saying the words *why*), "but because she probably wouldn't forget it for the rest of she life." She leaned forward, swung her feet off the table, and started to knock her chest with her fist. "How you could forget somebody's face when you was there with them the day they dead?" She was speaking quickly now. She belched once, then a second time, then another, and when her cheeks puffed out and did not suck back in, she motioned for me, quickly, to go away. I ran to the basement, cursing, that now of all times puke had taken the place of her words. I brought a pail and placed it at my aunt's feet. She threw up into it, and as I held my breath, I thought of the old cousin and how I had pressed my ear to that bathroom door, and how, now, for the second time in my life, I have had to listen to a relative spew fluid from their body for the sake of gaining another piece of the grand puzzle.

Through the words garbled with vomit, I kept saying, "Uh huh, uh huh, huh," moving my hand in small circles on her upper back – she said that Rani was the one to take Chevy and Junior to school on their bikes on that fateful early morning. Then she took a deep breath, and when she thought she was done, she threw up some more, saying in between heaves that it was the last time everyone saw Junior, and that was when things changed. Everything, really.

18

"No," says my mother. She holds up a palm as if stopping a force. Briony and I hang our coats back on the wall and stand there in our winter boots. Cece's quivering eyes dart from us to our mother to Auntie Moira, to us to our mother to Auntie Moira. Our mother's eyes roll sideways to the wall, the one Rani sits behind. "No," she says again, louder. "Nobody going anywhere. Sangeetha is a grown woman, she could take care of she self. If she want to come back, she will come back. Leave it for now."

"Leela," Auntie Moira says. The tiny hairs on her arms raise from the draft that seeps in from under the front door. Our mother turns toward her sister. Auntie Rani turns up the volume on the TV. Auntie Moira, mouth agape, looking between the wall and my mother, forgets what she has to say. Her parted lips seal. Uncle Bass puts his hands on her shoulders. My mother closes the front door.

*

In the late afternoon, Cece and I revisit an endearing pastime of our youth: we bake a cake. Betty Crocker's Super Moist chocolate cake from a box, the one we've always baked since we were children which made us feel like future gifted chefs.

Cece cracks the eggs, I measure the oil and milk, we fight about who has to hand-mix it. I lose, I mix it for eight minutes, which Cece says was really only five, she opens the oven door, we cower from the blast of heat, slide the pan in, and sit down at the kitchen table.

I ask how school is going and if she likes her professors. She says it's going okay, and yes, she does like all her professors. Really? All of them? She says, yeah, all of them. I ask her what she wants to do when she graduates later this year, and she tells me she doesn't know how a B.A. in Sociology will really help her find a job, but maybe she should have thought about that before. I tell her to go easy on herself, nobody at any age knows what they're doing, at least not for long, and she says, as if she hasn't heard me, that after university she might get a college degree for social work. I tell her that is amazing, that is so great, that is a wonderful idea, and she should definitely do it. She smiles at me, tucks her hair behind her ears, and looks at her feet.

We head to the living room where the television is still blaring and Auntie Rani's coffee cup and saucer are on the table. I turn down the TV and Cece lies down on the couch, her bony ankle hanging off its edge. I take the saucer and cup into the kitchen.

"Cece," I say, once back in the living room, "you know what we should do?"

"Mmm," she says with her face buried in a cushion.

"We should take the cake over to Posie's when it's done."

"Yeah," she says, turning over to face the couch. "Yeah, that's a good idea."

She falls asleep.

*

When she hears someone approaching, Auntie Moira stops talking and makes her way down the attic stairs. As the distance between us closes, the approach of an awkward silence heightens. She breaks it first.

"You see your Uncle Bass?"

"He went out for cigarettes."

She nods her head. "You all baking something? It smelling nice."

"A chocolate cake. Cece and I are going to take it over to Posie afterwards."

She arches her eyebrows, like I have said something controversial. She says okay and we brush past each other, her rose oil scent mingling with the cocoa heat that spreads throughout the house. She makes her way to the guest bedroom and closes the door behind her.

*

My mother's room has always felt like a treat to step foot in, even now. Whenever I crossed that threshold separating the attic hallway from her room, I felt as though I was trespassing not into another world, but another dimension. Within this confined space of off-colour wallpaper, hazy notes of floral baby powders, the urn, and face creams like puddings left open on this or that dresser, there lay a different set of rules from the rest of the house that could only be entered on the grounds of trust, and usually, by appointment. The Room that my mother and father had once loved each other in did not have this air of restriction and formality. There were times – and what brief, fleeting times they were – when Briony and I (Cece was still turning in the womb) would be lying on their bed, daydreaming while our parents talked around us of bills or dinner or gossip back home. My mother might be putting on her earrings – when she used to wear earrings – and my father might be slipping a t-shirt over his head. It was as if there were no other rooms in the house that we could talk or read or nap in (naps were always dreamless, deeper, on our parents' bed). When I think back now, we must have loved The Room because of the smell, because it was all of our smells; my father's soap that he never fully washed off the back of his neck, whose residue lingered on their pillows; my mother's Elizabeth Taylor White Diamonds perfume; the cheap Calgon Hawaiian Mist Briony used to unsuccessfully cover her smoking habit; my own scent, of candy inspired lip-glosses; the remnants of cinnamon and saffron that stuck to our clothes and roamed through vents; the clear apple freshness that strolled in from the backyard. All of it mingled and fused into something that could not be dissected, it was undefinable and inimitable. Ours.

My mother had taken nothing up to attic when she abandoned The Room, except for clothes and toiletries and the crib Cece was to sleep in. With the widower's pension she received every month from the government, plus the small maternity leave pay from the small office she worked at as a receptionist, she had made Briony order a new bed, a new dresser, a new laundry basket, a new everything. In the immediate aftermath of her husband's death, the furniture the delivery men brought up to the attic remained in its original condition for weeks; everything was kept in its plastic wrapping, including the mattress she slept on, its rainlike static crinkling down the stairway into our rooms at night. Briony and I would sometimes find her coiled up in a ball, even as swollen as she was with Cece, her hands wrapped around her head as if she were ducking from hail. When we brought blankets from our rooms and placed them on her, the next morning we would find them flung to the ground. In time she got better though, my mother. She had to, for Cece.

*

My mother sits on the edge of the bed flipping through her phone-book. The air has a scent of lavender. Tucked into an ornamental piece of wood is a tea candle's flame, surviving. The cordless phone lays next to her and I look at it like a gun, like something I need to snatch away. The floorboard creaks when I step toward her, she looks up at me through her wiry glasses sitting low on her nose, then back down.

"Oh, boy," she says. "Is only three o'clock and it feel like a whole week gone by."

"I'm worried about Auntie," I say. She steupses at me, turning the pages of the phonebook.

"Is nothing to worry about, Cassandra. Ain't I say she's a grown woman? You know how much time Sangeetha leave home when we was children and come back a few days later like nothing happen? Plenty time."

"What, like a dog?" I want to say.

"She probably sitting in a Tim Hortons or Subway right now." She laughs. "And she wearing she slippers. She was always dramatic. People probably looking at she like she crazy. They wouldn't be wrong. She was just trying to make a point, that's all. She will be back home this evening."

"No." I clear my throat. "*No*. I mean Auntie Rani."

She stops turning the pages, then resumes, flapping each page hard against the previous. "Well, that is not really something I could help with."

I saw you guys under the apple tree, I say in my head.

"I will talk to Sangeetha when she come back," she says.

I want to say I'm scared, but I'm not sure if there's a point.

"What if she doesn't come home?"

"Ain't I say she will come?"

"What if she doesn't though?"

179

"Cassandra, leave me. I have other things to worry about."

The need to sleep and forget rushes through me, and fatigue droops over my body. I yawn long and loud.

"Cassandra, please," says my mother, "Cover your mouth."

*

Evening falls. As the sunlight dwindles, a bitter wind shrieks past us as Cece and I stand outside Posie's door, shrugged in our jackets. I hold the cake in both my palms, the heat of it warming my gloves and my chin. We had asked Briony if she wanted to come as we were leaving, but she said, "No, I'm good," and went back up to her room.

I click my tongue as we wait for Posie to answer our knocks and take stock of the porch: vast and long like a ranch, it is barren of furniture, save for two old wooden deck chairs, one with a thick, worn copy of a Nora Roberts' *Red Lily* wedged between its planks. The wind chimes hanging from a low beam knell against each other to the tune of *Amazing Grace*.

"Huh," I say. "I didn't even know wind chimes could do that."

"What's that?" Cece says. She peeks through the frosted glass of the door.

"That wind chimes could play a song. Did you?"

She nudges me with her elbow and straightens up. Through the frosted door, we see a nebulous form shifting toward us. Posie opens the door, and seeing my sister and I behind it, smiling suddenly as if for a picture, says, "Oh. Well, hello."

Not sure who should speak first, Cece and I remain quiet. A moment too long passes. "Hi. Posie," I say. "We're from across the street."

"Oh, yes. I know," she says. "How are you, girls?"

"We, uh," says Cece. "We... baked a cake for you."

"Oh," Posie says, her face softening. "Oh, how sweet of you girls. Cassandra," she points a crooked, pink finger at me, "and Cecelia?" she says, narrowing her eyes at my sister. "Did I get that right?"

"Yes," I say smiling.

She nods. "Well, why don't you girls bring the cake in and set it on the table? It looks heavy on that platter and I'd hate for you to drop it."

"Ummm," I say. Cece and I look at each other; we had hoped our good deed would require nothing more of us. "Sure," I say.

Inside, heat bathes my face. It feels like a balmy summer day in the dark corridor, and I blow out a puff of air as if climbing uphill.

"Oh, I know," Posie says. "I need it to be this hot or I just can't get anything done. Let me take your coats, girls."

The three of us fumble between who should hold the cake, and in the end Posie takes it. Cece and I remove our jackets, put our gloves in their pockets, Posie hands the cake back to me as I hand her my jacket, and she lifts the heavy coats onto the coat rack. As she does, my sister and I position our hands behind her as though she might fall; Posie's legs, through her black tights, the same kind that my sister and I are wearing – cheap and comfortable – look like two thin branches broken off from our apple tree.

"Oh, let me get that," I say too quietly, but then the coats are hung. She wipes her eyebrows with her fingers.

"Woo," she says. "Okay. The kitchen is right this way. Follow me."

Coupled with the black tights, Posie wears a powdery-blue, knitted sweater that runs to her mid-thighs. Her hair, which I had thought was white when we watched her from our porch a few days ago, is actually a very light pale blonde clenched in a tight bun at the nape of her neck like a newborn's fist. Her outfit seems youthful for a woman her age; up close she looks to be in her mid-sixties or early seventies, and her glazed blue eyes with a brown spot of melanosis in each one, match the blue of her sweater. Cece trails behind me quietly, and I can tell her curiosity matches mine. There's a feeling like no one's home and we're all intruders tiptoeing through the dark. All the lights on the ground floor are off, and our way through the hallway to the kitchen is guided by the day's last remaining light. The house has a smell, like all houses do, of fresh laundry, slow-simmered tea, and something familiar that I can't make out – leaves or herbs or something aromatic and chemical. The floorboards that creak under our featherweight are the same shade of blue as her sweater and eyes, as is the carpeting of the stairs. In the kitchen we discover that this is Posie's preferred colour. The cupboards with their soft grey handles, the tasselled cushions of the kitchen table's seats, the hand towel hanging lopsidedly off the oven's handle, the pot cloths on the stove burned in their centres, the sink's sudsy sponge – all robin's egg blue.

"You can just place the cake here, Cassandra," says Posie. I set it on the round kitchen table that has only two chairs, one of them pulled out like someone has just walked away.

I put the cake down, and not knowing what to do with my hands, I smile at Cece, who smiles at Posie, who smiles at us. Her lips are thin and pink, glossy with saliva, and she has a mixture of grey and brown eyebrows, one naturally higher than the other. Her eyelids look heavy, and at an angle, they sheen with oil. Her laugh lines run deep as do the dimples on her cheeks. Fine lines sprout from the corners of her eyes and reach her temples, and the skin under her eyes is thin and grey-blue. Two prominent bones like tongs extend from her beneath neck as if holding up her chin. She is a beautiful woman.

"It is really very nice of you girls to bring this cake," Posie says. "Did you bake it?" Her voice is soft, but not fragile, and it does not tremble like her knees had when she hung our coats.

"Yes," says Cece. "But it's not from scratch. It's just box cake. It's our favourite, though."

"Oh, that doesn't matter if it's not from scratch. Most people can't tell, anyway," she says, winking at us. She clasps her hands in front of her. "Why don't we cut it so we can enjoy it together?"

Without waiting for us to answer, she walks to the cupboard, takes out three teacups and saucers, a knife and four forks from the drawer, brings them to the table, and puts the kettle on. She scrapes another chair from a back room into the kitchen. We sit at the table eating the cake and drinking masala chai tea.

"I was sorry to hear about your cousin Chevy," Posie says.

Cece and I stop mid-chew.

"Thanks," says Cece. "We're really sorry to hear about Nina, too."

"Thank you, honey." She blows on her tea and takes a sip. I feel a slight breeze on my neck and look over my shoulder. Posie says, "My mother was very old, as you know. Though, you girls might be too young to remember her. Do you remember her? Anyway, she was very old." She takes another sip of tea. As she swallows, she waves her hand around. "Many people were coming to the house. They're still coming to the house. In the hours after she died, I mean. Bringing food – like you have – and checking in. Especially after the funeral. It's nice of them, really, so nice, but there's only so many words you have, saying the same thing, over and over and over. God, that almost made me wish I was dead, too."

She laughs dryly, and seeing our flat faces, stops. "I'm sorry," she says. "I didn't mean to be insensitive and imply that you're intruding. Not at all. I just meant… we're both in the same boat, you and I, and you've probably experienced a little bit of that too."

"It's okay," I say. "It's hard. I'm sure people stopping by every hour can get pretty exhausting on top of everything else."

Posie nods. "Yes. Exhausting. But it's more difficult when the death

183

is unexpected. And when they die very young, like in your case. Chevy was only… forty years old or so?"

"Forty-nine," says Cece.

"So very young." She nods for what seems like a long time.

"How old—?" begins Cece as Posie says, "He was—", and Posie holds up her palm. "You first, sweetie."

"I was just going to ask how old Nina was," Cece says.

Posie smiles, like my sister has conjured a long-forgotten memory. She takes her time to say, "My mother was a hundred and two years old," as though it's the first sentence of a long story. I would have sat and listened if she began to tell it, but she says nothing more.

Cece gasps in childlike wonder. "Wow."

"But I was going to say," says Posie, "that Chevy was a really nice guy. He used to help me and Mother with our bags if he saw us from the porch, and sometimes if Daniel – Daniel next door to you – hadn't already shovelled our snow, Chevy would do it for us and sprinkle salt. He always did it with such care. He never rushed it, and he didn't just sprinkle a little bit of salt. He used to go to *town* with that salt. I think he hated the snow just as much as I did," she says, laughing.

"He did," Cece says. Our plates and cups are empty now, and we sit with our hands in our laps.

"He was such a nice man. He really was," Posie says, looking at the floor. "But, *c'est la vie*. I hope you girls and your family are keeping up well."

She gets up to gather the plates and the cups, and when Cece and I both stand to help she asks that we please sit down. She returns to the table and says how she's watched us grow over the years, and how tall (we are not tall) and beautiful we are now. She asks what we have decided to do with our lives.

"I'm studying Sociology at York University," says my sister. "I

184

graduate soon, but I'm thinking of going to college for another diploma afterwards. I'm not too sure yet."

"Well, that's already very impressive, Cecelia. So young and already you have a degree, and then another one after you're done. How old are you? Twenty? Twenty-one?"

"I'll be twenty-three soon."

"Oh, my mother could tell you some stories about women pursuing degrees back in her day. She was born in 1917, remember." She taps the table four times – one tap for each number in the year – as she says it. "A whole other world. You're very lucky, you know, to be so young and free." She smiles at me. "And you, Cassandra? What do you do now? You don't live at home anymore, do you?"

"No," I say. My hands are folded on my lap like a little girl at charm school. "No, I live in London now. I'm doing some writing over there. Writing and working freelance."

"Ah," she says. "What kind?"

"Mostly copywriting for agencies. Newsletters, blogs, social media, that kind of stuff. Boring, really."

"No, honey," she says, placing her palm on the table. "I meant what kind of writing do *you* do?"

I shake my head. "Oh. So stupid of me. Creative writing. Fiction. It was a hobby that turned into something, I guess. I read a lot when I was a kid."

"Fantastic," she says quietly. "That's fantastic." She smooths her hair and sighs. "Oh, my mother, *oh*, she loved reading. She started reading full-time after she retired and got all of her books at the library or in those – what do they call them?" She puts her index finger to her lips, and says, "Oh, they're called little free libraries – have you seen them around? These beautiful little boxes outside of people's homes. They look like birdhouses, except instead of feed, there are used books in them, which I guess is a *kind* of feed. My

185

mother just loved them. She would take a book, leave a book." She stops and smiles. "If you'd like, you can take a look at her bookshelf. Probably lots of authors you'd recognize."

"Thanks. I'd love that."

After a few more polite exchanges, Posie thanks us again for coming and wishes us and our family well.

"This, too, shall pass," she says.

Down the hallway on the way out, Cece trips over Posie's slippers and falls to the floor. Stifling my laughter, I help her up, and she tells me to shut up under her breath while Posie kicks them out of the way. We take our coats from the rack, and she waves us off like we're her children.

"That wasn't so bad. That was even... kind of nice?" I say on the short walk back.

"It was kind of weird is what it was," Cece says. She nuzzles her neck deeper into her jacket. "She doesn't seem sad that her mom just died."

"Of course she was sad. She couldn't stop talking about Nina."

"I know. But she was, like, smiling and stuff, and talking normal, like nothing happened. And the house looked so normal, too. Like, it wasn't messy and nothing looked old. It looked antique. If she was really sad, like, *really* sad, wouldn't she be too sad to clean up? I don't know. It was just weird. I think she's in denial or something."

"Yeah. I know what you mean."

What my sister means is: no one in our family has ever mourned that way. They have not looked back on a life, not even their own, and smiled, the way Posie had when she said, "My mother was a hundred and two years old." Posie did not tuck away the past and divulge pieces here and there, that, like vanity books on a shelf, might open a hidden door and reveal skeletons. In that blue house, no one is emboldened by the dark, creeping in corridors at night, saying the things they cannot say in the light – things they had been holding on to for far too long and needed to exorcise from their conscience and place on another's. And most of all, we would not talk about death over tea and chocolate cake, we would not leave the sequestration of our rooms where we talked to ourselves, looked at old pictures, misremembered memories, imagined them, even, and extracted from them what we needed to make the days more bearable.

19

According to a Google search, a woman who is pregnant can lose up to three hundred hairs per day – two hundred more than the average daily hair loss of a woman who isn't. The hair could sometimes fall out in small tufts, said one website, cascading away from its owner like tumbleweed if the mother was extremely stressed. The associated image, with a black bar across the eyes of a young woman with supple skin, showed the strands on her head dangling like dead threads of an old weeping willow.

In the photo box, there is a picture of Auntie Tippie on the living room couch in Macaria. Her eyes are closed but I'm hesitant to say she was sleeping; with one arm hanging off the couch and the other flung over her eyes, it looks more like she'd passed out. There's a cloth tied around her head, a solid red one with its tail end snaked across the pillow. The skin around her bones – her cheeks, wrists, knees, and ankles – once firm and succulent, looks sagging and thin. When I was very young and had asked my mother if Auntie Tippie was sick when the picture was taken, my mother took one look at it, then looked away. I saw her swallow. She shook her head sadly as though in apology. "No, she wasn't sick. It wasn't like that. That wasn't a nice time. Your Auntie Sangeetha did tie that around she head, and your Auntie Tippie just lie there and let she do it like she didn't even know Sangeetha was there. She didn't— stop going through that box and come help me fold these clothes."

When Auntie Tippie was pregnant with Junior, wisps of hair fell from her head, little by little. Weeks passed, and she began to see more of her scalp than ever before, having now to loop her hair tie around her ponytail four times rather than the usual two. This did not bother her to the extent it might some women, especially Indian women, for she had since Blues given up on love and vanity, relinquishing herself to God and fate, allowing the future to make decisions for her. When Junior died in March 1982 on Main Street, only five blocks from my childhood home in Macaria, and three blocks from the school, Auntie Tippie discovered that she had not surrendered herself at all. In the wake of Junior's death, the shallow pond of happiness she had allowed herself in motherhood not only dried up and drained itself with a guttural gurgle, but grasped at her ankles and sucked her into its muddy depths. There blackness brought to light emotions she had not yet known slept within – where in her heart had these devious darknesses hid? It is almost futile to use words for that *thing* which words evade, to shape what has no shape, to that which the body simultaneously contains and expels. Any effort to structure it begins failing; it has no boundaries, it does not colour within the lines. This thing is grief, and grief is like an inside joke: you have to have been there to really *get* it.

A bumbling attempt to seize that weeping beast, anyway: hollow yet occupying; a light tremor that thunders in the bones; dark, but like light, explosive within; a collapsing star caught in a black hole, stretched and spun and thrown never to be caught again; trying, forever; shock, not as a reaction, but a constant state; she scared her sisters, the way they could see the white all around her iris, how she walked with her arms stuck out at her sides and her fingers spread out like ice water had just been poured over her; the fusion of daytime and nightmares until they were indistinguishable; the body feeling everything, the body rejecting everything – what body?; finding the sense in nonsense, finding the joke in sense; laughing when nothing was funny; someone digging the nail of their thumb, hard, into her arm to see if she was there; they could light a fire under her feet, she would let herself burn; a whole tree could fall onto her body and bones shattered, she would lie comfortably beneath it, gladly, lulling herself asleep to its familiarity. The feeling was endless, these words could roll on forever, they would not matter, what could words undo, words don't matter here, what was done was done, words, words, words, here she remained.

My Auntie Tippie lost ninety percent of her hair when Junior died.

20

But I keep secrets about my family *from* my family, too.

My sisters and I have never really warmed to Auntie Moira. (Cece was often excluded from these sorts of observations on account of the fourteen-year age gap between her and Briony, and her sensitivity.) We always felt that Auntie Moira never really let her guard down, that she was always in acting mode with a fixed script of lines, gestures, and reactions. We thought it might have been because everyone except Auntie Moira had eventually moved up to Toronto and lived with us. Yet there was still something – some inconsistency – we couldn't quite put our finger on. One day she would be firm with us, slapping our hands away from second helpings of food, while on other days she would tell us to eat more, we were all skin and bones. On most occasions, both back in Trinidad and when she flew up for the summers, it was like we – "the children" – were not there at all, even when we addressed her directly. Briony and I came to the conclusion that she did not like children, but then we thought, no, wait, she adored Chevy and Junior, so we adjusted our theory and over the years came to a conclusion: she did not like girl children.

In our peripherals, we often found her eyes on us, moving upwards from our socks, all the way to the high point of our ponytails. I believe Auntie Moira had the same opinion of me as I did of her – that I was plain and uninteresting and what was there was there – but of Briony, and specifically, of Briony's body, she did not approve. Briony, full-figured by the time she turned twelve, had breasts and ass and lips that were plump and pert. Even when she wore large clothing, her body betrayed her, jiggling if she laughed, or sneezed, or made any motion that was not sitting still. Once at Maracas Beach in Trinidad, Briony and I wore matching one-piece bathing suits, and when grown men glared at Briony (I was seven, she was twelve) like they had never seen a female in their lives, Auntie Moira yelled at her when our mother was a safe distance away, telling her, like a jealous high school girl, that she must want attention if she was running and squealing all over the place.

Another time in Toronto, she told Briony that only women who took money wore lip gloss, and Briony said it wasn't lip gloss, "It's Vase*line*," touching the top row of her teeth with the tip of her tongue on the last syllable. Another summer, Auntie Moira complimented Briony's wedge heels as she saw her walking out of the Florence Street house, and when Briony said thanks and left, Auntie Moira wore a half-smile, half-frown like she couldn't decide how she really felt. It became that in the presence of our mother and aunts, Briony and Auntie Moira were cordial enough, but once left alone with me and Cece, Auntie jumped a generation a rung below and turned into Briony's rival sibling.

Now Briony and Auntie Moira don't say much to each other, and we do not talk about her as much as we used to. Naturally, I take Briony's side in most, if not all, matters regarding our aunts. But there is one thing I have always felt guilty about not sharing with my sister, and that is how Auntie Moira went to the National Archives of Trinidad and Tobago and retrieved the newspaper article of Junior's death and mailed it to me.

It was a measure of desperation.

I was on the fourth floor of the Scott Library of York University working on some essay or other, when, jolting a fellow student out of sleep, I called myself an idiot, asking how I could be so stupid all these years. There would have to be records, I thought. It was a child's tragic death – of *course* there were records. I pushed aside my textbooks, opened a new tab on my laptop browser, and typed in "newspaper archives trinidad". In seconds, I was on the National Archives of Trinidad and Tobago website, and in minutes learned that the Archives stored newspapers published from 1825 to 2007. I straightened up, then hunched back down, clicking through to the newspaper collection. I was discombobulated, teetering between excitement – from scrolling past headings like "Historical Gems" and "Records Management" – and anger, feeling like I had been robbed of years of my life having never known this source. Just as soon as I found the website, the thrill of discovery was taken from me; once I was on the newspaper collection webpage, there was nothing more to click. The webpage had a reference code, some information about the collection, like the names of major newspapers and the condition of the records, but that was it. The desperate digital native that I was, expecting instant, accurate information with little to no research, I triple-clicked plain text that I knew wasn't hyperlinked, thinking it might be an administration error, that the website was just not displaying webpages properly. Once I read near the bottom of a page the suggestion to bring a sweater if visitors were planning to stay a long time, I realized that the National Archives of Trinidad and Tobago, where the news of my little cousin's death was stored in a locked filing cabinet, was in a cold room across an ocean, in Port of Spain, Trinidad.

I could not travel to Trinidad on my own, nor could I forget what truths lay in that cold room. I thought maybe I could fly to Port of Spain, get a hotel for a few days, find the article, and fly back. But the horror of someone bumping into me on the streets saying, "Eh, you looking like Leela daughter. Ain't you's Leela daughter? You well looking like she," and reporting back to my mother was enough to cross out that option completely.

Auntie Moira was the only one I knew in Trinidad, and the more I came to understand that she was my only option, the more I convinced myself that she was the right one. She could say yes, she could say no. I played out both scenarios, and then a third, highly unlikely one in my head.

In scenario one, I would explain the truth of why I wanted the article, that I just wanted to know a little bit more about how Junior died, and for nothing more, I just wanted to *know* for myself. She would say okay, fine, mail me the article, and we would both agree not to tell anyone else, because, really, what was there to know? Plus, my mother would yell at us both (I would make a point to mention this).

In scenario two, she tells me no, she calls me boldface, and tells me that I'm lucky she's not going to tell my mother. If she tells my mother, my mother, being *my* mother, will take my side, scold me in private, and we three would never speak of it again.

In scenario three – and this would never happen as it would require Auntie Moira to truly show herself – she would tell me there is no need for her to mail the article, she can tell me the entire story herself.

In the proceeding days before I called her, I hardened myself for scenarios one and two and agreed to accept the consequences of whichever one played out.

I retrieved her number from my mother's phonebook. The phone rang four times before she picked up, and hearing that the voice on the other end belonged to me, who had never dialed her phone number in my entire life, asked what was wrong and if everyone was okay. I told her that everyone was fine, nobody died. Then she asked me if I was okay, and touched by even the slightest concern from her, and hearing the melody of a voice that never left home, I softened, and became honest. I told her I was okay. I asked how she was doing. She replied she was fine. Our ellipses hung in the dead air.

"Auntie," I said, "I have a favour to ask." I had written what I was going to say on a piece of paper, and cold-calling my own aunt, I said in one breath that I was interested in our family history, specifically Junior, and that I knew he was difficult for everyone to talk about, so I thought this – the article in the archives down in Port of Spain – might be a more respectful way of finding out more *and* preserving a part of our history. "Because," I went on, "why should only the archives have it? It's ours, isn't it? We should have it, too, no?"

She was quiet. I was tempted to ask if she was still there. I thought the phone might slip from my clammy hands, and switched it to my right ear, wiping my left palm on my jeans. I could hear Uncle Bass in the background talking, his voice muffled behind a closing door. Auntie Moira still had not said anything. I felt like minutes had passed and that if this did not work, I would begin to cry and plead like a child.

Finally, she said, "Yeah. Okay. Yeah."

"Really?" I said, and she said again, "Yeah." Perhaps feeling the weight of responsibility as the adult in the conversation, she cleared her throat. "I understand where you coming from."

I said thank you, took a deep breath, and then said thank you so much in a tone higher than my original voice. I gave her the address of the archives and restrained myself from pushing my luck and telling her exactly what was needed so as to avoid any errors. The only thing I specified was to make sure to find the news in at least two newspapers, please. When we were finished talking logistics, a lull widened between us, not because we didn't know how to say goodbye, but because one of us had to say: this stays between us. Putting aside the script I had written, my confidence solidified by the trust I placed in my aunt, and she in me, I told her the article was for me, and me only, and there was nothing I was going to do with it other than read it. She said okay.

Two days later, Auntie Moira texted me two pictures of articles ran in the Trinidad Guardian and the Trinidad Express. I texted her thank you with a period at the end, and three minutes later, sent her another text of three blue heart emojis. She replied with a red heart, large and throbbing, and then I did the same.

I began to feel that Briony and I were wrong about Auntie Moira. After Auntie had sent me the articles, when Briony said something mean or critical about her, I would respond with, "She's not so bad" or "It doesn't bother me," and Briony would just stop and look at me like gibberish had just come out of my mouth, and say, "What the *fuck?*"

*

But the call with Auntie Moira made me too brave. One call led to another, and on the next and last one, I was neither the caller nor receiver. I listened to one of my mother's calls. I don't mean I overheard it, like I was in another room translating whispers and key words, but that I picked up the landline phone in the basement and listened to her and a cousin, who was not really a cousin, have a conversation. I had heard my mother say Tippie's name earlier, so I spiralled down the house in one fluid motion, down the attic steps, then the second floor's, then the basement's, turned on the television to MuchMusic, muted it, picked up the phone, and lay down on the couch with a bag of ruffled chips on my stomach. Pompously, I didn't bother to cover the receiver with my hand, thinking they wouldn't mind if I serendipitously joined the conversation had I been discovered, given how well it had gone with Auntie Moira. They talked and talked. I slid a single thick chip into my mouth and crunched down on it. No one said anything, like "Eh, you hear that?" perhaps thinking it was the other who was eating. I went on to hear this cousin, Dimple, say that she often thought about how Tippie seemed like she had gotten a lobotomy after Junior died. She said when she think about it, it make she very sad, she dream how Tippie was there walking on the road late, late at night. I listened to the whole thing – all of it. My mother, after twenty minutes of Dimple talking, said, softly, that she remembered it all, too, and began to cry. Dimple and I listened on the other end. I felt a well of guilt in my stomach, swallowed the chip, snapped out of my arrogant spell, and quietly hung up.

I didn't do anything with the articles, nor did I tell anyone about them. When I had first received the pictures from Auntie Moira, the weight of my phone in my pocket felt heavy every time I walked past someone in the house. I thought I might confess every time my mother and I, or Briony and I, or even Auntie Sangeetha and I, stood too close to each other. Terrified, I avoided my family in the kitchen, in the hallways, in the living room, as much as I could, for weeks, claiming that I had not heard them call my name if I was beckoned.

Still, I suppose I wanted to make it all the more real and less like myth; I printed the images of the articles which both had the same school picture of Junior – the child for whom "death was swift." I cut out the excess white of the printed paper. As though Junior were my own son, I folded the article and put it in my wallet, and over the years, as it wrinkled and wore behind receipts and dollar bills, I deluded myself into thinking they were not copies, but the original articles themselves.

In pockets of the day, I went to the park and read the articles on a bench. When I was on the bus listening to music and looking out of a window, I would pull them out and run my thumb over them, mouthing the printed words like a psalm. I reread them at night under the dim glow of my phone before falling asleep until I knew both the articles by heart and didn't need to look at them to see them anymore. They became more proof than pictures that this thing had really happened. This happened to us. Instead of carrying the physical weight inside my pocket, I then carried the weight of knowing. At night I dreamed about it all.

21

Cece's birthday is tomorrow. I don't imagine we'll celebrate much this year, at least, not in the literal sense of the word. We'll acknowledge the day, we may cut some cake. No one has been speaking much, least of all Cece, and Auntie Sangeetha has been gone for two days.

On the day Auntie Sangeetha left, all slippers and tracksuit trotting down Florence Street with her head held high, when it approached evening, my mother and Auntie Moira came into the downstairs living room where Briony and I watched *Wheel of Fortune* in the dark. As if believing we were still children distracted by the happy sounds and colours coming from the television, they looked out of the window, leaning forward with their hands crossed behind their backs, mumbling to each other. "You know Sangeetha. She probably staying in some twenty-four-hour café until someone come to look for she, waiting to be rescued." My mother, replying to herself, "But you know what kind of people does be in those cafés at night? Maybe she check she self into that small, little hotel and tell them she promise to pay them back later. Sangeetha have that charm, you know." Auntie

Moira only looked through the window, turning her head from left to right as though on patrol.

Briony and I had exchanged knowing glances. "We'll take a walk around," Briony said, like we might find our aunt sitting on a stranger's stoop like an orphan. "We could ask if anyone's seen her."

"You crazy?" said my mother, turning from the window.

Briony, wide-eyed, held her palms up in surrender.

"Should we… call the police?" I said. I looked back and forth between Briony and our mother. Everyone else looked to my mother.

"No," she said after a moment, turning back to the window. "No. She know is Cece birthday. She wouldn't miss it. She never miss it. She's fine. She just being she dramatic self. I know she. She will be back soon." Then she said to Moira, "But send Bass out, nah. Let him take a little walk around and just see. It wouldn't hurt."

Auntie Moira went upstairs and returned a few minutes later. "He going now," Moira said, and my mother nodded.

Uncle Bass, with disheveled hair and pillow creases sketching his face, came down after ten minutes, passing Briony on the stairs as she headed back to her room. My aunts and I watched him in the hallway as he put on his winter coat, scarf, toque and wool socks. Auntie Moira said he should make sure to keep his phone on him and have Google Maps open in case he got lost. Watch out for any black ice, she said, to which my mother replied, "Oh, God, Moira, that melt away long time now." Uncle Bass told Moira to ease she self, he was only going to be gone for half an hour, kissed her on the cheek. My mother and I looked away – she looked at the shoe rack, I at the wall. He walked out the door, first turning left down the street, then changing his mind and turning right. When he disappeared out of view, Auntie Moira looked so worried I thought she might run to the porch, pull from her pocket a laced handkerchief and wave it in the wind.

We waited in the living room watching the bonus round of *Wheel of Fortune*, each of us dryly taking turns at guessing the puzzle. Auntie Moira guessed something ridiculous, and when my mother said, "Moira, how it could be that? They already call all the vowels," she didn't guess anymore. When the evening news aired, none of us reached for the remote. There was a bungalow fire somewhere in Etobicoke, in which no one was hurt, and a car crash in Scarborough in which everyone died. Politicians said things, citizens said what they thought of those things on their way to work. Uncle Bass came back an hour later with his shoulders hunched up to his ears, saying between shivers that he didn't know how we could live in this blasted cold, that he didn't see Sangeetha around, and no, he didn't ask anyone. He said he would try again tomorrow. My mother told us not to worry, that Sangeetha, though immature, was an adult, and she knew what she was doing. We all went to sleep before half past nine. Later that night before I closed my eyes, I texted my sisters in our group chat what our mother had said verbatim. Neither replied.

The next day, Cece came up to the attic for the first time since I'd been home and told me she was worried. She thought we should call the police just to be sure. "Auntie doesn't have a cell phone in case she needs to call someone," she said.

I repeated what my mother had said on the previous night, and that Uncle Bass was going out for walks, too. Cece looked at me bug-eyed and left the room.

On hearing her room door close, I googled the number of the pharmacy that Auntie Sangeetha has worked at for the last few years. A woman picked up on the fourth ring.

"Good morning, Maynard's Health."

"Hi," I said. "Hello. I'm looking for Sangeetha. Is she working today? I just wanted to let her know that she forgot her wallet at home and thought she might need it. Sangeetha Rampersad."

The woman said, well, there was only one Sangeetha working here, then asked who was calling. When I said I was her niece, she said, "Oh, another niece. Okay, no, listen, I can't be giving out this information to just anyone. I'll tell you what I told the girl who called this morning. Sangeetha is not in, and – oh, sorry – hold on. Is this Cecelia again?"

I said yes.

"Oh, Cecelia, sweetie, I'm *sorry*. It's just very busy here. It's Betty."

I said hello to Betty and asked how she was doing.

"Same as this morning, honey. Sorry, I can't talk too long. I have customers lining up here. But no, your aunt still isn't in. Remember? I told you this morning? She asked for two weeks off?" She paused. "I'm sorry if I sound condescending. I know things must be hard at home right now. I know in times like these you forget things you've already done and start doing them all over again. I understand, honey. Time just mixes itself all up, doesn't it?" She tutted. "I'm sorry, sweetie."

I said thank you and goodbye.

Throughout the rest of the day, I heard the front door opening and closing in hourly intervals. People were going on short walks alone. I tried to catch one of them, running down flights of stairs two steps at a time, rushing to tell them I will come with, just give me a minute, let me grab my coat. But my family are a stealthy bunch. I hadn't heard anyone's bedroom door open, the creaking of stairs, or the light patter of outdoor shoes, and by the time I reached the front corridor, breathless, I only saw a coattail slithering into the slimming shard of daylight behind the closing door.

*

But Cece's birthdays have always been a thing. In the fervent days preceding it, we wake up with a sense of purpose, mainly due to the fact that our mother assigns each of us, even Auntie Rani, a chore in preparation for the festivities. My mother does not do this for anyone else's birthday, not even for Chevy when he was alive, to which Briony and I never took offence. We said to each other that Cece was the baby of the family, and we hated the attention, anyway.

On the day before Cece's birthday – today – our mother begins with ablutions. At the break of dawn, she swings her feet over the bed, brushes her teeth, washes her hair, blow-dries it, ties it in a ponytail, then puts on her cleaning clothes and marches through the house as if everyone is awake. By seven, curtains and bedsheets and tablecloths are already tumble-drying, and by nine, each room in the house smells like a sudsy summer breeze. The hardwood floors on the ground floor are all mopped and shiny, so that by the time we wake up and come down for breakfast, we have to be careful not to drop any crumbs or spill any milk lest we be threatened with mopping the whole floor once over again. Typically, we wake to my mother and Auntie Sangeetha vacuuming and beating the dust out of the couches with the broomstick's pole. But on her own this year, my mother's slow thwaps sound punishing, like she's following the tick of a metronome. The vacuum runs on low, its dust-trapped spirits moaning out of the opened windows. There's nothing she can do about the faded paint and the chipping edges of the kitchen counters and cupboards, but she wipes them with something chemical that smells like fresh lemon and mandarins; through a trick of the nose, they appear brighter. Any missing bulbs in the kitchen and living room chandeliers have been replaced with the help of a small stepladder.

Briony and I grunt a greeting to each other and walk down to the kitchen. Cece, up before either of us, hunches over a bowl of cereal with her hair hanging in her face so that I can't see the spoon move from the bowl to her mouth.

"Happy almost birthday, gaw-geous," I say. I move her hair back to kiss her, and startled, I draw in a small gasp. Under her eyes a pale crescent of blue has sunk into her skin, and her cheekbones, once rounded as rosy apples, are carving their way out of her face. The bones in her chest, which I see down her sweater, show themselves as rake throngs as she breathes in and out. I say nothing, I lean in again, and kiss the peach fuzz of her cold cheek with my eyes open.

"Thanks," she says. When I move away, she shakes her head so that her hair falls back in her face. Briony nudges Cece's shoulder and calls her an old fart. Milk splashes out of Cece's spoon onto her sweater, and she looks down at it like she's having trouble placing what just happened. She says thanks, grabs her bowl, and pushing her chair backwards with her body so that it squeals against the polished floor, goes up to her room.

"Who can blame her?" says Briony. She makes a cup of instant coffee and drops two slices of bread into the toaster. "Who would want to celebrate their birthday now?"

"No," I say. "I can't blame her." I sit down in Cece's seat and prop my head up in one hand. Briony pours me a cup of coffee and, sitting across from me, looks surprisingly naked. It takes me a moment to realize that my glamorous sister is not wearing one piece of jewellery. Aside from a pink tourmaline ring, her birthstone, on her middle finger, she wears no earrings (not even the subtle tiny topaz stones she wears to sleep), and no necklace, no bracelets or watch. Not even her sweater has a brand name stitched across its centre or a logo in its corner. We blow and sip our coffee.

"I guess I'll clean the bathrooms," Briony says.

"You?" I smirk at her. "May I ask why?"

"Ha-ha." She shrugs. "I don't know. Ma's cleaning everything. I thought it would be nice to help. Is that so hard to imagine?"

"That's sweet. I'm sure Ma will appreciate it."

She rolls her eyes and continues to blow into her coffee, her lower lip resting on the cup's rim.

"What? I do. I think she would."

"Cas," she says, lowering the cup from her face, "I think you're the only one who thinks that *anyone* would appreciate anything in this family."

I tilt my head to the side and tut in a mocking sympathy. "Oh, Briony. I think they appreciate things. I just don't think everyone is good at expressing it."

She swallows coffee and says in a hoarse voice, "You've been gone for too long."

"They've been through… things. Things that don't compare to what we've gone through. And I think that sort of… beats people down."

"Okay. Sure. But it doesn't mean we're not entitled to our own feelings."

"When did I say that? I didn't say that."

She points her toast at me. "You kind of did."

"I didn't."

She nods quickly, smiling sideways at me.

"I *didn't*," I say, raising my voice. She dodges my kick under the table. The drone of the vacuum waxes and wanes as my mother pushes and pulls it across the basement steps. I lower my voice. "I just think we could be a little more compassionate. Then maybe we would stop expecting so much, and just…you know what I mean?"

She raises her eyebrows at me and bites hard into the toast. "How did we go from cleaning the bathrooms to this?"

"Well?"

"I don't know what you want me to say."

"Useless."

"Where's your compassion?"

"Don't."

She puts her mug down on the table and cups it. "Cas. One of our adult aunts has run away in her joggers and house slippers. That's not normal. She's fine. I'm sure she's fine – she's a resourceful gal and a lot smarter than she pretends not to be – but people – people, like *Cece* – are allowed to feel whatever they want. It's exhausting to keep looking back. Honestly – don't roll your eyes, listen! – too much compassion can make you fucking dead inside, okay? You need to have compassion for yourself, too? Otherwise you leave no room in you to live your life? It's fucking *exhausting*," her voice heightens to falsetto here, "to keep looking back. It is. I'm sorry, it is, and that's the truth. You're always putting everyone before you – not you, I mean people in general – not that *you* don't put people before you – what I'm saying is: trying to understand why people act the way they do is fine, to a point, but eventually you have to just stop and start doing your own *thang*. You've got to *ride* your own *vibe*." She gyrates in her seat. "It sounds like a load of shit, like I just watched a TED talk or something. Only you can bring this out in me, by the way. But take it from your big sister, okay? I've been there. If Ma appreciates something, fine. If she doesn't, tough luck for a bit, but then, fine. If Cece feels like shit, fine. Let her."

"We're different, Briony." Her tourmaline ring winks at me.

"Oh-ho." She guffaws. "Quite."

I reach across the table and grasp three of her hot fingers, one of which has the ring. She stops laughing, looks down at my hand, the same as Cece had done with the splashed milk on her sweater, and back at me.

"Yes?" A pause. The hum of the vacuum and the crackling of

sucked dust surrounds us. "You got something you want to say to me?"

I push her hand away. I kick her under the table and she kicks back, and we are kicking, kicking, whisper-cussing, one calling the other an ol' tantie, the other accused of being a child, until one of Briony's claws latches onto my sock, and pulling it off with swift force, leaves the burning trace of a fresh tingling scratch. I want to say, "I guess you can't shoplift pedicures," but she is holding hot coffee.

Rubbing my calf, I ask, "Do you think she'll be back today?"

She sighs. "I don't know. If she doesn't, that's a whole next thing. I don't even want to think about that."

We hear the vacuum turn off, and soon our mother is hauling it up the stairs like a piece of carry-on luggage. I go to her and take it, and she wipes her forehand with the back of her hand.

"Cece come down to eat?" she asks.

Briony and I nod.

"Okay," she says. She looks around the kitchen with her hands on her lower back and her chest pushed forward. She is wearing her serious cleaning outfit: dollar store flip-flops, black linen pants and an orange t-shirt that says *I paid off my student loans and I all I got was this t-shirt.*

"Okay," she says again. "Is almost ten o'clock and allyuh just wake up? When you finish eating, allyuh go and get Cece a cake and some chicken for me to stew. I want to finish it by five this evening." She turns to go, then turns back and says, "And get the cupcakes, too. From the good bakery. And don't forget to get candles for the cake. Pick up a bottle of sweet drink and some cheese, too. And some Canada Dry. That should be good, I think." Briony is typing it all down in her phone. "Yeah, that will be enough. Everything else I already went out the road and get."

"Um," I say, "Do you need any help cooking?"

My mother looks at me, briefly, and obviously unconvinced that I could be of any help in a kitchen, until she realizes she is one woman short. "Yeah," she says. "Yeah, you go help me in the kitchen today. Moira could help, too. Good. When Sangeetha come home tonight, she will see you and Moira had to help me because she decide to make a whole big thing out of nothing. Allyuh go and get what we need now."

"Okay," I say.

"Okay," says Briony.

*

It's a balmy four degrees above Celsius, so we wear our lighter jackets. Unlike Uncle Bass on his solo search party walks, who wears a wool fisherman's turtleneck, a twice-looped scarf up to his eyes, and a pair of thick fingerless gloves that gives him the air of a toddler, Briony and I have long become accustomed to the chill settling into our brown skin.

"Woo," says Briony, fanning herself, "we are in for one *helluva* summer this year. It hot, boy!"

Laughing, we decide that Briony will get everything but the cake and cupcakes at No Frills, and I will go to the "good bakery" in Bloor West Village. "Or you can get the cake and I can go to No Frills," I say.

"No, who cares?" says Briony. "I'll go to No Frills." She pulls out her phone, puts in her earbuds, nods upwards at me, and walks away.

I decide to walk toward the train station, take in the old neighborhood and venture down memory lane (this time trying to keep it to post-1980s), and see who has the same garden ornaments from ten years ago, whose minivans still have the same dents in their sides, who hasn't yet taken down their Christmas decorations, and who decided to move in and knock down the old place not knowing the history of this neighborhood. My feet instead carry me diagonally across the street, and soon I am knocking on Posie's door.

There is barely a breeze; the wind chimes tinkle out "Amazing Grace" in staccato like a child learning to play piano. The curtain behind the frosted glass pane with an infinity sign carved into it, which I hadn't noticed before, moves aside after a few moments. I make eye contact with Posie, smile and wave. She looks at me deadpan, lips straight, the corners of them downturned, then breaks into a toothy smile and opens the door.

"Cassandra, hello." She is wearing the same outfit as when I last saw her, black tights and the baby blue sweater, but instead of her hair tied in a low bun, she wears it like me, in a thin and light ponytail. "How are you?"

"I'm good. Sort of," I say. "I just… actually, I just wanted to stop in and say hello again." Though nothing is funny, I laugh. "I was thinking about your mother's bookshelf and how I never got a chance to look at it. Is that weird? I hope I'm not bothering you. I can come back another time."

"Oh, well." A pause. "That's very sweet you. And no, it's not weird at all." Posie steps back. "Please, come in."

I step inside, smiling, smiling, smiling, then not smiling when she goes to close the door behind me. I look around as I take off my mittens in the suffocating heat of the house. I peer down the hallway into the kitchen directly, and the stairs that lead to the second floor where not too long ago I watched Posie from my attic window, sitting behind the curtains alone. I take my shoes off and hang my jacket as though I'm a regular visitor.

"Just this way," Posie says. "I'll put on some tea for us. Is chamomile okay?" I nod. "Go on into the living room and make yourself at home, Cassandra."

"My mother loved Margaret Laurence, as I'm sure you can tell," Posie calls from the kitchen. The clattering of wares and pouring of water allows me to delay my replies.

"Yes," I call back. "I can see that." I run my finger over the spines of Nina's books, Nina's old fingerprints, Nina's last touches, even, meticulously slotted into a seven-foot antique alder bookcase. I bring my face closer to the books and smell them, then remembering Nina is dead, snuff out the earthy scent and withdraw.

"I think she read everything by her," called Posie. "I think she saw a lot of herself in Ms. Laurence. I, myself, never read her – I'm not a big reader – but my mother would always tell me about her books after she finished reading them."

Posie brings two floral cups of tea on little matching saucers into the living room. She places them on the table and sits on the blue corduroy sofa, and when I go to join her, she shoos me back to the bookshelf. "Oh, go ahead and browse. I insist."

I obey, and scan the shelves with my eyes, sipping tiny sips of the scalding tea.

"My mother was never without a book. Every week she was reading a new one." She chuckles. "She said if there wasn't a book on her nightstand or somewhere around the house with a bookmark in it, she felt idle in everything she did."

"I like Margaret Laurance, too. May I?"

She nods and I pull out a copy of *The Stone Angel* from its top shelf.

"I think I was the only one in class who was actually enjoyed reading *The Stone Angel* in high school. In everyone's defence though, it is pretty hard to read a dense text about a 90-year-old in a nursing home when you're seventeen years old."

We both laugh lightly.

"One time, in school," I say, turning around to look at Posie, Posie perking up for the anecdote, "our English teacher assigned us a project for it. We had to either collect a bunch of items that Hagar – that's the name of the woman in the book – would keep in one of her drawers, like a flower or a brush or a card or whatever. Anything that we thought would have meaning to her. *Or,* the other option was to write letters that were from Hagar to other characters in the book."

"Oh, my."

"I was the only one in the whole class who wrote the letters and I had to read them out loud. I loved the book so much, I felt like the letters were from me. So it was… mildly traumatizing."

"Well," she says, leaning forward, "if you were the only one, that must have meant you were special."

Suddenly I feel young, and stupid. "Yes. Maybe."

I fidget with the handle of the teacup and tap my fingers against it. The wind chimes outside knock against each other.

"Does that ever get annoying?" I say.

"What's that, dear?"

"The wind chimes."

"No, I can't say they do. They don't bother me."

"Posie?"

She says nothing.

"Can I please talk to my aunt?"

Her face doesn't change.

"I… I know we don't know each other very well. At all, actually. But, please. Can I talk to her? Everyone's worried at home."

She closes her eyes, takes a deep breath, and lets out a long, bleeding sigh. Her face returns to the face I had seen behind the frosted glass pane of her front door: serious and honest.

"When you get older, you'll understand, honey." She smiles, sadly. "You'll understand that sometimes… sometimes, you don't need to ask someone what's wrong, you can tell just from the look on their face and *know*. Because you've been through it, too. It's a terrible to thing to know, you know. It's a terrible thing to know."

I keep my hand on *The Stone Angel* like I'm taking an oath. She groans as she gets up, bearing her weight down on her trembling arms as she lifts herself.

"Your aunt and I – oh, we go back. We go way back," she says, walking out the living room. She shuffles down the corridor in her slippers, hunched over now, muttering to herself like she doesn't need to pretend anymore. She loosens her hair from her hair tie and lets it fall to her shoulders, running her fingers through its ends. "We met at the pharmacy if you can believe that, very soon after she moved up here to help your mother with you kids. We hit it off instantly." She knocks three times on a closed hallway door, then disappears behind it, switching places with my aunt.

"You's a sneaky one, you know. Just like me. I always know that."

I put the teacup down on the coffee table.

"How you know I was here?"

"Tomorrow is Cece's birthday. Are you coming home?"

"I know tomorrow is Cece's birthday, Cassandra," says Auntie Sangeetha.

A pause. She crosses the threshold into the living room. She picks up Posie's cup of tea and takes a sip. "I wouldn't miss it. I coming home. God, how I hate chamomile."

Although she has been gone for only two days, it feels like weeks have passed, and seeing my Auntie Sangeetha in all that she is, grandiose in body and soul and heart, she looks weakened outside of her element. She's missing her makeup; she looks pale and small-eyed, but her skin looks plump and prepped. Posie, in the two nights they've been together, as though at a sleepover, must have lent her some cream or another. Her hair hangs freely, brushed and airy. She is wearing a sweater that doesn't belong to her, pink and pilled, and too tight for her in every way. The rolls of her stomach ripple as she breathes. Heavyset that she is, her chest is pushed up almost to her collarbone. She does not hide any of it. She did not bring her hands to her neck to cover herself, or clutch at the sweater's neckline like she does at home. She is wearing her jogging bottoms, and beneath her slippers a brittle stem sticks out.

"Whose sweater is that?" I whisper, moving closer to her.

"I don't know, I didn't ask," she says, sipping the tea.

"Oh, my God. Are you wearing Nina's clothes? Is that Nina's sweater?"

Looking down and holding the teacup frozen at chin level, her eyes widen like there are spiders crawling all over her. "I don't know," she says. "I didn't ask. It... it could be Posie sweater."

"It's too big to fit Posie! That's Nina's sweater. You wearing a dead woman's clothes."

She again looks down at the foreign cloth that has temporarily taken her in, then drops her shoulders and shrugs, resumes sipping the tea. She stares blankly at me like Briony does when she's about to say something sarcastic.

"What you come here for? You come here looking for me?"

"Yes. Obviously."

"That sweet, baby. Everybody worried at home?"

"Yes, Auntie. Everyone is worried at home."

"Everyone?"

Before I can say anything, she says, "Well, I coming home tomorrow. Don't worry."

"In that?" I hold my palm out.

"I not going to stay long, anyway."

"What do you mean you're not staying long?" I sigh. "Auntie, what is it that you want?"

"Rani could apologize to me."

"And what if she doesn't? I—" I take a deep breath and hold my hand in prayer to my nose. "Auntie, it's Cece's *birthday*. What – you going to come back here and shack up with Posie?" She shrugs over and over while I talk, inspects the design of the floral cup, acts impressed. "You listening to yourself?" I talk louder, Posie can surely hear me. "Huh? You going to come back here and live with Posie like she your mother? That is what you plan to do?"

"Look who come back home," she says. Then pointing a pinkie at me says, "Watch it, eh, Cassandra. You still talking to your auntie."

Neither of us say anything, both looking to the floor in the opposite direction of the other.

"How you know to find me?"

"I didn't know you and Posie were friends. Good friends, it seems."

"Well, right. How you did know I was here?"

"I don't know how I knew. I just… felt like you were here. Like I could smell you or something. I just had a feeling."

"That sweet, baby. That real sweet. You's a nice child, coming to look for your auntie." She puts the teacup down on the coffee table, walks toward me, and brings her palms to my cheeks. "Don't worry so. Tomorrow I will come home and Rani will apologize to me. She must." She kisses my forehead. "Okay, baby. Go now."

22

But what she was doing all down so by that road, so late at night, all by she self?

He tell the police he did not drink, he was only a little tired. He was coming home from a late shift, and had just, *just* bought the car after saving up for nearly two years. Two years! It was not even a new car, and it was his seventh night driving it, he said. But it wasn't like he never drive a car before, he drive them he whole life. He was a valet at the big hotel downtown, for *God* sake. The two policeman look him up and down, and they could see he was a reasonable man. He wasn't allhow, he was still wearing he uniform, minus the hat that swerve from the dashboard into the passenger seat when he did come to a screeching halt. He uniform was still looking smooth, smooth from when he iron it earlier in the day. He was speaking with calm and articulation, a rush logic, but logic all the same. It was clear the man – just a boy, really – was real shake up.

She did wander into the street at about one, two in the morning. Any later and it would have been approaching day, that side of the earth would have been turning its sleeping face toward the sun, and he would have seen she. Any other time and he would have seen she, he say to he self. Any other time, any other time, he keep saying to he self. He was not drunk – if only he was drunk! That would have make everything more understandable, and it was a simple thing to tell people. "She get hit by a drunk driver." That could be the whole story, done and done. There wouldn't be any questions after that. Unless – *unless* – people knew the specifics of the situation, that she was out walking at night, with no shoes on she foot. In which case, they would definitely say, "Well, what was she doing all the way down along Main Street, quite near Arouca, so late at night on she own? Ain't she living all the way back by Macaria?" And then they might pause, look into the distance, and say, "Wait, nah. Wait." A quiet gasp, a palm coming up to they chest. "Ain't that is right where Junior get hit? Oh, God. Oh, God, oh."

And what everybody would say then? What they would tell they neighbours, and they children? What would we tell *we* children?

What would we tell we self?

Go on, young man, said Avi, one of the two policeman.

Officer, he say. Officer, she come out of nowhere, man. You have to believe me. He say this with deep apology, on the verge of crying, as if just realizing what he do. One minute he was driving, he say, *nooooo*body was on the road, not even really other cars, except other men like he that was working the late shift, and all the streetlight was working, except maybe one or two, but he not blaming that, that nothing new, he could see everything good. He have perfect vision. He did get he eyes check only a few months ago. He have perfect vision, he say again. He eyes bulge out.

Okay, said a policeman.

He see these streets for years, day and night, day and night. In fact, he said, he sick of this street, but is the fastest way home. He know this street so good, he could tell you if… He look around the street for something specific, and he eyes land on a garbage bin. He could tell you if a garbage bin move from they place, he said. He pause. He just wasn't expecting anybody to come out from behind the trees, right onto the road with they back turn. She didn't even turn around, man.

While two of the paramedics was checking she on the road, one of them walk back to the ambulance and turn off the flashing head-lights. The young man start to talk fast, fast now.

It was like she was sleepwalking or something, he say. She didn't look like she was drunk or anything, she wasn't stumbling or stag-gering or struggling to walk or keep she balance. She just look like she was dreaming and walking at the same time, that is what it look like to me, from the back, anyway. All I see, he say, in my headlights was a flash of beige, from that ol' looking dress she wearing, but to be honest, maybe that was the yellowness of the car lights. And I see a flash of bright red tie around she head.

If the young valet did turn around to look at where she was lying down on the road now, he would have see that the red cloth was knock off she head, and she wasn't wearing a beige dress, she was wearing a pinkish dress. But he didn't turn around.

Officer, he say, running both he hands through he hair, keeping he hands on he head, I didn't even have time to honk my horn. It only then at the last minute like she snap out of it and she turn around and scream and cover she face.

The police write it all down on the side of the road. The man start to cry into he hands. Two of the paramedics pull a stretcher down its ramp and unfold a white sheet. He wasn't going fast, the man say through his hands, and the police agree. They was nodding. This is how fast people does go, it wasn't like he was speeding, he keep saying. He start to tell the whole story again.

When they bring him into the station, this twenty-something-year-old man with no prior record, they say among themselves that it didn't look like a homicide, or even manslaughter, he was driving on a main road, and it wasn't he fault that this lady walk out in the road.

Is a shame, and is sad, truly, say Avi at the station when the young man was being held in the back room. Because, Avi say, because *that* is the same lady who lose she small, small son only a few months ago. Yeah, she looking a little bit different now. Oh, God, boy, she looking *old*! But that is she. And now, he said, and *now*, somebody going to have to tell the family *this*, and it not going to be me. *I* was the one who take down the details of that small boy, Avi said. *I* was the one who had to drive the dead boy's aunt and he big brother home. They face was white, white, white, like…like…like this piece of paper (he held up the piece of paper they write down the driver's information on). And *I* was the one that had to tell this same lady, who get knock down and dead now, that *she* little boy was dead – eh, *fuck* this, man. What is this shit? What kind of *shit* this is? This is not the kind of thing I sign up for. Violence and crime and drugs – okay! I could deal with that – that is what I come to do. But this? Nah, man. I's not no *mystery* detective. I's not no *Sherlock* Holmes. He was crying now. I look like I does carry a magnifying glass and notebook in my blasted pants pocket? I look like I does want to stay up at night drinking in my chair, home alone, like I's some old, old man that want to figure out why things does happen to people so? Nah! Nah, man. I tapping out. *I* not going through that again. Not me, boy. Not me.

All the policemen, about ten, fifteen of them in the room, was looking at Avi because he was in the middle of the room and holding up both he palms like he was the one under arrest. People at they desk stop what they was doing, and it sound like even the

220

phones stop ringing, like crime take a break just for this one man monologue.

What happening? one policeman whisper to another.

Avi having he first breakdown, he say.

Another policeman come up from behind Avi and put he hand on he shoulder and Avi jump.

Cool it, Avi, he say to him. Cool it.

Allyuh, Avi say, allyuh going to have to find *somebody else* to tell the family about *this woman now*. I ain't going to be that family grim reaper. First (he clenched his first and stuck out his baby finger), I was the one who had to tell the family about the little boy, and now (he stuck out his ring finger – no ring), you telling me I have to go and tell this same family about this woman? Nah, nah, nah. Not me. Call in the boss, if allyuh have a problem. Or fire me. None allyuh could fire me, anyway. It not going to be me, boy.

Avi, man, say another policeman, nobody say you have to tell the family. One of we could go. Just gone and sit down and rest your head. Gone now, gone.

Avi walk back to he desk. He sit down, lean back in he chair, and fold he arms across he chest. He shake he head back and forth, back and forth, like someone was asking him over and over to do this one thing and he keep saying no, no, he not doing it. Not me, boy, not me. In the room behind him, through the closed doors, everybody could hear the valet crying, and somebody say, oh God, man, somebody gone and hush that man up.

All the policeman in the room look at one another, then slowly, they went back to doing what they was doing before; chatter rise back up, and crime come back to ring they ass on the phone. One policeman say to another that Avi was young, and he should not have been the one in charge of telling the family about the little boy in the first place. If two people could break down in one night so, imagine how the family going to take this news? Boy, the type of job we have, no amount of money could pay we to forget.

But I know Avi, the policeman say. He wouldn't let anyone else tell the family. He will want to tell them properly. He just need a little bit of time to ease he self up.

This is what does happen when people see thing, the policeman say. You can't blame them for acting so. Is human. Is a terrible thing to know, man. Is a terrible thing to know.

PART III

23

"This one summer – remember this? – Cece and I were catching apples in our buckets, playing that little game we played. And then Chevy threw an apple into the Einhorn backyard. When he gave me one to throw – it was gross and rotten – I threw it through their clean window. Remember I told you about Einhorn?" I pause with my finger still on the record button.

I'm sitting in the backyard on a plastic picnic chair under the naked branches of the apple tree, hunched up and swimming in Briony's winter jacket and Cece's old jogging pants. Smoking a cigarette I found in the coat pocket with a lighter, I bow my head away from the house to the ground, and blow smoke into frozen mulch. With my ankle on my leg making the number 4, I watch the old Einhorn house.

It would be six in the morning in London now. I try to think of something else to say so but failing, I lift my thumb and the message whooshes and lands in Ines's chat box.

The back windowpane of the old Einhorn house is, of course, fixed. It's been more than fifteen years since Chevy and I threw rotten apples into their backyard (though, by no means is the passing of time any indication that broken things will be repaired). They don't live there anymore – the Einhorns, the man – and the back of the house is now painted a healthy bran-muffin brown by its new inhabitants. A child, cold be damned, swings away in a swing set next to a jungle gym I might have pined for as a child. Even now its primary colours, juxtaposed against the white and grey and dead browns of an ebbing winter, make me sad and jealous.

Back then, Einhorn was forty-something years old. He was balding, as men his age will, and wore thick-rimmed glasses, as men his age do.

He worked a job in an office, I assume; he wore a tie and dress shirt and pants when he left the house, and carried a briefcase.

It was around the same time that single red dime-sized dot disembarked from within me and punctuated the end of my life as a child. I was tender and confused all over. When watching comic book movies, I felt akin to the villains after their transformations – Mr. Hyde, the Hulk, the werewolves. I told Briony I felt like a monster, and that a boy at school had said to a group of boys in front of a group of girls that no one should trust anything that bleeds for five days and doesn't die. Briony had gotten up from her chair and paced the room back and forth, whooshes of air coming out from her mouth. She told me to give it time, that what I was going through was not a mutation, it was a metamorphosis. She added that I should ask the boy at school if he trusted his mother.

I wore shorts and tank tops all the same, but now men looked at me. My mother noticed, as did Auntie Sangeetha, as did Briony, and as if I were on fire, they threw Briony's hand-me-downs on me, clothing that draped off my bones so loosely that if I held my hair back I looked like a pretty boy. I didn't care; I liked knowing that Briony had once worn these and that her smell was still on them; I felt they lent me her confidence. But there was that two-week period in between wardrobe change when my clothes were too small, and where the world saw me before I did.

The boy on the swing looks bored. I suck on the cigarette, and boldly, blow the smoke up into the sky. Then I get scared and wave it away.

That young summer, I had been standing on the porch waiting for the half past five ice-cream truck to park in front of our house, as it did every day without fail from June to August. I had the exact change for a vanilla-dipped-in-chocolate-sauce ice cream cupped in my hand, shaking it in my fist to the beat of "Clint Eastwood" by Gorillaz. I had put the weight of my body on one leg; I learned on television that's what girls did when they were waiting. I was wearing a cropped red-and-white striped shirt, and red shorts with a bow-tie drawstring at its center. I was waiting and waiting, shaking and shaking the coins like maracas, playing the song in loop in my head, when slowly the song faded. I stopped shaking the coins, and with it my new flesh, sensing Einhorn in my vicinity like a fawn who stops drinking from the rippled river's edge. Putting my weight on both my feet then, I turned to see him looking at me through his open glass-screen door. He was just returning from work, and had his suit jacket folded over his arm, the proper gentleman that he was. Holding his briefcase in one hand, and the screen door with the other, his mouth was parted, the lower lip slowly making its gawkish descent to form an unsightly double chin. His eyes were glassy. He did not wave. I did not wave. Minivans were parallel parking, skateboards were grinding by. Parents were walking hand in hand with their small, jubilant children.

I folded my arms across my chest. I wanted him to go inside his house. I wanted to shout across the few houses between us (the brown screen divider, by bad luck, was rolled down that day), "*Go inside your house.*" I would not, and did not, want to be the one who walked away, the one to admit that I was doing something wrong simply by standing there in my new body. Like the child I was, I thought, I was here *first*. Chevy walked up the pathway with a grocery bag in one hand and the other in his jeans pocket, and neither of us – me or Einhorn – noticed him. As Chevy approached the steps, he said, loudly, louder than I'd ever heard him speak, "What the *fuck* you looking at, man?" I jumped, and looked up behind me, thinking he was talking to me. But he was looking Einhorn straight in his glassy, beady eyes, which, when I turned back to him, wide-eyed as if I cared about his safety, were now blinking back to life. I could hear Chevy grinding his teeth, and I was scared – not for myself, but for Einhorn. Did he know that Chevy did not speak, and that when he did, it was serious? Did he know that the voice of the silent rang a thousand times louder when the sound barrier was broken?

"What—" said Chevy, and he dropped the grocery bag and ran into our house. Einhorn fiddled for his keys, he found the right one, and scurried inside. His screen door hung wide open, and like a cartoon, Einhorn's arm reached out from inside and pulled it shut. Chevy returned with a plank of jagged wood, like he had torn up the floors inside. He ran down the porch steps and I wanted to yell, "Chevy, no!" I didn't. Chevy ran across the neighboring lawns in leaps, and I saw Einhorn's screen door open again. Instead, his daughter Janet rushed out onto the porch. Chevy stopped in front of their house. I dropped my hands to my side. Chevy didn't say anything to Janet, nor did Janet to him. She only looked back at her screen door as though confused why she came out in the first place. The ice cream truck's jingle turned the corner. Chevy disappeared from my view. I leaned over the

228

porch railing and saw that he was walking back to the house, calmly, but breathing hard. He came up the stairs and did not look at me. He threw the wooden plank in the corner of the porch, picked up the grocery bag and went inside. Janet and I, both on our respective porches, looked at each other and shrugged, and when she went back inside, I went back inside, too, dashing my ice cream money into the mail tray, and succumbed that year to a mostly indoor summer.

My phone vibrates. A message from Ines says: When are you thinking of coming back? Honestly feels like you've been gone for months.

The kid on the swing is in full throttle now, and I wonder if he's going over a memory of his own in his head.

I type out that I know, and I might be here for two more weeks, maybe three. But then she'll ask for what, and I won't know what to say or want to say it. I backspace and tell her that I'm not sure, but probably sooner than later.

My mother calls out the back window of the second floor. I do a little dance in my chair, sit up straight, and drop the cigarette. She sticks her head out of the window's slanted frame.

"Cassandra? Cassandra, is that you there?" she yells, as if she hasn't seen me in years.

I wave and smile.

"You get the cake?"

"Yes, Ma!"

"You get the cupcakes and chicken, too?"

The boy on the swing looks over to me and up at the window to my mother. I wave to him, but he doesn't wave back.

"Yes!" I yell to my mother, then, "I mean, no! Briony got the chicken. I got the cupcakes!"

"You get the scones?"

"What scones? You didn't tell me to get any scones!"

"I see scones on the kitchen table."

I shake my head and shrug my shoulders.

She nods once and disappears.

The day Chevy and I threw rotten apples into Einhorn's backyard, sparked something in me. It was the same steely feeling of invincibility I would have years later when Auntie Moira agreed to send me the articles about Junior and when I listened in on my mother's phone call. That night, all those years ago, I went back to the backyard for more. At eleven o'clock, in my pyjama shorts, tank top and flip flops, I had hurled apple after apple – the healthy ones, too – they were firmer – at the Einhorn house like one of those tennis-ball machines with an endless supply of javelin pitches. I did not stop. I did not think about Janet. I cussed, with great ease, all the words I knew. Most of the apples landed on their back deck with a dead thud, but two or three made it through windows. When there were no more apples on the ground, I was breathing heavily, sweating in the summery, still air, and made eye contact with a dog perched on a fence some houses down. I rotated my shoulder in circles like a baseball player, and when a light came on in the Einhorn house, I ran to the tree and hid behind its trunk. A figure, tall and broad – it was Einhorn – stuck its head out of the back window on the second floor. One hand rested on the sill, the other held a brown apple. He looked into our backyard, but he could not have seen me, dark-skinned under the moon, another contour of the night. The dog was still looking at me, and I looked back at it threateningly should it decide to bark. Einhorn pulled his head back into his house and closed the window softly. No one said anything to us the next day, or the next – not to my mother, not to my aunts, not to me or Briony, and certainly not to Chevy, even though we were the only house on the block with an apple tree. I had cackled into the night and felt powerful, and tall like the tree, like I could threaten the man, taunt him, torment him, and he could do nothing about it. Because what could he say, if I brought my face close to his, like one of those tough guys in the movies. What could he say when he felt my breath on his face when I said, "What you going to do about it, huh, punk? What you going to do about it? I have a Chevy – what do you have?"

*

My mother is right – there are scones on the kitchen table. An assortment of goods have been laid down for my sister like a shrine: a black forest cake whose nucleus is enclosed by cheese and soda; pink and yellow birthday candles; pink coned hats; a disposable plastic tablecloth patterned with balloons; a bottle of Peardrax, Canada Dry, and Coca-Cola.

They have started without me. Auntie Moira washes the chicken in the kitchen sink, the smell of raw, fresh chicken turns my stomach, and my mother douses rice with soy sauce in a wok that takes up the stove's four burners. The tap is running, oil is sizzling, glassware is clinking, cupboards are opening and slamming shut, and in this sensory symphony under the command of the maestro that is my mother, I feel like everything is going to be all right. It plays the most soulful of songs. I forget everything that came before and this is all that remains. Something chimes against something else, and mesmerized, I turn my head in its direction. It falls to the ground without a sound like a shooting star, light tailing its edge. What did she mean when she said she wouldn't be staying long – is that what she said? Did I hear her right? Auntie Moira is looking at me, saying something to me about the star that has fallen.

"Did Auntie Rani buy the scones?" I ask. "Because Briony wouldn't buy the scones, she just wouldn't. She would just get exactly what she went to the grocery store for, and walk on by everything else on the shelf, not thinking if we needed anything extra at home. I doubt that she even pulled out her wallet. I should ask her later. Yeah, I'm going to ask her later."

Is Auntie Rani home? She is so quiet. All of the time, she is so quiet.

I bring my hand to my brow like a woman in a migraine commercial. Who am I in this symphony? *Am* I in this symphony? I've left home.

Auntie Moira takes a step toward me, I hold out my hand to indicate: don't come any closer.

Have I left home?

My mother dashes salt into the wok; it crackles like applause.

Can I ever?

"Cassandra, just pass me that onion there."

A pale and cratered cabbage sits lonesome on a side table like a moon with dusty planets of potatoes nearby. My aunt flogs the raw, blood-clotted chicken limb, with a mallet and it begins to double, triple, quadruple by the sink. How much chicken did Briony *get*? The ketchup for the stew is slogging its way down the upturned bottle on the table, taking a long time, a tortuously long time, for its drips, dense like stones, to hit the plastic.

Could I do this, too? I hold on to a chair. Could these comforts – these strokes and plucks across carcasses and carbs, this domestic bliss without men – eventually extinguish, or even answer, my questions? Could I settle into our story like a principal player instead of a voiceover, and, finally, understand it all? Could I add sugar and pepper sauce to everything and make it all better? Could I change anything? Did I do enough? Auntie Sangeetha said she was coming home, but not for long? What does that mean? How does that work?

"Cassandra, the onion, please."

How is that going to work?

Auntie Moira taps my mother on the shoulder and says something and points to me.

"Cassandra – but how you looking *so*?"

*

Blots of black and electric yellow explode beneath my eyelids. I open my eyes and the ceiling is warmed by a light from a corner lamp. I turn my head and see two pairs of legs, one skinny and standing, moving slowly from my head down to my feet, the other thick and curvy, sitting crossed legged in a chair. Something crawls up my leg and I kick it off, flailing my limbs, grabbing at my clothes. A papery brown ball glides across the room.

"Cassandra, relax yourself."

My mother, the vertical pair of legs, goes over to the scrunched-up ball and it crinkles in her hand. I realize that my mother is jharaying me. I close my eyes and drop my weight into the mattress and smile inside. She runs the crumpled paper bag, fragrant with peeled garlic and hot bird peppers at its center, over my head, all the way down my stomach and legs to my toes, warding off the evil eye and any demons that have entered my body. I get goosebumps as the paper lightly tickles my skin, like when Briony and I were younger and used to play that game where she cracked an invisible egg on my head. She would trace her fingernails on my scalp, down my shoulders, down my back, singing to me in monotone, "Let the yolk drip down, let the yolk drip down, let the yolk drip down," before sticking a knife in my back and demanding that I let the blood drip down, let the blood drip down…

233

I fold my hands at my pelvis, and when my mother tells me to turn over, I splay out like a starfish as she jharays the back of my body.

"Okay," she says. "Briony, gone and burn this outside."

She takes the ball from our mother and leaves.

I roll over again, a happy kid, and my mother brushes the hair from my face. "How you feeling, baby?"

"I feel fine." I sit up on my elbows to see Cece standing at the door. My mother lays me back down.

"Lie back down. Just take it easy for now. You eat this morning?" says my mother.

"No, I forgot."

"How you could forget to eat, Cassandra?" Her hands are still dusted with flour from cooking. She rubs her thumb on the inside of my arm, and coupled with the scent of peppermint permeating Auntie Sangeetha's bed, I begin to feel sleepy.

"Okay," says my mother. She smooths her hair and t-shirt, leaving trails all over her like war paint. "Cece will bring you down some water and I go make a sandwich for you. Just lie down for now. You hear me?"

"I already have the water here," says Cece. She steps forward and hands it to me, and my mother leaves the room.

"How come they brought me down to Auntie Sangeetha's room?" I say, sitting up on my elbows.

"They couldn't carry you up two flights of stairs to your room," Cece says.

"True." I take a gulp of water. "Briony could have done it, though. She could have thrown me over her shoulder and taken me up, no problem. That woman build *strong*, boy."

Cece laughs, but it's a laugh that comes out as a single breath through her nose.

"But yeah, makes sense," I say. We both look around the room. "Are you excited for your birthday?"

She sighs and rolls her eyes. "Everyone makes such a big deal about it." The white splotch from this morning's spilt milk is dark and caked on her sweatshirt.

"You're the baby of the family. Everyone loves ya."

"I know, I know." She gets up and paces the room. "It's just... it's not really the best time to be celebrating, you know?"

I nod.

"Like, I called the pharmacy this morning and they said they haven't seen Auntie either."

"Yes," I say. "Yes, but, Auntie asked for some time off, so the pharmacy wouldn't have seen her, anyway."

"So where would she go then? She was wearing friggin' slippers. And it's cold. And she doesn't even have a wallet or money or anything." She turns toward me, holding out her palms like I might pull the answer out of my pocket and hand it over.

"Cece, believe me," I say, looking into her eyes. "Auntie Sangeetha will turn up."

"Turn up?" She scrunches her face.

"No, no, I don't mean turn up, like, oh, her *body's* going to turn up somewhere, like in a ditch or something."

She looks at me, I look back at her. I smile briefly, utterly unconvincing. The smile drops, I drink from my glass. I look around the room and blow air through my puckered lips and finger a few bottles and trinkets on the dresser next to the bed. Cece sighs and pushes past Briony as she walks in.

"Excuse *you*," Briony says. She turns back to me and takes hold of my foot at the end of the bed and shakes it. "Leave it to you to faint before a big event. Drama queeeeeen."

"I'm sorry, I'm not currently taking any visitors."

"Feeling okay?"

"Yeah." I shake my head and roll my eyes. "Honestly, I just didn't eat anything this morning and was just stressed, blah, blah, blah."

"If you say so."

"Did you burn the paper bag?" I say, smiling wide.

"*Yes.*"

"Where?" We're both giggling.

"In the backyard. I started coughing a lot because of the peppers. And we wonder why the neighbours don't invite us to barbeques." She laughs, then says, "Like I give a shit what they think."

"Yeah." Our laughter wanes into dreamy sighs. "Hey," I say. "Did you get those scones? The ones on the kitchen table?"

"Yeah. Cece likes them. I thought being her special day and all."

"Oh."

"Mmhmm."

"I thought Auntie Rani maybe bought them."

"Mmm." She sighs, looks around the room, and slaps her thighs. "Right. Ma wants me to do some stuff. You coming up?"

I tell her I will be up soon, that I want to lie here a little longer and rest my head. My eyes follow her out the room as I wonder if Auntie still keeps her diary in the chest of drawers.

*

Auntie Sangeetha's room, for all her theatricality, is uninspired, resembling a freshly cleaned motel room from the seventies. Below a small mirror on a chest sit the essentials: a half-used red Revlon lipstick, liquid and kohl pencil eyeliners, white face creams, talcum powder, foundations that are two shades too light. Pushed up against the wall is the bed which has no blankets or duvet, just two loose, white sheets spread over the mattress and one pillow at its head. If I stand on the bed, I can peek out the window and, like a gopher, see the ground outside. The single chair in the corner of the room is taken from the kitchen set upstairs and looks more interrogative than conversational. All the little flourishes of hope – the little fiddle-leaf fig tree by the closet, the cluster of African violets on the window sill, the jewellery and scarfs hanging unevenly from their stands on her dresser, swaying in whatever breeze came down from the window – are now gone. In the bulb's stark light sitting on a side table and undressed of its tasselled lampshade, my slanted and stretched shadow is cast on the wall, tossing sweaters and pants from my aunt's drawers like something out of a film noir movie. I allow my eyes to scan the room as I run my hands along the bottom and sides of the drawers.

I slam the fourth drawer shut, cursing, swearing that it used to be here, and move on to the last.

Perhaps it's a little late to mention, though by no means an obscure note, that my Auntie Sangeetha did not like Toronto, not when she moved here in 1996 to help my mother with my sisters and I, and not now, more than two decades later. Like Chevy, she found the streets too clean, lacking personality and soul, and wondered aloud in the early days of her transfer if painting the houses with colour – real colour – was banned across the city. When we used to wander the Junction where sometimes my mother, my sisters, and Auntie Sangeetha would eat at Swiss Chalet on the weekends, I would point to the distance just beyond the intersection of Keele and St. Clair. "See," I told her, "not all of Toronto is spotless." We lived on the clean side of it, and across the way we saw plastic bags and newspapers blowing in the wind, roads cracked and potholed, tiny restaurants with flashing neon signs and grimy windows, and even grey stratus clouds advancing in the distance. Cars backfired and men yelled things in short, jolting bursts that made us tense up. But Auntie Sangeetha said she wasn't looking for dirty *necessarily*, she was looking for *personality*, then said a bunch of abstract stuff, like she couldn't pinpoint what she was trying to say. The more I thought about it, the more I wondered if what she was looking for was not a place, but a feeling: home.

Sometimes we would walk in the Junction, just the two of us, when I was much younger. I would hold her hand as she visited almost every store in a two-block radius buying flowers, sleeping pills, and lottery tickets – one each for the past, present, and future, she said. Often, she was asked by store clerks to repeat what she was saying (Auntie Sangeetha had a thicker accent than anyone else in the family, including Auntie Moira who lived in Trinidad all her life). When she repeated what she had said, she didn't change the way she said it, not by enunciation or pace, but would simply stop fiddling in her purse for change, cease to blink, and speak with an exaggerated flair, an almost Southern American, Blanche DuBois twang, while I looked up at her, smiling and holding her hand. I knew no other Trinidadians, or any other person for that matter, who spoke like my Auntie Sangeetha.

I find the diary in the last drawer. I sit lengthwise on her bed, prop her pillow behind my head, cross my legs, and lick the tip of my finger.

I'm not a terrible person. I'm just trying to understand.

My aunt has had this diary her whole life (Auntie Moira's gardening journal she decorated with flash fiction and broken sonnets notwithstanding; Auntie Sangeetha wouldn't have written anything there unless it was open to interpretation, her feelings disguised as enigmatic

238

prose on account of Auntie Rani's routine supervision). As I flick through its browned and toughened pages, dried up and thick like bark, I see the entries I already know: her first piece written at six years old at two in the afternoon. (I am forever thankful for the teachers who taught them the habit of recording the time, day, month and year.) Little Sangeetha draws things that children draw: flowers, birds, people and the sky in supernatural conditions. When she is eight, her parents die, and on paper at one in the morning, she returns to the literal world; her entries become less of drawings and more of words and questions. *How? Why? Who decides? When I will see them again? Will I? I still don't get why. Why?* Drawings of circular faces with impossible frowns, drooping tulips with dripping tears, the sun divided in two pieces with a straight line as its mouth scatter the pages – she is still a child. Then, there are fifteen or so pages ripped out from the book, leaving jagged insides at its center like teeth, gnawing off the beginning of sentences that leave me with words that have no use to me on their own – *the, we, so, night, for, it, was.*

She begins writing again when she's ten. Auntie Tippie has just given birth to Chevy, and in hopeful, almost hesitant words, she documents the arrival of her nephew hesitantly as if not quite trusting the happiness he promised. *Tippie had a baby boy. She name him Patrick. I do not know why she choose that name. He is very cute.* Week by week, she writes more and more, each entry five sentences or less as if written in a hurry, accompanied now by happy hieroglyphics; exclamation marks, grinning faces, smiling ladybugs, small hearts around Chevy's name, and all the things he was learning. *He crawling fast now. It sooo sweet to see. He cheeks so pink and fat!!!* The tulips now stood up straight and grinned, the sun's rays extended through the words. Three years later when Junior is born, she writes more confidently, factually, like Junior is her own second son and she knows all the ways the baby will grow. *He not walking yet but it will take time.* She begins to trust life again.

In her teenage years, she moves on to write about, yes, love. She starts pencilling poems in kohl, and over the years they've smudged between the pages so that when I tilt the book, the poems glisten as though preserved with clear nail polish. It is in kohl that she wonders what love means, then a few weeks later, returns to the page to concoct a definition on her own. *Love is not knowing what time it is. Love is sitting next to someone and feeling the happiest in the world. Love is not being able to see anyone else beyond they face. Love is a seal between two people.* A few more months pass, she writes that she doesn't know what it means anymore, and like many of us, comes to define love by what it is not. *Love is NOT throwing it away on a whim because you mad. Love is NOT being able to go days and not think of the other. Love is NOT avoidance. Love is NOT not apologizing and just letting time pass, just letting me slip away.* The initials *F.N.* stand in place of the person who first broke my aunt's heart.

The next entries, years later, are deduced to recipes with instructions so poor they can barely be called that. The metric for the red bean's brown sugar is "not too much" instead of the traditional tablespoon. "A good amount" substitutes the exact number of tamarinds needed for chutney. The only directive for the chokha's baighan is to "mash it up good" before the recipe moves on, with or without the cook.

The last entry of the book is dated one month after Junior's death, three months before Tippie's. Sangeetha would have been twenty-two.

Sunday, June 13, 1982, 1:12 a.m.

A blue ballpoint dot pressed to the paper a few lines down.

240

Then, nothing.

No names, no explicit lamentations, no maudlin confessions, no damning of the gods, no questions – no words.

Just page after page after page of blank, white, devastating space.

24

My high school science teacher, Ms. Symanski, the one who taught us about the splitting of atoms, used to get heated when trying to explain space to us. From behind a long counter of Bunsen burners, test tubes, and plastic models of body parts, she would pull out a stool and sit down with her head bowed and her arms folded at her chest as though beginning a skit. Her first line was: "Space is… boundless." She struggled to get each word out, speaking slowly as though confessing something tragic, and the showmanship of it kept us fifteen-year-olds, and the potheads at the back of class, entranced. "Space… is the extent in which objects and events have relative position and direction. *But*," she said, holding out a finger, "many modern physicists think that space is not defined by its relation to something else. They believe that something should not be defined by its *emptiness* and its relation to another thing." She paused. "It's possible," Ms. Symanski laughed, "that these physicists are personally offended that something they admire so much should be defined by nothingness – that space, in all its awesomeness of black holes and supernovas, etcetera, etcetera, is reduced to only what it is *not*. In simpler terms – stay with me here – these modern physicists think that space, even though it holds everything, and *does* have a relationship with everything *in it*, is a separate entity on its own."

She stared at our blank faces.

"You don't have to be a physicist to have an opinion about space. Jason," she pointed to Jason, "has an opinion, or at the very least, some loose understanding of what space is." Jason looked shifty-eyed around the room. "He, and you, probably don't think about it any more than you do the meaning of words like 'the' and 'but.' But that's the glue. How can something empty hold everything together?" She got up off the stool and went to the blackboard. "I believe what you think about space is what you think about life. Think about it. If you don't yet know how you feel about life, ask yourself what you think about space. And that will be how you feel about life. If you haven't really thought about space, well, honestly, you likely haven't thought too deeply about much of anything."

"I'm confused about space," said one confident boy, and everyone laughed.

"That's fair." She waited for the laughter to subside.

"Both theories about space can be right," she said, her voice higher, more optimistic. She put one hand in her pants pocket. "Personally, I think space is a separate thing *and* defined by its relation to the things around it. But can anything, really, be a separate thing in the presence of other things?" The teacher made her eyes wide. "Is space purely contextual?" My friend tilted her notebook toward me. *my mind is exploding right now lol.* I smiled without looking up. I was writing it all down.

She wrote on the blackboard: *Is space a separate entity from everything else?* She dropped the chalk on its ledge, dusted her hands, and turned back to us. "I told you what I think, now tell me what you think. Write something down, a single sentence or two, then put the paper on your desk. Don't write your name on it. I'll collect them and read out loud everyone's answers. You have ten – make that five – minutes. Lin, put *away* your phone."

It took me ten seconds to write down, *nope not possible*. I ripped the page out of my notebook, folded it, and semi-slammed it on my desk. Then in my notebook I wrote the names of my family and circled them in slanted blobs, drawing a line from one person's name to the next. Where dates of birth and death were missing, I put a dash followed by question marks. I greyed out Tippie's and Junior's circles, who like dead planets, remained in my family's trajectory with the full effects of their gravity holding us in place.

When Junior and Tippie died in 1982, my mother, pregnant with Briony, did not stop crying for four months straight. Morning, afternoon, evening, and night, she wondered where exactly pooled within her a bottomless reserve of tears, why she had not yet shrivelled up and died from dehydration. I know that my father, his heart breaking with my mother's, found it near impossible to move her from Tippie's room to their own new house, just down the street from her sisters like she had demanded.

"It not good for the baby to be around so much grief, Leela," my father had said.

"The baby is not around grief," said my mother. "She growing inside it."

When Briony was born, it was said that neither mother nor child cried in the hospital. Like the Big Bang Theory, it happened quickly and silently, a soundless creation in which glorious life came to be. My mother, limp and tired and depleted from the chronic pain of eternal grief, had squeezed Briony out in four pushes, falling into a deep sleep before even the umbilical cord was cut. Someone had taken a picture, likely my father, when a nurse handed Briony to our mother for the first time. The photograph shows my mother passed out and double-chinned, both arms straight at her side like she was playing dead, and Briony, naked and slimed and still connected to my mother, staring directly into the camera lens, fists and feet curled, screaming with the might of new life…

…The line from my mother runs to Auntie Moira who found solace in the arms of a man down from San Fernando. He had been pestering her to marry him for years, and one week after Tippie's death, she called him and said, "Yes, okay, come and get me. Now. We could marry." She hauled her few dresses and shirts and shoes, and she cried and cried, saying she was sorry, she was going to get married, it was about time, anyway. Wasn't she, at twenty-four, practically a hag? No one congratulated or stopped her when she said goodbye, when she moved out only a few days later, although I suspect my family weren't much of anything at that point. News could have reached that Pitch Lake had turned into truffle honey overnight, and they would have reacted all the same. Auntie Moira has been with Bass ever since, though she never did marry him…

…And over to Auntie Sangeetha, who, when she cried did not hold her hands to her face, but spread her arms out on beds and couches, or simply slunk to the ground like a wind-up doll whose motor had run out. She began wearing heavy ink-like kohl eyeliner atop and beneath her eyes, and with that very same kohl, wrote a three-line poem about the cruelty of life. (I was once snooping around for spare batteries, and found a torn piece of crinkled paper in one of her drawers that read, "You take he, you take she, but you forget to take me!")…

…The lead of my pencil skirts to Chevy, twelve years old. He could no longer be in the same room with Auntie Rani or look her in the eye; both had been with Junior when the truck struck him down and rolled over his… Both had seen it. Up until Chevy's last living day, it proved challenging for him and Auntie Rani to be in the presence of the other, to speak beyond the everyday niceties of mechanical words for the sake of words, if Chevy bothered to speak in the first place, which he didn't. It's what Ms. Symanski would call "covalent bonding", pairs that maintain a stable balance between both the attractive and repulsive forces between them. The deaths, their common nuclei, had both bound and separated my aunt and cousin, heightening the awareness of their new relationship, and what they had seen, what they couldn't unsee. Something mutated in them that deathly day, and surged and shook at its breaking point like the thrashing needle of a speedometer; in each other's company, unable to confront or forget it, they turned away from each other altogether. For one whole year, after Junior and Tippie's death, they did not speak a word to each other or anyone else...

And so started the dance. Cells in a petri dish repelling each other. When Sangeetha looked at Rani, she saw Tippie's eyes. When Chevy looked at my mother, he wondered where his own had gone, and why. When my mother looked back at Chevy, she had no words, just a clenched heart whose valves could only be released by turning away. If Chevy was in the room, Auntie Rani would leave, if Auntie Rani was in the room, Auntie Sangeetha would leave. When my mother, still laden with grief, visited her sisters with newborn Briony, Auntie Rani would seldom say hello. When she walked into a room, my mother, Auntie Sangeetha and Auntie Moira would change the subject, and Auntie Rani knew it; she knew that no one ever entered a room right at the breath of a new sentence. When my mother spoke to Chevy – when she could finally look at him again – she no longer spoke to him in the rough and stern way that Trini mothers do out of love. Quietly, she left him little toys from my father's snacket, chocolate and chips from the SuperSuperMarket, coconut suckahbags that sagged and melted on the kitchen counter, undrunk. Auntie Moira brought Chevy his favourite fruits and vegetables which their garden used to grow before she left and it wilted in her absence. Auntie Sangeetha showed her affection in female touches; playing with his hair, his ears, stroking his cheek, embracing him after he'd fallen asleep so that his neck and arms hung backwards like he, too, had died, leaving merlot lipstick on his forehead and cheeks.

With this safe distance between them all, the years went by. Six years after Junior and Tippie died, I was born right there in the Macaria where it all happened, and despite the sorrowful womb that nursed Briony into this world, she was a jubilant and gorgeous child. Cece, too. The little planets that we were, sucked into the vortex of everything before, we fell into place in our positions as the good daughters – the subservient daughters, the domestic daughters, the unopinionated-ask-no-questions daughters, the completely-normal-everything-is-fine-falling-apart-on-the-inside daughters – circling… circling what? Who was at the centre of this force? What was both pulling us in and passing through us? What was its name? Why couldn't we break free?

It was the past.

25

We always start with the cake. We're all wearing pink cones on our heads, standing around the black forest cake with its twenty-three candles flaring. The sun has already set, and in the dark our illuminated faces and bags under our eyes are ghoulish. Uncle Bass leads us in song. His eyes are closed, and his palm is held to his heart like he's singing the national anthem. He sings deep and slow, his voice oaky and operatic. In flat, cultish unison, we sing happy birthday to Cece who stands at the head of the table, transfixed by the candle's tall flames, wild fires in her eyes. Her hat leans to the right and the strap under her chin presses hard into her skin while she mouths the words with us, though just a touch too slow. When we're done singing, my mother tells Cece to blow out the candles.

In a smoky haze, Briony flicks on the kitchen lights, and after a disjointed applause, Cece and I cut the cake and ease pieces of it into each other's mouths. I'm smiling as I hold up her chin, like a mother feeding her baby. She lets the cake slide down her mouth. Her wet black eyes investigate my own. I want to pull her into my arms. When it's her turn to put the cake into my mouth, I have to move my head forward and edge the fork in myself. Briony clicks a picture on her iPhone. When I pull back, the fork remains in its place, hovering mid-air with Cece's hand. Briony clicks another picture. I move the cake to the counter, Auntie Rani gets plates and glasses from the cupboards, and Auntie Moira places forks and spoons onto the table. Uncle Bass scratches a chair across the floor and takes a seat at the table, and my mother brings hot food from the stove. I have left the front door unlocked.

Swivelling the taste of cake out of my mouth with water, I reach for potato salad. Uncle Bass goes for the curry chicken, Briony the stew shrimp, my mother the fried rice, Auntie Moira and Auntie Rani for the salad. Auntie Moira retreats until the salad is back on the table, Cece reaches for nothing. I slap some potatoes onto my plate, then hers. I ask if she wants me to pour her some Canada Dry. She says okay.

Uncle Bass talks about San Fernando and then the whole of Trinidad – crime, corruption, violence, drugs, guns, curfews, "The same thing over and over, nah", and I am smiling and nodding through it all, happy to hear about any place that isn't here right now. I swallow the sweet and peppery taste of my mother's fried rice that had me salivating and wandering around the house earlier, and ask Uncle Bass if Trinidad still smells the same. Briony crinkles her face and looks at me. "Smells the same as what?" Auntie Moira's shoulders rise and drop in silent laughter, and though I feel stupid, I ask again. Auntie Rani and my mother keep eating, Cece plays with her food.

"Oh, yes," says Uncle Bass. I smile. "Oh, yes."

"Do children still get hit at school?" I ask.

"Oh, I don't know about that," he says. "Moira, what you say? They does still give licks in school?"

"They must," she says.

"Do they still have those doubles stands in the savannah?" I ask. "Remember, Briony? When we used to go buy them and it took the whole of recess just to walk there and back and we had to eat the doubles really fast?"

"I can't believe you remember that," says Briony.

There's a rustling at the front door. Auntie Rani gets up and goes to the foyer.

I turn to Cece. "There used to be one or two shops in the school back home," I say. I speak quickly. "A doubles shop and a pholourie shop, and the pholourie used to be more expensive, even though you got fewer pholouries than you did doubles. Right, Briony?"

Briony looks at me like she recognizes me from somewhere but can't quite place my face.

"So we used to always buy doubles," I say to Cece. She looks back at me blankly. "It was one dollar for a doubles, and one-fifty for the pholourie, which was a lot back then. And we always used to want the pholourie because, well, it's pholourie. I don't know if it's like that anymore." I look at Uncle Bass and Auntie Moira, but they just scoop food into their mouths.

"Briony and I used to meet right at the beginning of recess, always at the same spot, and walk as fast as we could to the doubles stand. We had to go down the hill, across the savannah, then uphill. That field was massive. It was massive, right?"

Briony nods.

"Girl, you remembering all them thing?" says Auntie Moira. "How she remembering all them thing?" she says to my mother.

My mother asks Briony to pass her the stew shrimp.

Auntie Rani returns to the kitchen and smooths her pants before sitting down and eating again.

"Was there someone at the door?" asks Cece.

We all turn our heads to Rani.

"It was nothing," she says.

"You would have liked it," I say to Cece, tapping her arm, coaxing her face back to mine. "You would have really liked it."

Cece places her spoon by the side of her plate.

"Really," I say. "You would have." I turn to Briony. "Those were good times, weren't they?" She says yeah. "See? We had good times," I say to Cece.

Uncle Bass picks up the conversation, this time for the elders. He speaks of names we don't know – Pregs, Clock, Piglet (son of Pig, he clarifies), Spanish – and how they're all still there, which means they're alive and not much more. My sisters and I used to laugh hard from the belly when we heard names like these; we knew there was a stupid, simple reason for them; Pregs probably had a big, sloping forehead, and Clock was born with one arm shorter than the other. But today we don't laugh. We don't ask, they don't tell. I am still smiling like the lines are etched into my face, and when they chuckle, I chuckle back too heartily. Briony elbows my ribs. "What's wrong with you?" she whispers.

Cece asks to excuse herself, which is a rather formal and un-Trinidadian thing to do. I nicely tell her that she should take a seat and finish her food so we can open her presents. My mother agrees. She sits back down and scoops a large spoonful of potato salad into her mouth, then rice, then shrimp, until her cheeks can hold no more and sauce is leaking from the sides of her mouth. She takes a cupful of water to wash it all down. In a few minutes her plate is empty. Briony kicks me under the table. Then Uncle Bass starts talking about politics and I tune out. The time on the clock shows six thirty. Everyone finishes the final flesh on the chicken bones and remaining stems of steamed broccoli before piling their dishes into the sink. Uncle Bass keeps talking about the prime minister this, and the prime minister that, and I feel thankful for the banter of a seemingly unwitting man. I tell my mother to leave the dishes, I will wash them later. She tells me to slice the cake for everyone and bring the saucers and forks into the living room. We will unwrap the gifts and eat the cake at the same time.

*

When I used to live at home, my family, one at a time and spread over a few days, would knock on my bedroom door to drop off their gifts for Cece. Seeing whatever small parcel was in their hands, I would nod once like a mafioso, move aside, and let them ceremoniously place them on the bottom of my closet where they piled up. It was understood that I would wrap the parcels in pretty paper, top them with shiny bows, and forge their names on a tag or, if provided, a card. I have no idea how and when this tradition started.

Today, though, everyone has wrapped their own gifts for Cece. Misshapen and exorbitantly taped lumps that look more like damaged deliveries, form a small, slippery mountain on the coffee table, except for Briony's gift, which is a small box set aside.

Everyone is squinting like they've just woken up from sleep, and adjusting their eyes to normal light now that my mother has fixed all the chandelier's bulbs. Cece sits at the couch's centre, forward and upright in perfect posture, her hands folded in her lap. My mother and Briony sit on either side as her eyes scan the presents. Auntie Rani sits on the single loveseat, and Uncle Bass and Auntie Moira have taken two chairs from the kitchen to complete the circle. I am standing, leaning against the living room archway, eating my cake. My mother, as the custom goes, tells Briony to play some music. Briony sticks her iPhone into a portable wooden speaker thing and pulls up a pop playlist. Lady Gaga's "Poker Face" begins to play.

"Okay, sweetie," says my mother. "Go ahead and open Auntie Moira and Uncle Bass' present first." My mother tells Briony in a lower, more monotonous voice to take pictures.

Cece unwraps the gift as Uncle Bass and Auntie Moira smile expectantly. Inside the paper that unfolds like a flower when my sister pulls at its strings, is a green crew-neck t-shirt with a yellow bumblebee at its center and a speech bubble over its head saying, "Just bee awesome!". After a moment, my sister says thank you.

I look at the front door, now closed and its latch locked. While my sister opens Auntie Rani's present, which is only an envelope, I go into the foyer to open the door, poking my head outside, and feeling the wind slap my face. I go back to the living room, leaving the door ajar.

Auntie Rani has gifted my sister a year's subscription to Netflix. Cece smiles and gets up and gives Auntie Rani a hug, a real hug. Seeing them, my shoulders and face drop, and I feel the lids of my eyes weigh down, feeling, too, like an aunt. My mother purses her lips and reaches for Briony's present. Briony takes a picture of Auntie Rani and Cece hugging.

"Now mine, now mine, now mine," Briony says, and as though her words are incantations, the scene begins to set, the elements fall into place: a wind of some force comes through the front door, and like a poltergeist, blows my hair in every direction, the mail off the stand, and sends the chandelier rocking, its glass bulbs rattling in their sockets. It screams past us and up the stairs, slamming the bathroom door shut. Auntie Moira exclaims in a loud, exaggerated shudder, and huddles herself.

"Cassandra, gone and close that door," says my mother.

"But it's hot in here," I say.

"Is not hot. Please close the door."

I go. I hear my sister unwrapping something else, Briony talking in the background, explaining what the gift is and why it's great. Paper is crinkling and Rihanna's "Only Girl in the World" comes on. The neighbours' wind chimes on the other side of us tinkle sweetly and my aunt is walking up the front path toward me, the house, us. She is still wearing her joggers and Nina's tight sweater. Her belly peeks out from under it. I can see the goosebumps from here, then as she gets closer, that her nails are painted a fresh coat of deep violet. Her hair whips around in the wind like it has a life of its own.

Cassandra, the door! my mother shouts.

Through her hair, I can make out that she's wearing a little bit of a blush, a rouge too red for her face, and sheer amber powder on her eyelids that I can't turn away from. Face to face now, I ask if she's okay and tell her to please, come inside, it's cold, like she doesn't live here. She does not appear to hear me, and asks me to move out of the way. I tell her maybe she should calm down. She says to please, move out of the way, Cassandra. Move, please, now.

She walks the few steps to the living room, running her finger-nails along the wall, leaving broken trails of violet behind. Compost is stuck to the bottom of her slippers and like a bridesmaid, I want to trail behind her and pull it off. I quickly stick my head out the door and look down at Posie's house across the street. Her wind-chimes clank in the wind, the lights are all off, the porch remains desolate and neat. From the outside, it is just another house.

I turn around and Auntie Sangeetha is facing the living room. Someone has said something, maybe Cece, maybe my mother, but no one has come to console her or welcome her home. I can only hear Rihanna's voice. Auntie Sangeetha is looking down, then her head moves up, and I understand: Auntie Rani has stood.

You, she says.

Rihanna says that she is going to make you beg for it.

You, Auntie Sangeetha says again. This is because of you, she says.

I hear the couch creak; my mother is standing up.

I find the strength to move my legs, and like a shadow I walk past Auntie Sangeetha, and move into the living room unnoticed. I sit close to Cece, where a new iPhone sits in its glossy box on her lap. We are all looking at Auntie Sangeetha.

It 'cause of you Chevy stop talking, she says.

I close my eyes and turn my head to the side.

Sangeetha, sit down and shut up, says my mother.

You shut up, Auntie Sangeetha says.

We all look at my mother. She tilts her head to the side, and as though rewinding herself, walks backwards to the couch, places her hands back into her lap, and sits down.

Why you didn't protect Junior that day, eh? says Auntie Sangeetha. You could have protect them. You could have protect Junior, she says.

She juts her index finger in Auntie Rani's face, and when she flinches, so do we. Auntie Sangeetha's smudged nail polish sheens under the dim light of the chandelier.

Unless, she says, unless you didn't *want* to protect Junior. Unless you wanted to hurt Tippie. Unless you wanted to hurt Tippie *bad*. Everybody know why. Everybody here, back home – people did talk, *Rani*. I bet you didn't know that, *Rani*. That people did talk about how you was the one that wanted to be with Blues. People ain't blind, you know, Rani. You hated she, Rani. You hated she. You could have never have what she had, and you did know it. And you was jealous. And you was mad. Mad!

I fall back into the couch and let my body go limp. I will my body to fall into the crease, to reach out to my two sisters and pull them down with me.

All of this is your fault, Auntie Sangeetha says. The words pour from her calmly.

All of this – you, she says. All of this, because of you. You was jealous! And Chevy see it is – he see it! You does feel guilty? Eh? You does ever feel guilty? That is why you try to get in the coffin with Chevy? Is guilt doing that to you? It will do that to you for as long as you live. As long as you live, Rani, as long as you live.

Telling me, she goes on, telling me to leave the house like I's not a grown woman. Eh, we's not ten years old anymore, Rani. All of we grow up long time. You ain't see we's old woman now?

She laughs once, a hard *ha*. Ha! Telling *me* to leave the house, she says.

I look outside the window through the small opening where the curtains meet. The only light coming from outside is the flickering beacons of the street lamps. Rihanna continues to profess that she is the only girl in the world. "Turn it off," I mouth to Briony. Her lips are parted when she looks at me, her eyes dart across her phone, and her fingers fidget. The music stops.

It happens slowly, the realization of what Auntie Sangeetha has said. Someone should go to her, I think. Someone should go to Auntie Rani. All of us sit still, looking at anything but another's face. It is unclear what she's thinking. She is looking beyond Auntie Sangeetha, at the wall behind her youngest sister in awe, as if, finally, something she has long pondered has been made clear. She turns her face away from Auntie Sangeetha and places a heavy hand on her sister's shoulder. I feel everyone in the room straighten up. Uncle Bass puts his hand on the edge of his chair, readying to separate the two women. But Auntie Rani does not strike her sister. Rather, it looks like she is using Auntie Sangeetha to keep herself from falling. Auntie Sangeetha looks at Rani's hand like it's alien to her. Then she squeezes Sangeetha's shoulder, hard so that the fabric of her sister's sweater balls up beneath her hand. Before Sangeetha can react, Rani gently moves her sister aside and shuffles into the hall. Stumbling, she catches herself on the living room archway, and when she turns around to look at us, the colour from her face is gone. Then her eyes, glazed over, gaze down the hall at her bedroom as if it is miles and miles away. The hunch of her back has appeared to stop fighting gravity; she hangs more forward than I've ever seen her. Her lips, like Briony's, like mine, like everyone's, are parted. We expect her to say something. *To hell with us all,* she might say. *To hell with everyone.* But instead, the worst: nothing. She walks down the hallway. We hear her go into her bedroom, the click of her door quiet. Uncle Bass removes his hand from his chair's edge, and not knowing what to do with it, lets it hang by his side. Auntie Sangeetha turns her body, as if commanded, and follows Rani down the hallway. Uncle Bass stands up, Auntie Moira goes to grab him by the arm and misses, Briony and I sit forward on the couch. My mother and Cece remain in the same spot, Cece's fingers wrapped tightly around the box in her lap. Uncle Bass looks down the hallway, holding up a hand, signaling us to wait. When we hear nothing more, he drops his hand, sighs, and runs his hands through his hair. The basement stairs creak, then Auntie Sangeetha's bedroom door slams shut.

Later that night, when everyone has made their way into their own rooms, mine and my mother's gifts to Cece sitting unopened on the living room coffee table, Auntie Moira comes upstairs to the attic. I hear her tell my mother that she can't take on all this bacchanal, it's not good for her heart. She and Bass will be getting on a plane to go back home in a few days.

26

My aunts believe that we only need to look at our tongues to know how healthy we are. When we were children, my mother would line my sisters and I up against a wall on any day of the month and say, "Open." We would stick out our tongues, and she patrolled us, squinting into our gaping mouths as if we were hiding something down our throats, she moved her head from side to side and checked with the handle of a silver spoon, which clinked against our teeth, for lumps, spots, or discolorations. Sometimes she would grip one of us under the jaw, and caught off guard, nervous and scared that there really might be something down there, we whimpered hot air into her face. One of us might be diagnosed with a tongue too white (poor brushing), or too red (skipping vitamins), or bad breath (this was mostly Briony from smoking cigarettes she thought our mother didn't know about). But in the end, regardless of our defect, we all had to drink a curdling spoon of milk of magnesia to cleanse our blood. Briony and I always squirmed at its liquid chalk taste, gagging mid-swallow, then chugging a full litre of water like we'd just run a race. But for Cece, the taste of it always made her burst into tears and scream that she didn't want it, the milk dribbling down the sides of her mouth while my mother spoon-fed her a second serving.

Cece is the tongue of our family.

Like when she was six years old and saw Auntie Rani and Auntie Sangeetha fighting in the kitchen over the last onion. What had started as a small quibble – insults murmured under Auntie Sangeetha's breath, Auntie Rani ignoring them – turned into indecipherable shouts and nasty cussing. ("You muddahcunt" this, "you muddahcunt" that.) Auntie Sangeetha threw buds of garlic at Auntie Rani behind her back, missing, and dry green onion leaves that only fluttered to her feet like papier-mâché. When she picked up a bilna and came at Auntie Rani, Cece screamed shrill and high, until Auntie Sangeetha turned around and saw that her young niece was watching. Briony and I ran downstairs, meeting halfway in the second-floor corridor. She rolled her eyes and walked past me, and when we entered the kitchen, all seemed back to normal; Auntie Rani was attending to a sizzling pan, and Auntie Sangeetha was bent over a tearful Cece telling her not to cry, they were only playing, still holding the bilna that rested on Cece's shoulder.

Or when Cece was eight years old and began asking questions about our father. She asked how come we didn't make ice cream at home, here in Toronto, like me and Ma and Daddy and Briony used to in Trinidad. I asked her how did she know that we used to make ice cream back home. Like my mother, I was already hardened at the age of sixteen, and answered my little sister's questions – questions that rendered painful memories still alive and kicking – with single words: yes, no, maybe, sometimes. I lashed out at her then, turning around the inquisition, prodding as to why she was asking me so many questions, how was I supposed to know, I was only eight years old when all that happened. The look in her eyes was the same look she gave me at her birthday party when I eased the cake into her mouth: searching and hollow and hurt. She stopped asking me questions.

Or when she was eleven, and she saw for the first time – really saw – that Chevy was encased in a lifelong grief. He was watching television in the basement and Auntie Rani had just finished cooking. I was sitting at the kitchen table studying. Cece brought him a plate of food, which he accepted silently. I heard her ask him if he wanted anything to drink, and, of course, he didn't reply. My sister listed out the options as if trying to satisfy a customer. Water? Juice? Coke? Nothing. She came back up to the kitchen, poured three glasses of each of the drinks she had mentioned, and took it down on a tray. After a few moments of the wordless communication, that I myself knew so well, she came back up with the glasses of water and Coke and poured them down the kitchen sink. Then she washed the glasses, smoothed her hair and pants, sighed deeply but airily, like she'd just gotten a big chore out of the way, got a popsicle from the freezer, and headed to the living room to watch old episodes of *Buffy*.

For her sixteenth birthday, she was gifted gold earrings by Briony in secret. After the birthday party when everyone had gone to sleep, Briony texted me to hurry up and come into her room, and when I did, she and Cece were sitting on the bed. Cece was smiling, cross-legged and slapping her skinny thighs. Briony placed a box on Cece's knee where it wavered for a few seconds before Briony told her to open it. I was recording it all on my phone, smiling, too, when Cece hungrily unwrapped it and saw what was inside: two gold curves, so that when she wore them her ears would look like they were smiling. Briony said that they were coated with 18-karat gold and that they were very expensive. She watched Cece run her fingers over the earrings. "Nice, huh?" Briony had asked. Somewhere in a drawer or cardboard box or garbage dump, there lives that video of Cece on my old phone, snapping the earrings box shut, steupsing for the first time I'd ever heard, and tossing the box back into Briony's lap before walking out of the room.

Or, when she was eighteen years old, and I left her there – here.

The tongue of our family has been afflicted for some time now. We have not gazed down the mouth's well to check for lumps or spots or discoloration in years, we have not clinked the silver spoon against its teeth like a xylophone to hear if its notes are still in tune. We've grown too old for all that now. If we had, we might see that a disease has advanced, that it had long ago spread to the outer skin and now envelopes most, if not all, of the body. Or maybe it was already evident to us, and we saw it, and pretended not to see it, like a disfigured face. Maybe we hoped the symptoms would resolve on their own, that, if we drank enough milk of magnesia, we would be purged. Maybe we even said to ourselves, "The tongue is not unhealthy, the tongue was born that way. The tongue is sensitive. The tongue has always been that way."

The tongue has not always been that way.

27

If one of us is hungry and another is in the kitchen, we'll wait until they leave. We'll stay in our rooms or loiter in the bathroom a little longer than needed until we hear the fading patter of feet, a door closing, utter silence akin to the dead of night.

This is both old and new territory to us. It's a storm we've weathered before, though not to this extent. As if a plaque has been engraved in gold and nailed up outside each of our doors, we abide by it religiously: *Wherever she is, I will not go. Wherever I am, she should not come.*

Auntie Sangeetha, for example, will signal her occupancy that she's in the kitchen by shuffling her feet loudly, coughing, slamming a cupboard door. Then when one of us hears nothing more for about a minute or two, we know it's safe to enter. Multiply seven people (Uncle Bass and Auntie Moira counting as one) by five minutes in the kitchen to scoop out and microwave food, plus another two minutes to account for non-sounds that confirms the room is, indeed, free, equals up to about a forty-minute wait time to eat, three times a day.

To use the bathroom is easier. There's the universal rule – the universe being entirely contained and suspended in this house – that this basic need is more urgent. We only need to wait until the toilet flushes, or the shower stops running to know when it's available, so that with our toothbrush and towel already in hand, we can scamper off to our shift.

For three days since the words left Auntie Sangeetha's lips, none of us have roamed the common areas freely. The kitchen, living room, laundry room and lounge area in the basement still have rogue signs of habitation lying about; a throw sprawled half-way across the couch and touching the floor, an empty soda can on the coffee table, a hamper full of clean clothes.

My mother has been coming into my room from hers, asking me questions, hurried and desperate, borderline horrified, as if something critical hinged on my answers. Am I hungry? Have I been taking my vitamins? Do I need extra sheets or pillows? Is the draft coming through the window bothering me? Let me let her fix it. I answer her in grunts, not looking up from my book or notepad or just scrolling away at nothing on my phone. It's only when she's gone that I put whatever I'd been holding down on my lap, and look up at where she'd been standing, wanting her to come back and just sit next to me.

On the night it happened, around midnight, Auntie Sangeetha knocked on my mother's door. My room door was open and I was sitting near the window alternating between reading and watching an old small woman walk her old small dog. Every time the woman stopped walking, so did the dog. They would stop and walk, stop and walk; it was mundane and endearing, and brought foolish tears to my eyes. When I turned around, Auntie Sangeetha and I made eye contact across the hallway. She was standing on the other side of my mother's closed door, hands folded and head bowed as though waiting for counsel or forgiveness. I walked across the room. She watched me, her lips parted like she wanted to say something, or wanted me to say something, but when I reached the door, I looked back at her and shut it, the slim light from my room narrowing across her wide eyes.

The door and the frame, both slanted, don't align perfectly on my mother's door or mine. It was with no effort then that I heard her tell Auntie Sangeetha that "she take it too far" and "things like that was not meant to be said, not ever, in any circumstance." Auntie Sangeetha did not say a word, and I imagined her sitting on the edge of my mother's bed, black mascara leaking down her face. It was a sensitive time, that's all, my mother said. They was upset, they was all upset, she said.

For the next few days, I eat, shower, lie down, sleep poorly, and have ravaging dreams about being alone in a cave under a waterfall, or all of us on a crashing plane smiling serenely. I sit up, yawn, sigh, read and scroll through my phone scanning news and tweets, smiling at puckered faces, closeups of flowers and sparkling seas on Instagram, not liking or commenting on anything other than the odd meme that makes me feel something else for about ten milliseconds. Ines' question about my return hangs in our chat box. The world outside is a fabrication.

I have spoken only to Briony in the past few days, all three times in her room. For the first time in our lives, we've run out of things to talk about. When we don't know what else to say, we circle back and conclude our dwindling conversation with, "Crazy. This is crazy. Can you believe it? Can you actually believe it? Yeah, so crazy."

I've been texting Cece, but to no avail. She has not been online on any app, and I have not heard her come out of her room. But this is normal, I think to myself. That is her being normal.

Auntie Rani hasn't come out of her room either. At night I lie in my bed and zone out looking at the ceiling and thinking about what she's doing in her room, what world she's in, and how she'll come out of this. Is she staring at the walls, is she gazing out of her window? Is she lying in bed, crying herself to sleep? Is she planning revenge? Her room is directly above Auntie Sangeetha's. Does she stomp her feet at night so that dust from the ceiling falls into Sangeetha's own sleepless eyes? Does she unscrew the grilles of the vents and drop breadcrumbs into it so that mice might meet Auntie Sangeetha on the other end? Is she looking at the photo of Blues, rereading her unsent letter, wondering where in the world he might be, what other women, and children, he has damaged for the rest of their lives, and how it can be possible for someone to exist and move on and not know the havoc they've wreaked?

On the fourth day of silence, I walk into Briony's room without knocking.

"Have you spoken to Cece?" I ask. I don't wait for her to answer. "Come with me to check on her, will you?" I pull my hair into a tight ponytail.

"Why?" she says. She's looking out the small crack of window between the drawn drapes.

"There's a weird smell coming from her room." A pause. "She's right next to you. Are you telling me you don't smell that? How—" I swallow. "Please, just come with me. Please? I don't want to go alone."

"I don't want to."

"You have to."

I take her by the elbow and pull her down the hall. She is not putting up a fight. She begins to sob and moan saying no, no, no.

266

28

The police say to my mother that because Cece is an adult, obviously, she can't be reported as a missing child. Instead of driving up on the curb with their flashing lights, they've parked in an empty spot in front of our house like they're staying for dinner, and greet us on the porch. When my mother hears this – that Cece will be treated like an adult – she tells them no, *no,* she *is* just a child, then collapses. I catch her in my arms, and she is moaning, moaning, turning her head from left to right, mumbling beneath her breath. "Cecelia, Cecelia, oh, Cecelia, where she there? Ain't she was just here? Ain't she was in she room this whole time? Find she, nah, find she. Allyuh go now, nah. Allyuh wasting time, talking, talking. Gone and find she. Cecelia, oh, God, I go dead, just let me dead now, Cecelia, my baby, Cecelia…"

I hold her up under her arms. My aunts stand on the other side of the screen door watching us on the porch. When they had come out of their rooms – Auntie Rani from down the hall, Auntie Sangeetha from the basement, and Auntie Moira from the second floor – they merged at the epicentre of the foyer, not acknowledging each other. I hear Auntie Sangeetha say, "Oh God Lord Father, what happening now?" But when they see my mother fall into my arms, they tell me to "Bring she inside, bring she quick."

"Officers," I say, looking past them to the neighbouring houses and holding my destitute mother like a bag of laundry. "Why don't we take this inside?" Briony stays on the porch calling Cece's friends and we make eye contact. She mouths to me, "Nothing yet."

My aunts make way as I drag my mother onto the living room couch. Auntie Sangeetha holds out her hands to help, I shift my mother's body away from her. I tell my mother not to worry, everything will be okay and that I'm going to talk to the police now. Her eyes are squeezed shut like she's trying with all her might to die. I tell her I will be right back and smooth her hair, and she sprawls herself out, her arms become restless, moving across her body, from her head, to her face, to her stomach, a leg dangling off the couch like a strewn puppet. I grow afraid that she's going to scream that unbearable animal scream I'd heard at Chevy's funeral. I tell her again I'll be right back and that I'm close by in the hallway.

I stride past my three aunts and Uncle Bass, who has now joined us.

"Cas, girl, what happening here?" he asks.

His hands are on Auntie Moira's shoulders. I walk to the front door, and like a policewoman behind a two-way window, rap on its glass for Briony to come inside. Two people from two houses across the street are suddenly on their porches, checking for mail, reading a book, taking out the garbage.

One of the police officers, tall and thin with a thick mustache that makes him look older than he really is, asks us to tell him everything. The other one, a woman with greying blonde hair, writes everything down the mustachioed one says. As I speak, she moves her eyes around the living room and foyer and over each one of us. She looks

268

at Auntie Sangeetha just a little too long, perhaps at her freshly drawn on eyebrows and stained scarlet lips.

"Um," I say, taking a deep breath. "Okay. Well, we smelled something terrible coming from her room."

"Who?" says the policeman.

"Briony and I." I point to Briony. "We're Cecelia's older sisters."

The policeman nods.

"We smelled something really bad coming from her room and thought maybe we would check on her. It—"

"What did you think it was?" he asks. "The smell coming from her room?"

"I don't know," I say sternly, looking him in the eye, hoping he can read my mind. *You know how people get in times of grief. Maybe she's been stranger, more isolated than usual. Maybe we've been brushing her off. Maybe we didn't check on her for four whole days.* The policewoman writes something down.

"We just thought we'd check in. We've recently had a death in the family. It's been hard on us." My aunts, except for Rani, look away. "She wasn't answering when we knocked, so we opened her door with a butter knife because it was locked. And then when we saw she wasn't in there, we checked everywhere else in the house, obviously." I pause. "It's just very unlike Cece to leave the house, just like that, without telling anyone." I drop my shoulders and rub my arm. "She... she didn't take her phone with her, and I... I don't know. Is that a bad sign?"

The policeman's face softens. "Okay," he says. "Let's take it step by step." He asks me to show him Cece's room.

In quiet procession I lead the way to the second floor, the two officers following me, then Auntie Sangeetha, then Uncle Bass, Auntie Moira, Briony, and Auntie Rani. My mother's moans weaken. When we reach Cece's room I apologize, scrunching my nose. Auntie Moira brings the neck of her sweater to cover the lower half of her face. Uncle Bass coughs and catches his breath. Briony and I hadn't had the chance to remove the milky, mouldy bowls, rotted bananas, and half-eaten slices of decaying cheese. The policewoman says they've smelled worse, then asks everyone except me to leave the room. Clothes and shoes and random objects are tossed on and around everything, making it difficult to tell what Cece has taken and what she's left behind. After they've looked around for a few minutes, not touching anything, but just looking, and now both writing, we go back into the hallway. Everyone herds backwards like little ducks to make room for us. Auntie Sangeetha is crying now, and Auntie Moira folds her hands on her chest. Auntie Rani moves past them and us and pokes her head into Cece's room as if she's never seen it.

In the hallway, the policeman asks if there's any reason why Cecelia should leave home. I tell them no. They ask if anything upsetting or stressful has recently happened in the house. I say no, nothing out the ordinary, just death. The policeman stares at me as I speak, the policewoman looks at everyone else. She writes something down on her notepad and I look at it. The policeman looks at me look at it, and I look away.

"So what can we do?" Briony asks through a red, stuffy nose.

"The thing is," the policewoman says, speaking for the first time, her eyes moving from behind me to my face, "is that because Cecelia is an adult, this isn't really a missing person case." Auntie Sangeetha gasps through her tears and says softly behind me, "How that could be?"

"We have to consider," the policewoman goes on, "that Cecelia might have *wanted* to leave, and as an adult she has the right to go where she pleases. Legally, she doesn't need to tell anyone where she's going."

"Officers, please," I say. "Cece is not the type to pick up and just leave. And she left her phone behind. She doesn't seem to have taken anything with her. Doesn't that mean something? Like, maybe she's not in the right mind and she's out there, just wandering about? If we're worried and have legitimate concern, isn't there something you can do to just find out if she's okay? I really don't understand." On the brink of tears, my chest moves in and out and Briony slips her hand into mine.

"Yes," says the policeman. "Yes, we were just getting there." He pretends to tap my shoulder. "If there's a legitimate concern for her safety, we can run a check on her and see if she's used any credit cards to track her. If she is, indeed, the one using the card. Then, if we *do* find her, we can talk to her and let her know that you're worried about her. If she wants to, she can get in touch with you to let you know she's okay."

"But," he continues, and he puts up a finger, "she can also decide *not* to get in touch with you. That's her right and her choice as an adult. I really need to stress that."

I nod. "If she doesn't want to talk to us, can you at least let us know she's okay?"

"If we make contact with her, we're going to have to talk to her and see what the situation is," says the policewoman. "If we can contact her," she says again.

Auntie Sangeetha cries louder, turns down the hallway, and goes down the stairs. Auntie Moira follows after her.

I give them our home phone number and Briony's cell number and tell them to call us as soon as they find something, anything. They ask for all of Cecelia's social media profiles and tell us to keep calling Cece's friends, and if we come into new information, we should call them, too. Downstairs, my mother wails.

271

29

"I looked in Ma's box, the one under the bed with all the pictures," she had said.

She was swaying from side to side and humming in the kitchen chair to imaginary music. "There's a *whoooole* bunch of pictures of you and Daddy and Ma and Briony making ice cream in a wooden bucket. Daddy's grinding it from the side with a handle. I didn't know you could grind ice cream." She smacked her lips to make small, popping sounds. "How come we don't make ice cream now? Do we have a wooden bucket? Can we make ice cream, too? Do you remember how?"

"I don't know," I had answered, not looking up from my textbook.

"You don't know what?"

"I don't know, I said."

"You don't know what? You don't know if we have a wooden bucket or you don't remember how to make it? We can look up a recipe online. And we can get the grinding bucket thingy off Amazon."

"I said I don't know!" She stopped smacking her lips and dancing in her chair. "I don't *re-mem-ber*. I don't know if we have a friggin' bucket, and I don't even remember making ice cream back in Trinidad."

She grew serious and narrowed her eyes at me. She stood up from her chair. "Fine. Fine, be like that. It's not like I give a fuck anyway."

She walked out of the kitchen and down the hallway, the outline of her small figure strutting and receding into the darkness where the bulbs had long blown out in the foyer. Then her little body's outline was set aglow by the burst of sunshine when she opened the front door to the outside world, where she ran, suddenly and startlingly, through it, onto the front walkway, across the street, and out of my view.

30

Nothing happens. Time stops. My beautiful sister.

31

On the second day, we all sleep with our doors open. Briony stays with me in the attic, and we share my little bed while our mother writhes on her own. We don't say much to each other, Briony and I. We just sit alongside one another, watch the small television on a low volume, look at each other, smirk sadly, constantly check our phones. From the next room, at ten in the morning, our mother screams – at us, we think, though she hasn't addressed us directly – asking why we haven't found Cece yet. She bursts into sobs and tremors, grabs at the walls in an attempt to tear the wallpaper off, succeeds, she grips onto Briony and I so that our clothes seams loosen, then falls to the floor, exhausted. Auntie Sangeetha and Moira wait at the bottom of the attic steps, too afraid to come up. When it's over, Briony and I whisper over the banister to let them know she's calmed down, and they go back to their rooms. This repeats itself every two hours, each occurrence feeling like a different day, draining us. On cue, my mother restarts the cycle at noon: the sobs, the tremors, the screaming, a new piece of wallpaper on the floor, bits of it under her fingernails, and so on and so forth. In the fifteenth hour, she adds a new step to her accumulated mourning: she pushes the window up over her head and screams into the day with every ounce of energy in her small body. She's locked her door with the little chain that hooks to the wall, and when Briony and I hear her wordless scream, we look at each other confused, then run to the door. We see in the space between the wall and thin link chain that her body is leaning halfway out the window. Then: "Cecelia! Cecelia! Where you there? Cecelia! You there? You could hear me? Come back!" followed by a sound not unlike a whale calling to its calf. Briony and I shove against the door and together we break the chain, ripping it and its lock from the wall's crumbly interior. We ease her away from the window by the shoulders, our mother shivering and hiccupping back to her bed. I tuck her beneath the covers and tell her to just breathe. Briony leaves. My mother softly cries herself back to a sleep where she talks to herself, asking questions, answering them. Briony returns with two pills in the palm of her hand. "They're anti-nausea ones," she says. "They'll make her drowsy." At the bottom of the steps: "Psst psst psst." I leave my mother, peer over the banister, and Uncle Bass shakes his head at me; no sign of Cece in the neighborhood yet.

Our mother wakes at four o'clock, her murmurs escalating, quickly and anxiously, into loud questions. We hear her feet hit the floor and scurry to the window, and again we run, again Briony and I cajole her back to bed. Briony crushes the pills into a glass of water and tells her this will help her get some peace, and by the time she wakes up everything will be okay again. She tucks my mother's hair behind her ears. Willingly, my mother takes them, her lower lip trembling as she brings the glass to her lips, Briony holding its bottom and tilting it up into our mother's mouth. She chugs it down too fast, water leaks down from the corners of her mouth to her neck. She doesn't bother to wipe her wet face when she lies back down, breathing heavily. Her mouth remains open. Briony wipes her face with the cuffs of her sleeves. We close the window. She sleeps until nine in the evening.

*

A guilt-ridden Auntie Sangeetha patrols the basement, and like a troll under a bridge she asks me three questions at the bottom of the stairs before I can pass. "You hear anything? You call them again? You call she friends?" Then she drops her shoulders, turns around, and sulks back to her room, throwing herself face down on her bed.

I follow her and make myself at ease, sitting on the lone chair. Except for the water heater in the laundry room that clinks every few minutes, there's no other sound in the basement. I wiggle my toes into the carpet, so cool against my soles it feels wet. From the ground floor window, I can see that today brings a clear blue sky, a perfect day for an apology. She turns onto her back, her body bobbing before resting into a calm, and stares up at the ceiling like a daydreaming teenager. I cross my legs and tent my index fingers to my nose, tempted to ask her what the hell was she thinking. She looks up at me from the bed, I raise my eyebrows in expectation. She sighs and lays her head back down.

"Well," she says.

"Well."

"At least she take she coat with she. I check the coat rack and the thick coat she does wear gone, so at least she have that. When I did leave, I ain't take one thing – not shoes, not jacket, not wallet – nothing. At least she had the sense to take a jacket with she. I should have had plan like that. If only I was that smart."

*

We stay up watching the news in the living room into the night, like the proper zombie family that we've become, except for Auntie Rani, who stays in her room. Auntie Moira and Uncle Bass, whose original flight was meant to depart today, have said they will not go until Cece has come home and they've seen her face again knowing she is well and alive. Uncle Bass doesn't mean to say "alive" and bumbles on to another topic. None of us are really listening.

When everyone heads to bed after midnight, I mute the TV's volume and make up a wry dialogue to accompany an old black and white movie. Auntie Rani appears at the archway, surprised to find me there, and sits down. I hand her the remote and she takes it, though she doesn't change the channel or turn up the volume.

Slouched across all three cushions of the couch with my arms crossed at my belly and my neck lolling to the side as if it's broken, we watch in silence. After a while I ask if she's okay. She tells me she has seen better days.

"These are dark times, I guess." I turn back and look at my aunt.

"Yes." Her eyes remain on the screen.

"Cece is okay."

"Cece is a smart girl. Nothing bad go happen to she so."

She coughs and looks down at her smartphone that has blinked alive, a cheap Samsung in mint condition. She scrolls through something and I go back to watching the television on mute.

*

The next day around noon, Uncle Bass goes on what now seems like a routine walk to locate another missing woman in our family. He slips comfortably into his winter boots, scarf, jacket, and hat as though he's been doing this for years now. Auntie Moira has not left her room to bid him farewell. From the living room couch where I'd fallen asleep overnight, I groggily ask him if he wants me to go with him. He tells me to sleep, darling, he can manage on his own.

My mother, having taken to self-inducing herself into brief, merciful comas with the anti-nausea pills, sleeps upstairs. As I sip my coffee, which I've been forcing myself to drink since my sister left, CTV News reports that a girl's body – a young girl, in her early twenties – has been found in Lake Ontario at Harbourfront, near where the yachts park year-round. The voices and images on the TV blur together and the hot coffee falls into my lap. I stand up and inch closer to the TV. They show the body in a white bag with water leaking from it onto the sidewalk cement. A faceless voice says that the authorities are in the process of contacting the family. A pretty news anchor with a solemn expression interviews the man who found the body floating toward a boat. "It looked like she was sunbathing on the water," he said, shouting over the wind. "Her arms and legs were spread wide apart, and her hair kind of looked like seaweed. If it were summer and she was wearing a bathing suit, you'd just think it was someone trying to get a good tan."

I run up to Briony's room and scream at her to check her phone, then call her useless and take it from her. I call the number the police gave us and am put on hold. Briony is saying into my ear, "What? What? What happened? Did someone call? What happened?" She shakes my shoulders. "I didn't get any missed calls though!" I turn my back to her. She begins to cry saying oh my god, oh my god, over and over. The policewoman, the same one who had come to the house, tells me yes, they've found Cece. Here my mother comes, down the attic stairs.

32

Memories are largely misremembered – by now I know this. The past is perfect, if I look back the right way. Blurry and bubbly, crescents of pink and yellow gleaming on the edges of moments, however small and few, when the unremarkable becomes remarkable, singular moments in time, in parks and living rooms, walks and dinners, the first times of first times I didn't know would be first times. Faces. Faces, especially. I don't believe at the end it's the sunset we remember.

But I did not misremember this: it was my job to throw in the sugar, whipped cream, and vanilla. Briony's, the evaporated and condensed milk. Our mother threw in the basic, less romantic ingredients: ice, salt, and regular milk, because that is what mothers do – make everything pleasant for everyone else. My father, because he was the man, turned the hand-crank for thirty minutes until everything had churned into ice cream. Cece had not yet been born, the only flaw of this memory.

I do not need the photographs in the box under my mother's bed to remember this day. In fact, the photographs in the box are the fallible memories. They have captured the moment, but not the feeling. For example, the colours are all wrong. The day was so much more vibrant, so much less stark than the polarity of a Polaroid. We were sitting outside, each of us on our own block of wood or brick, leaning over the bucket as though looking down a well. The clouds were white, the sky was blue, the breeze was light, the sun was there, but it was not hot. My father's backyard was patches of green grass on deep brown soil from which Briony and I used to pull earthworms. The photograph has not captured the slow tumble of my mother's hair falling in her face when she bent to scoop up the ice from the bag on the ground and toss it into the bucket. They do not catch the angle of the one crooked tooth Briony used to have when she was ten years old, when the only thing that used to glisten on her was not ruby or rose gold, but the childlike light in her eyes of a full life ahead. They do not capture the smell of vanilla essence carried on the travelling breeze past my friends' houses, strong, strong, and pure, putting everyone in a mysteriously good mood. They do not capture the beads of sweat on my father's forehead, or his desire to impress a woman who was already his wife. His skin in the pictures looked oily as though the flash might have been on, but it was perspiration from turning the bucket's crank over and over, grunting, pretending that he was not getting tired. He took no breaks and joked that one arm would grow more muscular than the other and people would start calling him Lopside. "They go say, 'Look, look. Lopside coming,'" he said. He flexed said arm, and when the muscle failed to stand, my mother slapped his arm and called him a fool, laughing, saying to hurry up, nah, the children waiting. When my father pulled the iron grill from the centre of the bucket, Briony and I would lick our lips dry and stick our fingers into the ice cream to scoop a dollop up into our mouths, my mother, too, all of us agreeing that the perfect formula of store-bought food could never compare to the oddities of homemade batter.

The photographs do not capture any of this. I could paint the details of it in skillful, boundless strokes of colour, and still, I would not capture it all. Were I to know all the words in the English language and wrote atop a mountain descending years later with epic poetry and prose about this one tableau frozen in time, still, words would escape me, leaving alive and trapped, without protest, this moment, and this moment only. In this memory, I could live, and die, happy, laughing.

33

The policeman hands us a crinkly, unsealed envelope that looks like a small stash of money. He tells me and Briony on the porch that he's sorry that there's nothing more he can do. Ultimately, he says, the important thing to know is that Cecelia is well and alive. These things happen in families. He tells us to consider ourselves lucky and asks if we saw the news this morning. I nod yes. He says, see? Be glad that wasn't your sister. My partner had to give some family that news, and that's no picnic. Can you imagine what that must be like for the family? Then he leaves, tipping his hat like a soldier as if we'd just lost our husbands.

Huddled at the kitchen table, my mother again put to sleep by Briony, this time with a tincture of three pills instead of the usual two and some nighttime Benadryl, Briony and I hold one side each of the single piece of paper torn from a notepad with a letterhead of Holiday Inn & Suites Mississauga West. My eyes scan it quicker than I can read.

Don't know who's gonna to read this first. Don't care. Writing whatever pops into my head. Sorry I didn't call. I'm fine. Not dead (I know that's what Ma is thinking). Not gonna do anything stupid. Just needed space. Still do. Not at Holiday Inn in Mississauga anymore. Somewhere else now. Can't say where cause you'll come find me. And need space. Quiet = suffocating. Churches and libraries = good quiet. Funeral home, hospitals, our house = bad quiet. Always walking on eggshells. Can't do it anymore. Walked around Chevy. Why? What were we so afraid of? Trying to figure that out. Tell Auntie Sangeetha mad at her forever. Her own sister? Fuck. What was she thinking? Guess she wasn't. But still. Auntie Moira and Uncle Bass, sorry too. Briony, I love you, but stop stealing shit. Do you think we're blind??? Do you have to wear it to breakfast? STOP and better yet stop giving it to us. Disingenuous. Tell Ma she's the love of my life. Tell her to sleep happy knowing I live for her and she will see me again and not to worry, I'll be back soon, sometime. Nothing bad will happen. Have money. Not a kid. Cas. You did not leave home to write. You left home to leave. My turn now. Mackenzie will be by for some of my things. Be nice. Don't fight her. Don't ask her a million things. Briony don't be an asshole to her. Just let her come and let her go. Auntie Rani should not forgive. Anyone say that kind of thing to me, I gone long time now. Exhausted. Love, Cece.

Briony, breathing heavily, drops her side of the note, turns around, runs up the stairs, and slams her bedroom door.

I hold the paper in my hand for some time. I sit down, stand up, sit down. Then I smooth it with my palm and stick it to the fridge with apple-shaped magnets at its top and bottom to keep it from blowing away.

34

And could she forgive her sister for those words? She and Sangeetha have not so much as looked at each other since.

The note ends up on the kitchen table at various points throughout the day as though being passed around by invisible hands; first at its center, then near the edge, then the opposite edge, on the floor, then back again on the table, its recipients receiving their few, harsh lines of truth. Then not feeling the note belongs to any single one of them, so that they might stash it away in some drawer or box, they let it be on the table and go back to their rooms, feeling somewhere between relieved, that Cece is okay, and offended, that she should think those things about them.

My mother sleeps more deeply now knowing that her youngest is alive, but is still slightly confused as to why Cece's decided not to come home. Not quite understanding the concept of space, she says there is plenty of room in the house. She takes literal heed of Cece's words as if obeying them to a tee might suddenly conjure her daughter back into her bedroom. She is the love of Cece's life, and vice versa, she repeats, though, I note, with one small addition. She will sleep happy knowing that Cece lives for her, she says. She seems to edit out and skip completely Cece's words to me, forever branded in my brain ("My turn now"). Unable to reckon with the true meaning of the note, perplexed and comforted at the same time, my mother falls into a deep hibernation until the night, storing up her energy for the coming days when Cece will be home, she says.

That same evening, I sit at the attic window in my room not knowing what to think about anything or anyone, and not knowing what else to do but look out at the old woman walking her old dog, when I see Auntie Rani go out for a walk. Cold smoke escapes her mouth and dissipates, she scrunches her shoulders to her ears. She walks slowly down the pathway onto the sidewalk and turns and looks back at the house, staring at the ground floor all the way up until she sees me. We make eye contact and hold it. I straighten up in my seat and smile a little, timidly wave without lifting my other hand from the window's bottom ledge. She smiles back, though sadly, and walks away and disappears around the corner.

Forty-five minutes to midnight, the rapping at her door, however small I try to make it, sounds like the stone of a gargoyle knocker in our house's somewhat less fatal quiet than a few days ago.

"Auntie, can I come in?" I whisper. Nothing. Then bedclothes rustle, footsteps approach, and I am before her like a child. She is wearing a long, black nightie, and not accustomed to seeing her arms, I stare at their sagged muscle and sinews.

"Oh," she says.

She opens the door with just enough space to let me into The Room, and even though she closes it quietly behind me, I flinch. The bed, a queen, is covered in a pale green sheet like the shade of a nurse's uniform, a quarter of it untucked with a matching pillow sunken at its center. A chest of drawers in the corner has nothing on it except the blue cloth bag, and on another chest with a large oval mirror lies a hairbrush, toothbrush, floss, a studded pair of gold earrings, and the cardboard box from which I look away, ashamed of knowing what lies within are the untold secrets of her heart. Peeking out from beneath the bed are three pairs of shoes lined up next to other that each look the same. There are no clothes on any surface – not on the bed, not on the single chair, not even in the laundry basket – or a damp towel hanging off any hook or corner. The only thing that looks foreign to the rest of The Room are the curtains my mother had hung up with my father once upon a time, a too-luxurious Prussian-blue drape with gold tassels holding it open. Three long rhombuses of amber from the neighbor's backyard light fall above the headboard, lending a holy aura of godliness to her cleanliness.

I sit on the bottom right corner of the bed, taking up as little space as possible. Except for the light coming in through the window, The Room is in total darkness; she makes no move to turn on a light. She sits opposite me, on the bed's other corner, and not trying to disguise how she feels or project any notion of accommodating niceties, simply looks at the wall.

After some time of us both trying to understand why, exactly, I'm sitting in her room at midnight (or maybe it was just me), I realize how foolish, and somewhat in character, it would be of me to sit there and say nothing, then simply leave. So, I summon the words.

"Auntie Sangeetha… she… says things she doesn't mean. She just talks. I guess you know that better than anyone else. I mean, growing up with her."

I shift a little, taking up more room on the bed. In the dim light, her stooped silhouette looks like a shadow under a streetlight.

"No one takes anything she says seriously. It's a weird time, with Chevy and all. And now Cece." I sigh and run my hands through my hair, feeling the start of a migraine flowing to my temples.

"I know," she says, immediately following my words. "I know."

Then, as if the words had been waiting on her tongue: "I did know something was going on. I old, but I not stupid. I know them three. You think that kind of thing bother me? But I didn't know it was something like this. Something like *this*." She holds her hands out as if preaching. "This is not something that will pass so easily. Maybe for them. But not for me. Not for me so."

In the dark I nod, and perhaps because we were more like voices than bodies, unable to see each other's faces and look into each other's eyes, I found myself moving closer to her, my hand finding her back. Hesitating to touch it but feeling her warmth, I lay my hand on her. Softly, I say, "What happened, Auntie? What happened the day Junior died?"

She puts her head in her hands.

35

March 1984

Blues,

I find it strange to write to you because I never write to anybody before. While I still living, this letter will not reach you. Is only after I dead this letter <u>might</u> reach you. Nothing good will happen from me sending it while I still living, and that's if I could even find out where you is in the first place. If anything good was to happen, it would have happen already and not because of a letter. But maybe that is something I just telling myself.

If this letter should reach you by chance... which never work in my favour before... and you wondering why I writing like a stupidee... is because I want you to feel like I talking to you straight to your face. I not writing how they teach we in school. I not cleaning up how I feel.

Plenty years gone. Plenty years gone. The things I gone through... the things I see... you wouldn't know... you couldn't guess...

But why that is important for you to know is because the things that happen to me is also things that happen to you. Is possible you don't even know what happen to Tippie and your youngest son, who did look just like you. We name him Junior because he come out real small. But this is not something I want to talk about in a letter to you. These are things that really should be said to your face and not by me self. The one who should be saying it to you... well, if you don't know what happen to Tippie and your son, come back to Macaria. Everybody know. Let them tell you.

Don't feel I talking to you rough. Don't put down the letter. You have a bit of rage in you, I know. I did see once when you was talking to one of the old woman on we street, the one who used to hate you. I don't know if you know we was watching or that you didn't care if anybody was watching. But I did see in your face the scorn for the old woman. You wasn't violent or yelling, but you was saying something hateful, I could see so even from far. Don't scorn me so. I's not an old woman yet. I only saying things you should know. And if nobody go tell you, how you go know?

What I want to say in this letter is from me and me only. Maybe Tippie did write you she own letter, I don't know. Maybe she send it to you and you didn't care. Maybe this letter go end up in your hands and you wouldn't care too, maybe you go throw it away in the dustbin. But I go be dead when you reading it, so what I care?

In a way, is sad when you think about it. Since I don't know if this letter will ever reach you, is like I talking to myself. Which is not something new to me. But, in a way, is good. Is only with myself I could talk honestly. Is only I alone who know what I mean when I say what I say.

That is, until I meet you.

Here is where I go write what I really feel in plain English. I's not a poet. What I want to say is… that is a real rare thing to meet somebody and feel like you know them and they know you within only a few hours of the same day. I never had that feeling before in my life. Even though we only went out for that walk once – remember? It was getting dark and you was explaining to me the blues musicians you like and when I tell you I never hear the blues you was shocked? And we start to laugh. That walk home feel like a lifetime, a whole next life, in a good way, eh. It was only a few hours and still I can't forget. Less than a day self.

Is a hard feeling to let go. I don't know how to explain it. Is a strange thing to fail to forget something you can't explain. But maybe that is the reason self I can't forget. And it does bother me. To this day, it does bother me. Well, is obvious it bother me – I writing you almost sixteen years since we first meet at the supermarket. Remember? Remember how we first meet? Please don't forget. Don't mind you meet plenty, plenty people since you and me meet and plenty thing happen to you and me since. Don't ever forget.

I myself could explain every detail of your face like I only see you twenty minutes ago.

So that is the first thing I want to say. I sounding like one of them people in them romance books Sangeetha (that is the youngest one) does be reading. But at least that gone out of my body.

The second thing I want to say is… what I want to know and what I will never know is… and I go say it in plain bold-face English so you can't mistake what I saying is… why it wasn't me. I not saying that as a question, I saying that as a fact. Why you walk with me in the sunset so? Why you ask me questions about my father, like you did care? Why you walk me home? Why you bring dandelions for me? You does bring dandelion and savannah flowers for everybody so?

It must be so. Because when I did come to your apartment after we didn't hear from you the first time, when you did gone and run when Tippie was pregnant with Chevy, your landlord did tell me you went to Caracas where you had sons. Sons! I did nearly swallow my whole tongue right there. You had children and you ain't tell nobody? Look I write down my question and answer it myself. You pick plenty flowers in your life.

Don't get mad. Don't stop reading.

I say nice things about you at the start. Is not like I hate you. I try to hate you. I's mad at you and everything for the rest of my life. But I don't hate you. I try so long to understand why you was the way that you was. I try to say to myself, maybe he had a bad upbringing, maybe he parents wasn't nice to he, maybe something real bad happen to him, like it happen to me, and that is just how he turn out. He just bouncing from here to there, here to there, not really thinking or feeling but just moving, moving, always moving so he don't have to sit still. I does think: what it is about sitting still that does scare this man? Why he always need to run? Why he need to lie so?

But I get tired. They was just circles I running in my head and eventually it start looking like one big zero. I sorry to say.

Maybe bad things did happen to you. But that is no excuse for what you do Blues. Look, me don't even know your real name and you's connected to my nephews, to my sister, to me. We's not strangers, you know. We's family now. I know I say is not my place to say these things, but the things you do, you do it to all of we. Is only as I writing I feeling the rage boil up in me so. I say nice things, okay, but you wasn't a nice person in the end. Sometimes you was, but look at the end, look how it end. You leave we so.

But we getting on. We getting on and that is good enough. But you absolve yourself of responsibility, you slap your hands clean from we like we was dust. And for that you must live in shame forever Blues. If not by your own recognition, then by we own. Gone and take a long hard look in the mirror Blues. Not that you need a mirror to see yourself. Is not how you sleep at night but how you <u>fall</u> asleep. A guilty conscience don't need any accuser.

I real hope that if you decide to look at yourself… and it never too late… you's never too old… if you decide to look at yourself, you must see yourself, and forgive yourself, so that a better man is born from the shedding.

I did see him once.

Love,
Rani

36

She making noise, oh, she making noise. Plastic crinkling, hurried footsteps back and forth, papery things sliding across the hardwood floor, the front door muting and unmuting the outside world, the inquisitive voices of men, the commanding voice of a sure woman. One by one, each of our room doors open. She has three cardboard boxes of all the things she owns, and everything else she carries in big garbage bags, two in each hand. My mother, thinking the commotion coming from the foyer might be the promise of the returning daughter, rushes down the attic stairs with a lively energy of thirty years prior, me following close behind. We meet Briony and Auntie Moira on the second floor, then peering over the banister, we see her carrying the round, full bags with such ease one might think they were stuffed with feathers, props only for theatre. Auntie Sangeetha, I am sure of it, is either lurking down the hallway from the top of the basement steps, or lying awake in bed, frozen with the fear of consequence.

Who of we could ask where she was going, what she was doing?

Who of we could blame she?

She kicks open the glass-screen door in one last show of power, slamming it against the porch wall, and in a single swift motion swoops down and picks up the last box, tossing it outside without a care as to where it might land. Two men come into view – movers in navy jumpsuits and baseball hats who look like car mechanics. I fine-tune my senses and fit the final clue: outside, an engine hums in the midday's overcast grey.

I fall out of line from my family and run down the stairs. Briony grabs me by the arm, but I wrestle myself free, my sleeve slipping from her fingers. I reach the bottom of the stairs just as the last box leaves the porch stoop, already en route to the truck, soon to be en route to location unknown. I look at her in pleading apology. She is already wearing her jacket and shoes. The wind from outside blows in and lifts up the hem of her coat as if tugging her to hurry. I crinkle my toes in my socks, hoping my standing before her will be enough for her to stay, to say without words: please, don't do this, not you too.

Last night, she had put her head in her hands. When she raised her face, she had not so much sighed as exhaled, long and deep like a last breath of life. I was waiting, listening. I was there for her.

Across from her on the corner of the bed, not wanting to rush her, I had let a few moments pass, my face tender and soft and expectant, my hand resting on the arch of her back, rubbing it in light, and what would soon make itself known to me, trespassing circles. I felt movement on the mattress and she turned to me, where in the dark of the night I could see the baring of teeth, white squares like gravelly stones, a face out of a comic book; in the low light, the wrinkles from the twist of her face were streaks of black, and I could see as she encroached toward me that her cheeks were hot and aflame. I felt the need to move my legs, stand up, go to the door, reach for the doorknob, but remained on my corner of the bed. You idiot, I thought to myself, her shadow enveloping me. Who do you think you are, moving between your world and hers, your world and theirs, with your New World *compassion* and *commiseration*, and your feelings of nothing you know, only know *of.*

She said something, words that I couldn't make out in her snarling delivery, and when she yelled them, explosive in the night, my legs found the strength. I shot up. I faltered backwards and made for the door in that same stupor. She watched me, her fists clenched so tight that it might have been the driving force of a vein made visible on her neck. She came so close to me I felt her raging spittle on my turned cheek, and as I grasped for the doorknob behind me, jiggling and turning it, she said to me, mocking my earlier question, "'*What happen the day that Junior die?*' What you mean by that? You mean, what *really* happen?"

My hand found the small unlock button below the knob, and I pressed it speedily like a panic button.

"What you trying to say?" she said. "Something else happen? That there might be some grain of truth of what that fool Sangeetha say? And now you come in here, in my room, to find out what *really* happen?"

"No," I said almost inaudibly. "No. That's not what I was saying. At all. I just… I…" I wanted to say that I just wanted to listen to her. But she was too tall, too angry.

"What happen is what happen!" she shouted. "What, you want details? Is that you want? Details?" My hair wavered in her breath. I shook my head and a tear trailed from my shut eyes.

"Disrespectful child."

My eyes remained closed.

"You's a disrespectful child. All allyuh. Disrespectful children."

The doorknob squeaked as I turned it.

"You going then? Go. Gone then," she said. "Go."

And so I went.

301

And the door hangs open behind her.

Not two days later, Auntie Moira and Uncle Bass leave, too, though with less dramatic flair. Their winter jackets and boots remain in the foyer.

The Room remains empty again; none of us go into it. She had left its door open, and it was Briony, I believe, who shut it. We wondered what she had left behind, where in the moving boxes and bags she kept the picture of Blues safe from creasing while in transit, where in her new home she would put it. Would she leave it out in the open, on display, now that she did not need to keep it in a dark corner? Or would she keep it in her wallet and take it with her everywhere she went, indulging nearby eyes, and herself, the assumption that a long time ago this was her husband?

The house gets bigger. And smaller. Briony returns to work early, and on the day Cece's friend, Mackenzie, who she had referenced in her note, comes over to collect some of her things, Briony wears all the jewellery she owns, it seems; when she walks back and forth between the bathroom and Cece's room, she jangles and jingles like a tambourine, wiggling her eyebrows at the poor girl, whom she believes with the utmost certainty will report back to Cece the vision she claimed to know so well of her vain, older sister.

Auntie Sangeetha I hardly see in the common areas during the day. When I come down to the kitchen at night for water, or to watch television in the living room when I can't sleep, or to just sit somewhere other than my room, Auntie Sangeetha will appear, her face before anything else. She has started to fill in her eyebrows with a thicker stenciled black, and wear a darker, almost bruised, plum blush. "Did I ever tell you about the time..." she whispers. Whereas before my hungry antennas might have raised and I would have pinned whatever she saying up on that bulletin board of my mind – the papers and strings and thumbtacks already amassing

302

the beginnings of dust – I now coolly indulge her, heavy-lidded, feigning a yawn, and patting her on the shoulder, before heading back to bed, and her murmurs blend into another sound of the old house.

My mother begins to linger longer in my room, looking out the attic window with me at the streets and people below, until one day she takes her place permanently in a chair near it. In profile rather than facing the window, long after I've woken up and gone to bed, she twitches her head at every sound or motion outside to see with an overlooking bird's eye who there goes by. She coming back, she coming back just now, she says, holding the note cupped in her hands. I agree with her. She will hold her hand out and before it even touches my head, I will duck under it so as to slide beneath her fingers better, close my eyes, and nuzzle against her touch. She tells me what fine, thin hair I have, silky, silky, and not to use so much hot water when I bathe.

In a cool bath, with my head cocked back and my feet up on the tub, I think of London unfulfilled, but, always, a plane ride away. I think about Chevy, and that if I could say anything to him it would be, I love you, I'm sorry, I was afraid. I thought about how the greatest mysteries of our lives are our mothers.

And how there, out there, there are two more pieces of me, of us, astray and detached from our gravitational pull, forging futures of their own, leaving home for the first time – one at twenty-three, the other at sixty-nine. She had broken free but at first needed to be broken. I will find them again one day – I will. I will look at her and she will look back. I loved them all, in their flaws and fears. That was all I could do and ask of them the same. When on some lonely day, when I'm not quite feeling myself and I expect the past to fill that void, I will remember this. Here I am thinking of better days, if they were ever really so.

Acknowledgements

First it started with the teachers, who recognize which children like to read, and which children need to. To the teachers in Trinidad and Toronto that took literature so seriously that it made me serious, too – thank you.

Then the libraries. To the Toronto Public Library for calling me to its quiet shelves as a child, then its desks as an adult as I journeyed throughout this book – thank you.

Friends who never tired asking after "the book", even though they'd never seen a word of it – thank you. It's no easy feat to consistently follow up with a thing that may or may not have existed.

To my editor Ore Agbaje-Williams: for her belief and faith and patience. You have changed the course of my life, and that of those who may come from me. I am forever indebted to you. Thank you.

A special thanks to those who supported (and calmed) a writer who'd never published anything before *Wild Fires*: my agent Abi Fellows, and Nikesh Shukla at The Good Literary Agency; Priyanka Sarkar for being an early reader; Diana Bryden and Laura Barnett as early mentors; Terri Carleton for her passion; and to my mentor Chelene Knight: I am so lucky to have met you.

Thank you Arts Council England, University of Oxford (St Edmund Hall and TORCH), the Oxford Centre of Hindu Studies, Curtis Brown Creative, Sangam House, Humber College, and the Festival of Literary Diversity in Brampton for their early support of writers.

To M., J., and Tim – who I am the most grateful to and for – thank you.